CHE VAMPIRE KEEPER

THE VAMPIRE

KEEPER

SABRINA STREET

STREET INK. *Publishing*

LOUISIANA

Copyright

Cover art designed by Mirella Santana: mirellasantana.deviantart.com

STREET INK.

13 Fox Chase Drive

Pineville, LA 71360

Copyright © 2014 by Sabrina Street.

Author Website: sabrinastreet.com.

ISBN-13: 978-0692312179

ISBN-10: 069231217X

First Street Ink printing: October, 2014.

Published and Printed in the United States.

DEDICATION

In loving memory of my supportive grandmother,

Barbra Street.

CONTENTS

Acknowledgement

I wholeheartedly express my gratitude to the many people who supported me through this creative journey.

A tremendous thank you to Stephanie Whitley Shultz and fellow author Ashley Weaver for the many years of unwavering friendship and support that they gave me throughout the creation of this book. They listened as I talked or (to them) argued out my plot, read chapters, made comments, and encouraged me to publish regardless of my prevailing fears of failure.

Also, a gracious thank you to Denise Marquiss for driving me north to explore and research the sleepy little towns of Transylvania and Epps, Louisiana.

I would also like to thank the assiduous Rayne Holmes for the countless copy edits and Jason Sinner for his magnificent proofreading.

Many thanks to Mirella Santana, my graphic design artist at mirellasantana.deviantart.com, for creating an amazing cover and then tweaking it to my every whim.

A special thanks to Lilo Abernathy, my guru media consultant, without whom I would have been endlessly googling "How to –."

Last but not least, I am grateful to have such supportive friends and a loving family, who always encouraged me to follow my dreams regardless of genre. I am truly blessed, for I would not have published my work without any of you!

Finally, I beg forgiveness to any whose names I have failed to mention. I'll get you the next time around.

Chapter 1: Mirror of Desire

Monroe, Louisiana

THE SOUND OF ringing interrupted the clatter of clicking heels on the concrete driveway. Hanna peered down at her small phone encased in pink marble and held up one finger to her companion before slowing her pace. Not far from the front door, her companion gave a polite nod and picked up his stride trying to grant her silent request. It didn't matter if he put one stride or two between them; their conversation would not be private.

"Hello," answered his young, thin, brown-skinned beauty.

"Hey, where are you? I'm ready to go!" screeched a female voice trying not to be drowned out by thunderous music.

With a little giggle she replied, "You go ahead. I already have a ride."

"Hanna! You didn't."

"I did," she confirmed, trying to smooth out a crease she saw in her short skirt.

"What about Dylan?"

"What about him?" retorted Hanna. Silence overcame the caramel vixen as she eyed her two-carat platinum ring, until she heard an exasperated sigh which prompted Hanna to exclaim, "Don't worry so much, Kerri!"

"Well, I hope it's worth it," her friend snapped. The hint of judgment was evident in Kerri's voice, yet unheeded by Hanna, who nodded with a smirk as she glanced at the tall, handsome man that stood before her, propped up against the frame of the doorway. In an attempt to ward off another possible reproach, she rambled off a bye and some vague promise to call Kerri later before instantly flipping the phone closed.

Hanna smiled warmly at her companion, who stood before her with an out stretched hand. She found herself hesitant to accept his invitation. Thanks to Kerri, her mind flooded with images of Dylan. Unable to remove her fiancé's face from her thoughts, she moved forward and kissed the handsome stranger on the cheek before nonchalantly excusing herself. "Maybe next time," rambled out of Hanna's mouth as she flipped her phone open and turned to wander away. Before she knew it, and barely a step away, she felt his chest pressed tight against her back while his hands roamed the more sensitive parts of her body. It only took a few moments before Hanna's facial muscles tensed and her jaw clenched as she lightly bit down on her lower lip.

The clack of her phone hitting the ground prompted him to extend his invitation once more. "Are you sure that you wouldn't like to join me inside?" he whispered, nipping on her earlobe. He was assured of her submission to his request when he felt her body melt into his embrace. Moving backwards slowly, with Hanna nestled in his arms, he used his leg to sling the door closed.

What am I doing? Hanna thought for a split second as he flipped her around to face him. With her back now against the closed door, she stared deep into intoxicating blue eyes while his hands cupped and caressed her. Soon, Hanna's fiancé and her lover's eyes were a distant memory, for her breathing became rapid and she firmly gripped the door handle. Wrapping her other hand around her seducer, cradling him close for leverage, Hanna tightened her clutch once her body begun to quiver uncontrollably.

He waited for her body to relax before removing his hands to let her black skirt fall back to its appropriate length. After Hanna enjoyed one pure moment of pleasure, he scooped her up and carried her into the center of living room. Craftily positioning himself behind her, he continued his seduction. He felt her shiver as he lightly brushed her sun-kissed hair over her left shoulder leaving the right side of her body exposed. He heard her mumble some words of approval, so he leaned in and whispered, "To give pleasure before receiving has always been my forte."

A smile crossed Hanna's face as he softly kissed his way from the back of her right shoulder to her neck. He let his cool lips linger on her neck a moment, before she turned her neck violently and demanded with a discouraging tone, "Don't leave a hickey!"

After releasing his mouth from her body, he replied, "You don't have to worry about that, My Dear." He watched Hanna's expressions in the oblong mirror across the room as a smile slid back across her face. She mechanically tilted her head, giving him the go ahead to introduce her to more pleasure. With one eye still on the mirror, he brought his lips back to her neck.

Hanna felt secure in his firm grasp as he passionately kissed her. She felt a warm fluttering in her stomach until his kiss deepened. "No marks," she reiterated, but this time he did not respond. Hanna's smile faded as she felt his passionate kiss turn rough. She tried to wiggle out of his grasp, but every movement made the pressure on her neck intensify. Her frantic eyes finally caught sight of them in the mirror. Her alarm turned to horror as her eyes met his and it appeared to her as if he was grinning upon her neck before she felt a painful pinch. Hanna's pulse rose at the sight of bright red blood leaking from around his mouth onto her shoulder. She tried once again with all her might to free herself from his grasp, but found herself too frail to gain her release. The only option she had left was to watch the life drain from her face while her attacker stared without emotion into her distressed eyes.

Chapter 2: Moving In

Transylvania, LA

IN ONE CITY, dawn had brought death, but in another it had brought the merriment of a new tenant. Jezalyn Williford beamed as she pulled open the door to Wyler's Rare Bookstore. She could hardly believe her luck, for she had found a job with lodging. Although her new abode was but an hour away from school, it was even farther from her grandfather, so she felt like the drive was well worth the sacrifice.

The store owners, Wyler and Ana, greeted her as she entered.

Ana, who had reservations about renting out the top apartment, faked a sincere expression of happiness, while Wyler, being the astute gentlemen that he always was, noticed Jezalyn had not carried in her luggage so he warmly extended his hand and requested Jezalyn's car keys. Jezalyn, swept up in her excitement over moving in, anxiously fumbled about in her pocket causing them to fall out onto the floor. She giggled somewhat nervously as she watched Wyler, a man who appeared to be in his late thirties or early forties with dark blonde hair and a short, scruffy beard, instantly scoop up the keys.

"I have them," he said before Jezalyn could react.

"Sorry," Jezalyn replied with a smile.

Wyler returned the smile, and as he turned to walk toward the parking lot he said, "Ana! Take her on a tour while I grab her things."

Jezalyn broke in before Ana could lead her away, "Wait! I'll help you!"

"No, I got it. Go ahead and check out the shop."

They watched the faded trunk of her car pop open, Jezalyn with her eyes still upon the trunk suggested, "Maybe I should go and help him anyway."

Ana gave her a silly smirk and made a follow me motion. "It is no use, dear; he won't take your help. He is a complete gentleman when it comes to things like that." Jezalyn's eyes lingered on her trunk and Wyler, but she did not persist. Instead, she quietly followed Ana as she began the tour around the store. She showed her the different sections of store; it closely resembled a setup of a library. There were sections for fiction, non-fiction, poetry, autobiography, etc. Ana grabbed a book off the shelf, cracked it open, and smelled; "Don't you just love the smell of old books."

Jezalyn, who never gave much thought to smelling books, wanted to find favor in her new employer and landlord nodded. Ana placed the book back on the shelf, before continuing with the tour. As they sashayed through the store, Jezalyn pointed to a section with no books "What's that over there?"

"That's the antique corner; it's Wyler's favorite area. You know, that is how we met."

With an inquisitive tone, the word "Really?" slipped out of Jezalyn's strawberry glossed lips.

"Um-hmm. The day we met, I had gone to an antique shop with Mother; she loved to window shop. Anyway, Mother had found a set of china. It was seldom that she found something she liked, but when she did she always had to have a discounted price. The clerk was not particularly happy with her approach, and on that day, it had caused haggling war between them."

"Oh," Jezalyn uttered, prompting Ana to continue.

"Oh yes, it went on for several minutes, and then out of nowhere Wyler pulled the clerk aside. When they returned, the clerk sold the china for cheaper than Mother's haggling price."

"Really!"

"Yep! Mother was so happy she sent me back in with an invitation for dinner, he accepted, and we have been inseparable ever since."

"What did he say to the store clerk?"

"I don't know. To this day, he won't tell me the exact details. Instead, he just keeps saying, 'I told him to act like a gentleman in the presence of a lady.'" They giggled as they walked toward the back of the store, and when they neared the register Ana asked, "How about you, do you have someone special?"

Jezalyn's cheeks pinked as she nodded. "His name is Blaise Blackwell. We met at school."

"Oh, I always thought high school sweetheart stories were so romantic."

"Me too," Jezalyn sighed. Although Jezalyn had not met Blaise until college, she was too enthralled by her surroundings to correct Ana's assumption of when they had actually met.

Since Jezalyn gave no further details, Ana showed her to her work station, which was a small counter with an

old register, before leading her into the stock room. Jezalyn
followed Ana around the counter and through a small
opening. "This is the storage area. No customers are
allowed in here." Bewilderment filled Jezalyn's now full-
sized green eyes, for there were piles and piles of books
and knickknacks.

Noticing her anxiety, Ana explained, "Don't worry,
my dear, Wyler does all the processing, so you won't be
working back here too much. I usually leave him to his own
devices, when it comes to this stuff."

Although Jezalyn's mouth simply responded,
"Okay" her eyes held a look of deep relief as she thought,
Thank God, that's a lot of books.

When Ana saw the calmed expression, she
continued, "Also, back there to the left is the entrance to
our underground flat. If you ever need one of us, just
knock."

Jezalyn gazed at her oddly, "Oh, I never heard of an
underground flat. Is it like a basement?"

Ana laughed, "No, it's a flat similar to the one you
will be staying in above the bookstore."

"Oh, okay," said Jezalyn whose face showed a hint
of confusion.

Knowing that it was unusual for Louisiana to have a
basement, Ana quickly added, "The old owners had this
place built with a bomb shelter and evidently they were
people of comfort. And, I prefer it over the upper
apartment, since I work mostly nights."

After giving further clarification as to why
someone would actually sleep in a basement apartment,

Ana guided Jezalyn up a narrow set of stairs. Once they reached the top, Ana extended her arm toward the door as a gesture for Jezalyn to open it. Jezalyn edged around Ana closer to the door, and just as her hand grasped the doorknob, it flung open pulling her into the room, for Wyler was trying to exit the dwelling. Jezalyn recoiled at the fright and lost her balance.

"Are you alright? Here! Let me help you up," said Wyler, standing over her with his hand presented.

She accepted his assistance, but as she took it, she noticed his hand was soft as velvet. She was puzzled, for Wyler's hands felt more like the soft touch of an infant than they did of an old middle-aged man. "I am okay. You just surprised me," and with a little giggle, she tried to recover, "I should probably tell you I am kind of clumsy at times."

Glancing around the apartment, Jezalyn found herself standing in a living room with two small couches: one on the left wall and the other situated directly in front of her. They appeared to be old with a worn, mauve floral pattern. To the left, the living room flowed into the dining room where a round wood table sat with four chairs.

The refrigerator sat on the right side of the wall that separated the kitchen from the hall; it was yellow and looked as if it belonged in the fifties. Jezalyn barely noticed the fridge because her gaze was fixed on the washer and dryer siting directly behind the table. "Do the washer and dryer work?" she asked, with enthusiasm.

"Yes. I know it seems out of place, but when we put them in that was the only place they would fit," said Wyler.

Ana rushed over and stood between the table and washer. "When he says we, he meant he put them in. I have this bamboo-folding screen downstairs," said Ana as she stretched her thin arms out to model the screen, "if you want you can have it."

"Yes. Thank you. I think a bamboo screen right there would give it a nice Oriental feel," beamed Jezalyn.

Wyler broke in, "One of us will bring it up later." Then pointing down a short hall in front of them, he said, "Through here is the bathroom and right there is the bedroom." Jezalyn took eight steps, and she found herself standing in front of two doors with chipped-white paint. The door to the left led to the bedroom, while the door straight ahead led into the bathroom. He gave her a moment to peek around and after which, Wyler continued, "I placed your things against the wall in the bedroom. Let us know if there is anything else you need?"

With a jubilant glow Jezalyn shook her head. "Thanks for bringing my things up."

Ana, ready to return to her own apartment, forcefully tugged on the tail of Wyler's shirt and said, "Okay, we will let you get settled."

They were exiting the apartment when Wyler stopped in the entrance and told Jezalyn, "Come down later. We will have a bite to eat and make you out a work schedule."

"Okay," replied Wyler's timid, yet excited tenant. Wyler flashed Jezalyn a friendly smile on his way out, which faded as he found a distressed wife waiting for him at the bottom of the stairs.

"I hope you're right about this," Ana blurted out with a furrowed brow.

"I am. Just think about the free time you and I will have. No more double shifts for either of us," proclaimed Wyler with an irresistible smile.

With a more relaxed, somewhat of a stern wide eye, she said, "Yeah, that would be nice. I'm just nervous because of what happened the last time."

Wyler moved closer and wrapped his long lanky arms around his disquieted wife. "Don't fret, Bunny; I've already spoken to Larkin," he said, trying to remove Ana's fears of another lodging debacle. Wyler felt her stiffened body slightly relax, so he continued, "Besides, I'm going over the expectations with her today." Ana's husband was unsure as to whether it was all the reassurance or cuddling that he now held a limber body in his grasp, but he was happy to grant her silent request as he bent down and kissed her tilted head.

After lingering securely in his loving embrace a few minutes, she pulled back urgently and requested, "When you go over the store policies, make sure to include the flat rules. She is already curious about our underground flat."

Brushing a strand of toffee brown hair from her face, he said, "I will, Bunny, don't worry so much." Pulling her close to him once again, and with a devious grin, Wyler whispered, "I will include the apartment rules."

She jerked back and stared at him, trying to counteract his little quip she stated, "Flat, apartment whatever so long as we don't have another episode." Although Ana had tried to mask her irritation, she knew she had failed when her husband's slight grin widened. Ana wanting Wyler to take her statement seriously reached into her pocket and retrieved a piece of paper, "Here! I made a list of rules to cover since I won't be here."

"I don't need a list. I think I know what to say to Jezalyn. I have been his Keeper for a long time."

Still holding the list out toward him, Ana used the one thing that she knew her husband could not resist, she leaned close and with a sweet murmur said, "I know you have, but it will ease my mind if I know you have it. Please take it—for me." As Wyler's hand embraced hers and the paper, she knew her tactic had worked when he gave her hand a tiny squeeze. As his hand lingered awhile, she said, "Thank you. I need to go change for work. I'll check on Larkin before I go." Then, she gave a sweet yet seductive smile as she spoke softly, "I will think of you while I am gone."

Wyler still found his wife's allure as intoxicating as the day he had first met her, so he instinctively leaned in and pulled her delicate frame close, planting a long kiss upon her before whispering back, "I will miss you too, my love."

***

Several hours later, Jezalyn returned to the shop counter where she found Wyler sitting with two plates of food. "Ah, there you are. I was about to come and get you. Have a seat; Ana made us some chicken spaghetti, green beans, and garlic rolls."

Jezalyn sat down, "That was nice of her."

"Yeah, she mentioned something about lemon chicken and rice for tomorrow."

"Oh, I can't wait!"

Without responding, Wyler bowed his head and silently prayed. Jezalyn took notice of him praying, so she bowed her head and thanked God not only for the food that she was about to consume, but also for her amazing new apartment and job. Upon hearing the word amen, Jezalyn raised her head and began to eat. After Wyler took several bites, he asked, "Did you get most of your stuff put away?"

"Yes, sir. I only have a few boxes left."

"That's good. You can put the empty boxes back there," he said, pointing toward the back room. Jezalyn nodded as she took a sip of her coke.

"Well, there are some policies, or more like rules, we follow here at the shop that you need to be aware of." With that, she stopped eating and listened attentively. "This is for our own safety, since we live on the premises; never let anyone in the shop before or after hours, nor let anyone come up to your apartment." Not having any friends in town, Jezalyn did not think twice about questioning the rule, so she nodded, and let him continue, "Also, there is a door in the back that leads to an underground shelter; it's off limits. We reside there full time now, since Ana has to work a lot of random shifts. If you need something, just knock. I'm sure one of us will be up shortly. Unfortunately, we are both sensitive sleepers," he confessed lightheartedly, trying to take the edge of the intensity of his tone.

"Oh, my grandpa is kind of like that. I think he has insomnia or something," replied Jezalyn taking another sip of her soda.

Wyler nodded at her statement. "That's it I think. Do you have any questions?"

Jezalyn shook her head; "I will not go downstairs or let anyone in unless the shop is open," reiterating his rules to show him that she understood before continuing with her food.

After Wyler finished his plate he said, "One last thing, we don't invite anyone in our shop or go out and pull people in off the street like other shops. We dislike browsers; they are nuisances. They mess up the shop and never buy anything. In addition, when we are not putting merchandise out, we generally stay behind the counter waiting for customers to come check out. Ana and I believe: if people want to buy something, they will buy it; they don't need someone bothering them every two seconds saying, 'come on in, look around, and let me know if you need help,' so don't ever use those phrases here. Okay?"

Jezalyn nodded as she took the last bite of her spaghetti, and thought, *This is going to be a cake job. I don't have to lure customers in or even try to sell anything. All I have to do is sit behind the counter and put books up. Yep! This is the best job ever!* As Wyler placed her empty plate on top of his, Jezalyn said, "Hey, Wyler. Do you have a book on Greek Mythology that I could glance at? I am taking this Mythology class, it started last week, and the University bookstore says my book still hasn't come in, and I have a paper due soon."

Wyler's face lit up at the thought of his books having a purpose to someone. "Yes. Since you work here, you can read anything that you find appealing, but don't leave the shop with it."

"Thanks! Um, may I take it back to my room?"

As he shuffled over to a shelf to extract a book he exclaimed, "Sure, I just don't want them leaving the property; it lessens the chance of something getting damaged or lost."

She nodded her head and took the book, "I am sure this will be helpful. Is it all right, if I return to my room? I still have some homework to do."

"Yeah, sure. We can make a work schedule for you later. I know it is overwhelming with the excitement of moving in, going over the policies, and getting your school work in order." With a yawn, Jezalyn thanked him for dinner and returned to her room with the book.

Once upstairs, she excitedly called Blaise to describe her new apartment and job. They compared her job to his student worker job at the school library. Blaise felt as if Jezalyn's new job would allow her the same liberties his allowed, which was to toil away on assignments, research, and papers. They continued to talk for about half an hour or so, only hanging up to allow the mythical legend of Athena and Medusa to soothe her to sleep.

CHAPTER 3: MY BLOODY TEA

JEZALYN STIRRED TO bright golden rays of sunlight streaming in between the slits of the old, worn blinds. No matter which way she turned, she could not seem to hide; the rays always seemed to pursue her face. She finally glanced at her watch and discovered, despite the sun-drenched awakening, she had overslept. After jumping in and out of the shower, Jezalyn wrapped her strawberry-blonde hair in a towel and rummaged through a few boxes. It only took her about thirty minutes to pull together a wardrobe selection of old denim jeans, a light green scoop neck tee, and a slim copper belt. Slipping one leg into the jeans, she stumbled back catching herself on one of the windowpanes. Her body quivered despite the warmth of sunbeams. Trying to shake off the chill, she continued to dress making sure to grab her black leather jacket before turning out the lights and heading downstairs.

"Good morning!" A smiling Jezalyn greeted Ana and Wyler, who stood beside the counter.

"Morning, did you sleep well?" inquired Ana as she continued writing on a slip of paper.

"Yes, I did. I even overslept, which is rare for me."

Ana looked up and, without a response to Jezalyn's comments, handed Wyler the slip of paper. "Is there anything else you want to add before I leave?" she asked.

Handing the slip back, he asked, "Could you get two bags of sugar instead of one this time?"

She snapped back, "I know I used the last of the sugar this morning, but do we really need two bags?" With a smirk plastered across his face, he nodded. Ana glowered, with slight irritation in her voice, "Sure, why not. I'll grab two bags." Ana smiled meekly and turned to inform Jezalyn; "I am going out to for groceries. The closest whole foods store is in Epps about twenty minutes away. If you need to pick up a few things, I would be happy to give you a ride and show you about."

Jezalyn, excited to venture out without receiving the third degree, from her grandfather, for a change, exclaimed, "Yes! That would be great. I'll grab my purse."

***

As Jezalyn approached them, clutch in hand, she overheard Ana tell Wyler, "You drink more tea than anyone I have ever met," letting out a giggle.

"That electric tea kettle was the loveliest Christmas present I have ever received," Wyler confessed, before grabbing Ana around the waist to pull her closer. He kissed her so passionately that Jezalyn turned her head so they would not see her blush.

At the end of the kiss, Ana glanced over and saw Jezalyn. "Hey! Did I tell you that we had to add a counter top sink to the storage room so that he could make hot tea all day?"

Before Jezalyn could answer Ana's question, Wyler asked her, "Do you like tea?"

Jezalyn did not know why she felt so nervous, but she did, so she promptly gave an answer to each question. Turning to Ana first, she said, "No, I didn't see the sink,"

And afterwards to Wyler, "yes, I love tea; Lady Gray is my favorite."

Excitement twinkled in Wyler's eye at the very thought of a cup of hot tea. After listening to her response, Wyler's eyes widened as he said, "Come with me." Following him into the stockroom, Jezalyn noticed over to the right, partially hidden behind several stacks of books, sat a small sink in the middle of a bar like counter. Pointing toward the sink, Wyler's eye's twinkled as they always had whenever he thought about a nice cup of hot tea. "There it is!" he announced. "If you ever feel like having a cup of tea, don't be shy. Help yourself!"

Jezalyn observed a microwave on the right and on the left were teacups next to an electric kettle. She said, "Thank you!" and with a grin held out a couple packs of sugar toward Wyler. "I found these in my bag while I was upstairs searching for my wallet."

Wyler, overly excited, took the packets and thanked her. Now with the prospect of having sooner than later a cup in his hand, Wyler turned to his wife and said, "Maybe we do only need one bag of sugar. Get whatever you think is best."

Liberated from her husband's previous demand, Ana politely responded, "How nice. Now you won't have to wait on me to return. Well, let's get on the road so that I can make it back in time for work."

He pressed her hand, "Okay, Bunny. Drive safely." Ana smiled, motioned for Jezalyn, and proceeded toward the same door they had just entered. She had left her husband standing happily next to his little sink.

Once Wyler made his tea, he locked the shop door and went down to his underground dwelling. From behind the kitchen table, all Wyler could see of his friend's six-foot frame was the bottom of his jeans and his brown casual shoes. He moved over to Larkin, who lay on the floor in his usual resting spot with his legs propped up on the couch staring at the ceiling. Peering down at Larkin's dark brown hair and stark white skin, Wyler said, "Hey, the new tenant brought down some sugar, so I was able to make a cup of tea." Wyler watched as his friend got up, bit his wrist, and meandered over to him.

Larkin had no expression on his face or in his soft, baby blue eyes as he placed his wrist over the teacup and let the blood drizzle into Wyler's tea.

"What day is it?" asked Larkin without taking note of how much blood entered the cup.

"It's Tuesday. Do you want something to eat?"

As Larkin removed his wrist from over Wyler's cup he said, "No, not yet," before sitting down on the couch. Wyler said nothing as he roamed over to the refrigerator, pulled out a bag of blood, opened it, and squeezed the blood into Larkin's favorite cup. It was not so much a cup as it was a square shaped ceramic mug that tiered out at the bottom. Although the outside of the mug was black, the inside was dark red making it impossible for anyone, even Larkin, to notice blood stains; it was for this reason alone that this mug was Larkin's favorite. Wyler warmed the blood before bring it over to him, "Here, drink this." Larkin extended his arm, took the mug, and brought it to his lips. Wyler took a seat next to him and sipped on his blood-spiked tea.

They chatted about the shop and the new books that Wyler acquired. When they had finished, Wyler asked, "Do you need anything else?"

Larkin still holding a full cup said, "No, but thank you. Now tell me about our new tenant."

Taking his own tea cup over to the sink, Wyler said, "Well, her name is Jezalyn. She is nineteen and she goes to the University of Monroe."

"Oh, what is she studying?"

"I am not exactly sure. I do know that she is taking a mythology class because she borrowed a Greek Mythology book to complete an assignment."

His brow rose a bit, "What legend is she studying?"

Noticing Larkin was taking a little interest in something, even if it was their new tenant, delighted Wyler so he asked, "I don't know; would you like for me to find out for you?"

"Yes!" entreated Larkin as he ran his hand over his well-groomed goatee.

As Wyler put away his clean cup, he heard his wife calling for him from upstairs, "I'll be right back. Ana is home with the groceries."

"Wait, I am tired of this," he said, holding the almost full cup of blood out and away from himself. "Bring me back some tea," demanded Larkin.

Wyler's head bobbed up and down in compliance as he ran up the stairs. "There you are, Babe," said Ana as she extended several bags toward him. "Can you bring these downstairs for me? I need to leave for work now."

"No prob." Taking the bags he asked, "Where is Jezalyn?"

"She went upstairs; she's putting her groceries away. She said she will be back down when she is finished."

"Good. I want to show her the ropes today," said Wyler, as he kissed his wife on the cheek to say good-bye, before turning to bring the groceries downstairs. He put the food away and told Larkin he was going back upstairs to open the shop.

"Do you need something to eat?" asked Wyler, but received no response.

"How about some leftover pasta?" asked Wyler once more for assurance of Larkin's comfort before returning upstairs.

He said, "No," and he shook his head. "I'll take the tea."

"Okay. Jezalyn is coming down soon, so I'll put a new pot on upstairs and bring it down once it's ready."

"Alright, don't forget to find out about that myth."

***

Jezalyn returned to the shop after putting away her groceries and found Wyler behind the counter. "Hey, where is Ana? I wanted to thank her for taking me to the store with her."

"She left for work, but I am sure she was happy to let you tag along."

Jezalyn smiled. "What do you want me to do today?"

"Well, first we need to make you a schedule."

"Okay!" replied Jezalyn enthusiastically as she took a seat on one of the barstools behind the counter.

Pulling out a sheet of paper from underneath the counter, Wyler asked, "When do you have classes?"

She thought for a second and responded, "I have a morning class on Monday and Wednesday; a night class on Wednesday; and the rest are online classes, so they can be done whenever."

"Let's see where we can schedule you," he mumbled, as he drew the lines to make a weekly chart.

"How was the book I lent you?" asked Wyler marking big x's through the portions of the day that Jezalyn would be unavailable.

"It was good," she responded glancing around the room still trying to familiarize herself with the shop.

"What myth are you working on?"

She fidgeted a little, "Oh, I am still trying to decide, but right now I am examining the relationship between goddesses. I'll bring your book back down as soon as I get it done."

"No rush. That sounds interesting. Which goddesses are you considering?"

Just then, the electric kettle sounded and Jezalyn responded, "Athena and Medusa. Hey, can I make myself a cup of tea?"

Wyler, continuing to make the schedule, said, "Sure. While you're back there will you pour a cup for me?"

"Okay, with or without sugar?"

Without even glancing up he mumbled, "Um. . ., any flavor and add two teaspoons of sugar please."

Jezalyn sashayed into the stockroom, grabbed a can that read *Blackberry Sage: Tea for Wisdom,* and popped it open. After placing a tea bag in two nearby cups, she added hot water, but found the sugar jar still empty. Grabbing the newly purchased bag of sugar, Jezalyn lifted the sewn string and pulled. She failed at her attempt to rip off the top. Jezalyn, being unable to rip open the bag, scanned the area for some scissors. Spotting a small knife sitting on top the microwave, she gave up the scissor search and grabbed it. Jezalyn placed her right hand on the sugar pulling the tab up where she wanted to cut. Then taking the knife in her right hand she brought it to the lifted edge and created an opening. The toothed knife weaved back and forth. After a moment Jezalyn removed the knife to reveal only a small jagged tear. Exasperated at her lack of success, Jezalyn pulled the tab up once more, gripped the knife and forced the knife into the bag. Astonishingly, the blade glided through the sugar bag like a hot knife on butter. Jezalyn immediately clenched her teeth tight as she let the knife fall to the counter. All she could do for the first few seconds was stare down at the sliced tissue on her palm underneath her thumb area. Recovering quickly from the shock, Jezalyn gripped her bloody hand as she inched it to the faucet trying not to leave a trail of blood droplets all over the sugar-grained counter. As she turned on the water, she called for help.

In a blink of an eye Wyler was in the stockroom questioning her, "What's the matter? What happened?"

Embarrassed about the incident, Jezalyn simply lifted her hand and let the blood do the speaking.

Wyler dashed across the room grabbed her wrist and applied pressure. Now with compression firmly applied, he quickly led her to his sorting counter nearby where he placed a handkerchief over the gash. "Sit right here and hold this tight. I got something downstairs that'll stop the bleeding; I'll be right back."

Wyler returned to the sink, turned off the water, grabbed one of the cups of tea, and rushed downstairs. Once downstairs, he placed the tea soaked cup on the table and shouted, "Here is your tea," to Larkin, who still hadn't moved since his request. Stretching to snatch a small old worn black bag off the refrigerator, Wyler said, "I'll be back in a minute." And, before Larkin could get up or respond, Wyler was back up the stairs and out the door to treat Jezalyn's hand.

She slowly pulled back the blood-soaked handkerchief so that Wyler could get a good view of the cut. After examining the wound he said, "Well, the handkerchief makes it seem to be worse than it is. I am going to put this powder on; it will make the blood clot."

As Wyler shifted the powder unevenly over the wound, Jezalyn commented on his little black bag. "I love your bag; it has a worn look to it. I love antique things."

Without glancing up, he responded, "Yeah, me too. I acquired it some years back. I use it to store first aid equipment."

"Oh, it looks as if it's quite old. Do you know how old it is?"

Watching the powder absorb the blood, Jezalyn's observation made Wyler almost cringe as he began to recall something that was old and long forgotten. "Yes I do," replied Wyler.

Jezalyn's eyes sparkled. "Really! How old?"

"It dates back to the American Revolution era."

"Wow!" exclaimed Jezalyn, "That's old." Still overwhelmed with anxiety over her accident, Jezalyn babbled on. "Oh, how did you know it was from the American Revolution?"

"I had it authenticated by a specialist."

Being intrigued with old things herself she wanted to know more, so she asked, "Did the bag come with a story, when you bought it?"

Realizing Jezalyn was probably not going to give up until she discovered the bag's history, Wyler decided to tell her all that he knew. "The historian discovered that it had been passed down to a war surgeon's son."

Jezalyn eyes widened, and she mumbled, "He did?"

"Yes," replied Wyler. "It was at an early age when the son had to join his father on the battlefront. His father sent for him to assist with the suturing of wounds and the extraction of projectiles. After a few years, his father graduated him from being his simple assistant to an equal counterpart in the field of removing lead balls and sewing up soldiers himself. Unfortunately, General Charles Cornwallis of the British army had captured them at the battle of Charleston. Luckily for them, Cornwallis's surgeon got caught in the crossfire, so the General offered them a less restrictive lifestyle in exchange for their medical services. Preferring not to be prisoners of war, they agreed."

"On no," squeaked Jezalyn covering her mouth with her good hand. Before Wyler continued, he produced a

comforting smile to put her at ease. Once he saw the
tension in her face lessen, he reported:

"After the battle of Charlottesville, the son was left
with nothing but his father's little black medical bag. It was
not during the crackling roar of war that his father expired,
but after the sound of exploding earth and whistling orbs
gave way to the moans and wails of injured soldiers. The
day was waning, for dawn was soon setting. Fighting
extreme fatigue, his father, moving some wounded patients
into his medical tent, tripped and fell into the tip of a
bayonet. The surgeon's son ran to the aid of his father, but
discovered his efforts were useless when he heard the blood
gurgling in his father's throat as he removed the tip of the
blade. Still clinging to hope, the son applied pressure
against the wound as he heated the metal blade that
penetrated his father. Unfortunately, the searing of the
wound would not be enough to stop the blood from
entering his nicked lung and he died in his son's arms.

Before the death of his father, the surgeon's son had
only observed amputations. He held his ears to block out
the maddening blood curdling screams of the patients as the
cold jagged steel blade of the saw tore through the meaty
flesh of its victims. Eventually, after his father's death, he
had to put his entire training into action. Now as the head
surgeon, he found every amputation endless and hard to
stomach. He tried to pretend he was hacking off a piece of
beef or swine, but the vomiting still came as the saw
crunched against the bone, but after a while the sound
faded and the removal of a body part was done almost
effortlessly."

The word, "Ew!" escaped Jezalyn's lips, but Wyler
did not stop.

"By that time Cornwallis had fell at the battle of Yorktown, the new young surgeon gained skill in the world of war and survival before regaining his freedom and heroically setting off homeward, with nothing but a few biscuits and his father's black medical bag."

"That's an amazing story," declared Jezalyn. "You have yourself a real treasure; it should be in a museum or something."

"Maybe one day," replied Wyler mindlessly as he doctored Jezalyn's hand. A few minutes had passed following the application of the powder. Her hand had stopped bleeding. Wyler grabbed an alcohol swab, brushed over the cut lightly removing the blood clot residue. Once it was clean, he dug in his bag for a bandage. As he dressed the wound, Wyler thought, *I haven't needed my father's bag since . . .,*

Examining her doctored hand, she graciously said, "Thanks, Wyler, it looks like a professional patched me up."

Her sincerity cut off his thoughts. And, being quick of mind, Wyler devised a believable excuse for delivering such expert care. "Thanks, I took a first-aid class with Ana a few months back."

Scrutinizing over her damaged hand, mortification came over Jezalyn at the thought of her accident; she let out a little giggle. "I'll go clean up my mess."

Wyler nodded his head in agreement, as he tossed his first-aid equipment back into the bag.

Jezalyn, hand all bandaged, placed the knife and cup of tea in the sink, while Wyler retreated into the shop. She thought, *I'm such a moron*, as she emptied the now opened bag of sugar into the sugar canister before wiping down the counter.

Wyler heard the phrase "all clean" come from Jezalyn's voice as she snuck up behind him.

He turned and said, "Thanks! How is your hand doing?"

"It's throbbing a little, but other than that it's good."

Wyler handed her a slip of paper, "Here, I finished the schedule. Let me know if you see any problems?" She studied it, but found nothing wrong. Wyler continued, "Since you have tomorrow off, your first day will be Thursday."

An "Oh" escaped out of Jezalyn's mouth followed by, "So does that mean I am not working today? This schedule says I am supposed to work until seven tonight."

He flashed a smile, "No. I think that's enough sweat and blood out of you for one day."

Jezalyn, still feeling somewhat insecure, gave an uncomfortable nervous laugh, "Well, since you won't need me, I'll head up to my room and lay down for awhile."

"Okay, but if you need something else—even for your hand—I'll be in the stockroom."

Wyler entered the stockroom as Jezalyn departed in the direction of her apartment. He put up the few dishes Jezalyn had washed before returning downstairs. Immediately after placing his bag on top of the refrigerator, Wyler lowered his hands in time to see Larkin approaching him.

"Here, let me take that," said Wyler as he reached for Larkin's empty teacup.

"No. I got it." Larkin stepped to the sink and washed his teacup. "I think that was the best tea you ever made."

Wyler caught off guard, since he did not make it himself, was not sure what to say and changed the subject. "I asked Jezalyn what she was working on in her mythology class, and she said something about the relationship between Medusa and Athena."

A spark of curiosity flickered across Larkin's baby-blue eyes, "Really! That's interesting."

"I thought so, too. I am going to ask her more about it next time she comes down."

Larkin moseyed back to his resting area, lay down on the floor, propped his legs up on the sofa, and said, "I am feeling weary. I think I will rest awhile."

Wyler gazed at him for a moment contemplating, *Tired? Larkin is never tired. Depressed, deliberately reflective, but not tired.* Then, climbing the stairs back to his shop Wyler declared to himself, *There must be something afoot here.*

ChApCeR 4: Che SCORM...

EZALYN AWOKE IN the middle of the night not to the sound of roaring thunder or the thud of rain pounding on the roof and windowpanes, but to the stabbing pain in her hand. She pulled off the bandage and examined the cut that appeared to be turning bright pink. Her foot felt around for her slipper and, once found, she made her way to the bathroom. Jezalyn ran her hand under the water and searched through the medicine cabinet above the sink for something to aid her hand. At the back of the top shelf, she found a small bottle of peroxide and a butterfly bandage. Jezalyn watched the peroxide fizz and bubble up as she poured it into her palm. She placed the band aide over the cut only after the once bright pink tissue turned white.

With a newly bandaged palm, Jezalyn returned to her bedroom where she rummaged around in her purse for something, anything to take away the pulsating pain. She found a small cylindrical tub of ibuprofen, took two, and got back in bed. She checked her cell phone for the time and noticed she had a text message. It was from Blaise sent at 9:29 p.m. A smile crossed Jezalyn face as she read a message that superseded her last response by about an hour, "I have to go. Class is at 9 and I still need to study for chem test. Don't worry about the accident. Feel better and try to get some sleep." She responded to his text, "Sorry, I fell asleep, I hope you ace your test tomorrow," before replacing the phone back on the nightstand. She tossed and turned, but she could not fall sleep. The rain had turned to sleet and it sounded as if someone was outside throwing gravel at her window. Being unable to go back to sleep, she decided to work on her mythology report.

***

Downstairs Larkin sat up and scanned the pitch-black room with his sharp, cat like eyes. Rubbing at the stinging sensation in his right palm, he searched for something, anything that may have caused the pain. After discovering nothing crawling near and finding nothing visually wrong with his hand, he lay back down and tried to clear his mind. He could not concentrate. All he could hear was the sound of the rain. The rain pounded so clearly in his head, and he thought, *It sounds as if I were standing outside. Why is it so loud? What's going on with me? Maybe I just need some blood; it will help me get my bearings.* Larkin rushed to the fridge, without even an attempt to grab a cup, seized a bag of blood and drank it quickly. He let the empty bag drop in the sink, before returning to the living room, and sat down on the couch trying to clear his mind. The loud thudding of the rain seemed distant. The sensation in his palm was starting to wane. *Ah! This is much better,* he thought, but subsequently as the loud thudding fell into the distance it was over taken by the chattering of a voice.

It was female, *I cannot go back to sleep with this storm. Why does it have to be so loud? Oh, it's sleeting.*

Larkin leaped off the couch and thought, *The pain. The loudness of the storm. The voice in my head!*

"Whose blood did they give me?" Larkin wailed.

He paced back and forth and thought, *Calm down; they know that I can't drink a living human's blood. They know the thoughts and feelings of humans will transfer over to me, until their death.* His anger grew until the rage was uncontrollable; he darted toward Wyler and Ana's room. When he entered the room he heard, *Medusa was once a beautiful woman who was forcibly taken by the water god Poseidon in one of Athena's temples.*

Wyler raised his head, "Is everything alright, Larkin?"

The words continued to run in his head, *Athena, enraged from the disrespect in her temple, turned Medusa into a hideous monster. Medusa's gorgeous black curls turned to writhing black snakes, her teeth became like fangs, and her eyes turned any man that she gazed upon into stone.*

As the thoughts went on, Larkin just stood there unresponsive, *Poor Medusa! She was robbed of any chance at finding true love. Even if someone had overlooked the curse Athena put on her, she would never be able to gaze intimately into a man's eyes ever again.*

Wyler eased out of bed careful not to wake Ana and placed one hand on Larkin's shoulder. "Larkin! Larkin! Is everything …"

"Yes, Yes. I am fine. I thought I heard something that is all. I only came in to check out the noise."

"Oh, do you want me to go upstairs and check around?"

"No. There will be nothing there; it's only a storm."

Wyler, with an alarmed face, said, "I forgot about the storm. I hope Jezalyn is alright up there. I was supposed to tell her about the winter weather advisory; it called for freezing rain tonight." After a little silence, he mumbled to himself, "I should've gone up after the accident."

The small murmur did not pass Larkin's astute hearing, so he asked, without being able to hide the tension in his voice, "Accident! What Accident?"

With anxiety in his face and voice he replied, "She was making us some tea when she cut herself. Don't worry; there was no need for a paramedic or doctor to get involved."

An intrigued Larkin abruptly questioned, "Where did she cut herself?"

"On the palm. She couldn't get the sugar bag open or something. Do you think I should go check on her? See if she needs anything?"

Larkin turned to go out the door, "NO. She will be fine. Go back to bed. If she becomes distressed, I will hear it and let you know."

After pulling the door closed tightly behind him, Larkin lent against it as his mind investigated the facts. *The violent thudding in my head—a winter storm, pain in my hand—a cut, rambling of the Athena-Medusa scene playing out in my head—a mythology class. . .* His eyes widened as he proclaimed, "It's the new tenant."

Larkin examined his palm and rubbed at his imaginary injury. *She probably cut herself right here,* he concluded, before pacing back over to the couch to take a seat.

He was pondering as to why Wyler would let him drink of her blood. *Surely he could not have known about the blood or he would not have given it to me—or would he.* Larkin's thoughts were interrupted, yet again by the babbling of mythology. *Perseus handed Athena the decapitated head. . .*

***

Upstairs under a pile of blankets, Jezalyn was finishing her report, *After receiving the head, Athena mounted it to her shield and so ended the Athena-Medusa saga.* Glancing at the clock, Jezalyn could not believe she had finished; it had taken her most of the night to type it. With only three hours before time to get up, Jezalyn jumped out of bed, grabbed her bag and stuffed her computer into it. She told herself, *Ugh, only a few hours' sleep. I better set more than one alarm to get in bed or I'll never make it to class on time tomorrow.* So, without further delay she turned off the lights and climbed into bed. Closing her eyes, Jezalyn had one final thought, which was more of a wish, *If only this medicine could take away the embarrassment of my accident like it had the pain."*

CHAPTER 5: IT'S ONLY A BOOK

LARKIN PACED AROUND the shop, but he did not pay much attention to anything. His mind was more preoccupied with what to do about Jezalyn. Larkin stopped pacing when he recollected an Old Wives' Tale about the bonding curse. Long ago, an old friend told him, *Rulers once used vampiric bonds to deliver punishment to any traitor or villain who had escaped justice. It was said, soon after a vampire drank one drop of blood, they went on a hunting spree killing everything in their path trying to rid themselves of the incessant babbling. Death of the living being is the only way to break the curse.*

Larkin began pacing again as he thought about his new tenant and how her fate closely tied with the folk tale. He could now see how other vampires could become wild assassins if they had to endure every human thought, dream, or emotion. Although Jezalyn was not anyone's direct victim, an unusual chance binding might yet bring her to the same medieval fate.

The pacing ceased, when Larkin finally came to the conclusion that he did not want to hear and feel her every thought or emotion. But, as far as he knew there were only two options to stop the constant chatter that would soon consume him like a dog with a bone. The first and most obvious would be to kill her, and the last to convert her, for it was always about self-preservation with a vampire, so taking himself out never entered his mind. Slamming his fist into his hand, he declared, "I must break this bond and decide something soon!" Now, he stood frozen a moment debating whether to kill or change her, until he realized that he had stopped in the middle of the mythology section.

Dropping to his right knee, Larkin removed a thick book cleverly hidden out of sight behind two large dictionaries on the bottom shelf. The book that he held might have been golden once, but now looked to be more like a dirty copper. It had a tarnished silvery clasp that extended from around the back to the front center of the book. When Larkin placed his ring inside the elliptical center, it flung open. He pulled open the cover and exposed the book's hollow shell that hid away what seemed to be an old ragged manuscript bundled together with a piece of frayed twine. Larkin stuck his hand in the book shaped box to remove the collection, but halted as the grotesque expression of "Ugh!" was released in his psyche.

**

Jezalyn awoke to the sound of a powerful female voice singing her a sweet ballad. She mechanically rolled over and pressed the dismiss button to turn off the alarm on her cell phone. *Ugh, it's time to get up already! I should have stayed on campus. Well nothing I can do about it now. I suppose I should get up and turn off the other alarm clock before it goes off too,* Jezalyn thought as she got out of bed and stumbled over to the dresser across the room, but she found the alarm clock was not illuminated. *Damn, I forgot to set up the alarm clock. It's a good thing I set my phone.* She reached over to turn on the light switch so that she could plug up her clock, but the light did not come on. She flicked the switch up and down several times before she burst out, "Why me!?!" Leaving the switch up, she teetered over to the window and pulled up the blinds. *Wow! That's Beautiful!* she thought as she took in the scene; the trees greeted her with a bow as they folded over from the weight of the icy layers that formed on the oak leaves and pine needles overnight. The ground was paper white except for a few leaves that peeked out from underneath what appeared to be thin layer of snow.

Jezalyn grabbed her computer and retreated to her bed. "I shouldn't get my hopes up. . ." She logged onto the internet and went directly to the local news site, "Yes! There it is."

The news bulletin read, *Due to last night's freezing rain, several public schools and universities are closed in the following parishes. . .* Her heart leaped and she clasped her hands together in excitement. "Yes! My school is closed!" she proclaimed as she jumped up and down on the bed.

She plopped down on the bed so that she could continue reading the forecast:

> *There are widespread power outages and electricity crews have been fast at work trying to restore power since the rain let up. It is advised not to travel unless unavoidable. Several patches of ice remain unsalted throughout the city causing many road closures along the I-20 corridor. At this time, closures are ramps and bridges along I-49 and I-20, and the DOT asks that if you have to get out that you take extreme precaution on any small bridge or overpass.*

She slammed down the top of the computer in excitement as the phone rang and with a little grin she excitedly thought, *It's Blaise.*

"Hello."

"Hey, did you see school is canceled?"

"Yep, I just saw it on the net. What are you doing up so early? I thought you didn't have class until eleven today."

"I didn't. I was up for soccer practice, but it's canceled because the field is frozen. I was about to go back to bed, when I thought about you having to drive in. I figured I should try to warn you before you got all the way up here for nothing. "

"Thanks, Babe, but I'm sure it wouldn't have been for nothing."

"Yeah, I think we could have found something to preoccupy you with," he uttered with a sensual voice causing Jezalyn to release a short giggle, which he imagined was accompanied with a sweet, yet bashful smile.

"Um, yes. I'm sure you could," she replied.

He paused a bit, "Perhaps, a quick visit may be in order."

With all seriousness, Jezalyn ordered, "No. You are to stay home; it is too dangerous."

"Sometimes it's worth the risk," he responded, hoping to make her blush. Although he could not truly tell her composure, her little chortle was enough to content him.

"So, how is your hand?" he asked, not waiting for a verbal response to his previous statement.

"I woke up in the middle of the night and it was really throbbing, so I put some peroxide on it."

"That was smart; it will kill the infection."

"I hope so! Anyway, it's feeling much better. I am sorry that I fell asleep on you last night. I must have been super tired."

"It's okay. I needed to go study for my chem. test anyway, which was a waste since school is canceled. I guess it's a true snow day for me," he said as he released a rather loud chuckle.

She giggled alongside him, "Well, think of it as less to study later."

"Yeah, I suppose. Well, I am going to take a nap. I'll text you later to see what you're doing on this rare snow day."

A huge smiled crossed her face. "I know it never snows here. That's why it's so awesome, because it never sticks."

"Yeah, it took a while for me to get used to the warm winters here; I was used to twenty degree winters in Wisconsin."

"Burr," said Jezalyn, pretending to shiver at the thought of a winter colder than Louisiana's average forty-five, fifty. "That's too cold for me. I think the last time it was this cold was when I was seven; it snowed so much we built snowmen and made snow angles." After pausing for a minute she realized she was babbling, which she felt was too soon to do at this stage of their relationship, so she added rather briskly at the end of her last response, "Well, I will let you go so you can catch up on your sleep."

"Okay."

"Text me later," she added, as a confirmation of their future plan.

"Okay."

Following the hang-up, Jezalyn threw the phone on the bed. Her heart felt like it was about to burst as she did a little dance of excitement. She stopped in front of the window to observe once more the beauty of the scene that lay before her. Jezalyn thought, *Yes, No school today! And I am off of work! Hmm, what should I do? Maybe Ana will have a candle I can borrow.* Jezalyn pulled her hair back and was about to put on her slippers when, out the corner of her eye, she saw the mythology book she borrowed from Wyler poking out from under the bed. *I should return this*, thought Jezalyn scooping up the book.

***

"She is awake. . ." blurted out Larkin as the silence in his head was broken. After a few minutes of being made privy to her prattling, he found himself wishing Jezalyn was still asleep, for whilst she was asleep there was silence since she was not a dreamer. *If she only slept longer!* he thought, letting the book rest on the closest shelf. Suddenly, he felt an unrecognizable sensation. Clutching his chest, he blurted out, "What was that?" Initially, Larkin thought, *she must be in pain*; however, after a moment of reflection he concluded that it was emotional not physical. *No, not pain. Excitement! I almost mistook it for anxiety.* Taking a few steps, he thought, *Whoa—that was a rush. I haven't felt excitement in a long time.*

The thrill took Larkin by surprise, leaving him unaware of his location, until he heard Jezalyn's footsteps approaching. He darted past the counter and back into the underground apartment before Jezalyn could take another full step. Pressing his back hard against the apartment entrance, Larkin realized he left the memoir box open on the bookshelf. Tugging at his hair, he muttered, "Ah! I forgot to lock my memoirs."

***

Upon reaching the shop, Jezalyn proceeded over to the area where Wyler had retrieved her book. Jezalyn scanned the book titles until she came across a few that seemed to be in her book category. Using her left hand to sweep back an opening, she deposited her borrowed book between *Ancient Greek Playwrights* and *Greek Myth and Legends*. As she turned to leave, her shirtsleeve caught the edge of Larkin's wooden book that resembled a box, and it fell to the floor. A clatter arose from the open clasp as it hit the floor.

"What was that?" blurted out Jezalyn. Looking down in alarm, an "Oh" escaped out of her mouth. *I hope I didn't break it. Wyler will fire me! He will kill me then fire me.*

Jezalyn glanced around as she quickly picked up the book and examined it, "This looks really old." After inspecting the front and finding no damage, she flipped it over to check the back. With the book flipped upside down, the clasp hung down to the side. She released the left side to grasp the hanging clasp when the top flipped open and the bundled pages hit the floor. "Oh no! I did break it," she cried. Once she picked up the bundle, she examined the book trying to find a quick fix, and discovered with great relief that she had not broken it. Jezalyn had, however, found the book's secret. It was not a book, but a secret box disguised as a book. *This is cool. I wonder who this belonged to*, thought Jezalyn as she examined the somewhat tattered bundle for hints. She noticed that the paper was old and discolored as if someone had spilled coffee or tea over it. The pages were thin and tattered around the corners, which could easily cause the edges to crumble away if mishandled. Jezalyn noticed the font style, *I think these ink scribble marks are handwritten,* which led her to believe that she was holding either an extremely old book or someone's journal.

***

Larkin did an about face so that he could crack the door open with ease. He pressed his forehead against the door to peer out of the small crack that he made. *She found it! Maybe she will be uninterested and put it back—Oh, please let her put—*

His thought were interrupted, *It is hard to see what it's about in this dim light. Hmm–, Wyler did say I could read anything, so I will take it upstairs where I can see better.*

Larkin found himself enraged at his thoughts being interrupted again. *I must get rid of her. I cannot have her interrupting my thoughts all the time. I don't know what is worse the interruptions or her emotions.* The sensation quickly faded before he could act on it, and Larkin now cringed at the thought of his memoir being read by someone other than himself. He thought, *I have to get them back. . .,* but Jezalyn interrupted him again, *What was I thinking. I can't read in the dark.* In all the excitement of finding a unique piece of work, Jezalyn forgot to go ask Ana for a candle. Once Jezalyn gently placed the writings on her coffee table, she ran back down the stairs.

When he realized that Jezalyn was headed his way, Larkin blurted out, "Shit! Shit!" *She is coming down here. Where is she? Do I have time to sneak out and retrieve them? Think, Girl! Let me know where you are.* He heard footsteps approaching, so he eased the door shut and dashed into Wyler's room.

Larkin pulled Ana out of bed, "Ana, get up. Jezalyn's at the door and she wants to borrow a candle. Give her the candle and tell her you are going back to bed. Say whatever it takes to get rid of her quickly!"

"A candle?"

"Yes. Here give her this one." Larkin grabbed a pink candle off the nightstand and pushed it into Ana's hand.

Ana, still half-asleep, mumbled something to the effect, "But this is my favorite—"

Larkin cut her off, "Just give her the damn candle."

Ana, completely awakened by his tone, took the candle, rushed to the door, and opened it.

Jezalyn stood in front of Wyler and Ana's apartment door with her fist raised about to knock when it opened. Caught by surprise and with her hand still slightly raised, Jezalyn uttered, "Um, hi. The lights are out and I was wondering if you have a candle that I could borrow."

Extending the candle toward her, Ana said, "I guess great minds think alike. I was just on my way to check on you. You saved me a trip—take this one." Jezalyn thanked Ana as she took the candle and proceeded to tell her about the weather report. Ana, trying to follow Larkin's directions said, "You're welcome. Well, now that you have the candle, I think I'll go back to bed."

"Okay. Well, my classes were canceled because of the weather. I just love snow days." Ana nodded, and as Jezalyn turned to leave she heard the door bang shut.

Ana returned to the bedroom, where she found Larkin and Wyler whispering to each other. Ana sat down on the bed holding her head submissively down. "I gave her the candle like you requested. I am sorry I questioned you earlier; I was half asleep."

Larkin said nothing, but glowered at Wyler. They both got up to leave the room. Ana observed their behavior. She had never seen Larkin this unnerved since the mishap with the last tenant. Her curiosity got the better of her, so she dared to ask, "What's going on? Larkin, is everything all right?"

They stopped, turned, and glared at her. After a moment's pause Wyler said, "We might as well tell her. She is going to find out eventually."

Larkin contemplated a moment more and spoke, "I can hear and feel Jezalyn."

"How is that possible?" and before Wyler could respond to his wife's alarm she blurted out, "Unless you drank her blood! When—Why—You drank her blood!"

Wyler swallowed hard before he responded, "Bunny, don't get mad, but we had a little accident yesterday."

Ana stood up and retorted, "What accident? Tell me what happened!"

Knowing Wyler would try to calm her before relating the story, Larkin took over and gave her a rundown of events so that he could get back to recovering his book.

"Wyler let Jezalyn make me a cup of tea. She cut her hand opening the sugar bag and some of the blood must have dropped into the cup. Not realizing that blood may have dripped in the cup, he brought the tea down to me. Now I'm connected to Jezalyn because I drank the blood-spiked tea. However, my main concern at the moment is not the incident that bonds her every thought and emotion to me, but my memoir she found and just brought back to her room to read."

"Oh, my giddy aunt! How did she get your memoir?" asked Ana as if that now took precedence over the inevitable outcome of Larkin having drunk her blood.

Growing irritated, Larkin answered, "It's unimportant how she got it. The important thing is to get it back—" Stopping abruptly, he mentally finished his thought, *Because it holds my dearest and darkest secrets.*

"Don't worry; she will probably think it's an old book. We should just relax. I don't think we should make this into that big of a deal," retorted Ana.

Wyler, seeing Larkin aggravated with the simple dismissal of the situation, told his wife, "What if she figures out it is a real journal? Do you know what kind of problems it could cause for us?"

Careful not to betray his own insecurities, Larkin interjected the simplest explanation, "I need it back before she discovers vampires are real."

It finally dawned on Ana what was at stake and she began to think of a plan to help reunite Larkin with his memoir. Larkin was having a hard time coming up with an effective plan, since Jezalyn's thoughts were still interrupting his.

*** *

Jezalyn was overjoyed to find the stove was gas and not electric. She made herself a cup of hot tea to drink before sitting down to read. Larkin, with concern in his voice, announced, "She's finished making her tea and is about to sit down to read."

Ana blurted out, "I got it! One of us can sneak upstairs and grab it when she comes down for work."

Wyler shaking his head said, "Nope. That won't work. She is off today." After a short pause, Wyler continued, "How about this? Larkin, you're bound to Jezalyn, which allows you to keep track of her thoughts, right? If you follow her progression, we will find out what type of book she thinks she is reading."

Ana responded, "Yeah, that's a good idea. What do you think, Larkin?"

Larkin stared at them, "Well, it's not like her thoughts are going to go away—unless she miraculously dies."

Wyler glanced over, "Well that's the other option. We could either kill or turn her. One or the other will have to take place eventually. Which one would you prefer?" Although the question 'which one you prefer' slipped out of Wyler's mouth with ease, he cringed inside. Wyler hated the thought of having to be so callous, but as Larkin's Keeper it was his job to provide all the options and follow through with whatever Larkin would decide.

However, Ana, unlike her husband, was unable to contain her emotion, and distressed by the nature of the sudden change in topic, she interjected, "She has family that would come searching for her."

Wyler said, "So did Julius, but we've managed to evade that problem and remain here at home."

"That's true," said Larkin with a smirk.

Wyler made a grim face, ready to have the unpleasant situation behind him, he asked, "So which will it be—immediate death or death for eternity?"

Larkin did not respond right away. He placed his hands on his head and rubbed his temples trying to think clearly. Only one thought came to mind, *I should have snapped her neck when I realized it was her blood that I consumed.* Without removing his hands he finally said, "I am not quite sure. First, let's get the book back. I will decide what to do with her afterwards." He paused a moment before ordering, "Just go back to bed. I will monitor her thoughts."

Ana and Wyler went back to bed as Larkin returned to his bed, or rather his usual resting spot on the living room floor. Larkin propped up his feet on the couch, closed his eyes, and listened to Jezalyn's voice echoing in his head.

Chapter 6: The Memoir

JEZALYN TOOK A of her hot tea as she sat down on the worn couch; it was surprisingly more comfortable than it looked. She carefully untied the frayed twine and lightly tossed it to the other side of the couch. She gently laid the bundle on the cushion next to her, picked up the first page, and began to read.

***

After leaving Wyler and Ana in the bedroom, Larkin returned to his normal spot on the floor, propped his feet on the couch, closed his eyes, and listened to Jezalyn's voice as it echoed in his head.

It was during the War of the Roses that we met her. She was the most beautiful creature I ever beheld. She had long, wavy auburn hair that fell against her heart shaped face and flowed over her shoulders and down her back. Her honeyed skin set off the most stunning emerald eyes that I had ever seen on a woman. I was so enamored by the exquisiteness of her beauty that I would do anything that she asked of me, so when she asked me to become her Keeper I did not refuse. I gladly gave my life and soul to make sure she was not harmed or presumed to be a witch.

***

Jezalyn could not make out the next few paragraphs, so she put the page down and picked up the next one as she thought, *I wonder, what a Keeper is? And, is she really a witch?*

***

Larkin never heard anyone relate his most confidential personal feelings. "Just keep reading about my once beloved and you will find out," he mumbled answering her question. Soon, the sound of Jezalyn's voice returned.

My brother returned home and discovered her. He was about to turn me in for harboring what he thought was a witch, but before he could, I placed a small seed of doubt in his mind. Not wanting to falsely accuse his own brother, he agreed to go down and meet Isadora in person. He introduced himself to her as a distant relation. He did not give his name, Theron Drythe, in case she should turn out to be a witch and later report, out of anger, against him in court. Either way he found her as beautiful as I had, so he decided to devote himself to keeping her safe. Every morning she brought us a special tea. She said the elixir had magical abilities, like the beloved fountain of youth, that would not stop us from aging, but make us age more slowly. We aged only one year for every ten as long as we drank at least a sip or two of the special tea every day. Life as a Keeper was thrilling, for every day was met with the sweetness of sustainable youth. It was within a short period of time that my devotions turned to tender admiration, but I was in no hurry to secure her affections since I now had time on my side. I was more subtle with my actions of love, while my brother was more forceful at declaring his.

***

Jezalyn soon found herself at the end of the page. *I wonder who she will choose,* she thought as she eagerly scooped up the next page and continued to read.

I brought her flowers today. They were not her favorite flowers, because spider lilies are not in season. I gathered ordinary lilies, placed spiders on them, *and left them on her little table while she was out. When she returned to her room, they were the first thing she noticed. I watched her reaction from the window as she giggled and smiled at the token.*

***

Jezalyn paused and Larkin realized that he was holding his breath and his heart was pounding. The tension in his throat seemed to move to his stomach, but he was able to dismiss it with the sound of Jezalyn's voice, though not for long, for Jezalyn was about to reveal the first reassurance Larkin ever received from the woman he most ardently admired.

When I went to bed that night I found a folded handkerchief under my pillow. Once unfolded, it revealed the impression of red lips. I lay there with it clutched to my chest dreaming of what it would be like for her lips to be upon mine.

***

She paused again and Larkin felt his heart pound and his breath quicken. He could feel a pressure building in his throat and the pit of his stomach, a familiar but bittersweet sensation. *Oh, please let her tire of these recollections. They are resurfacing too many old feelings that I thought were dead and buried. . .* and his plea was unheard, for her thoughts once again interrupted his. Larkin soon realized her thoughts were of him and his brother. He listened to her analyze the recollections of his personal journal. Jezalyn thought, *I knew it. I would have gone for the more subtle one also, who wants someone forceful and full of themselves. People like that feel they are more deserving, so they just take, take, take, and never give.*

Suddenly a flood of nostalgia washed over him as he remembered the sweet tokens of love that passed between them, time seemed to intensify their love. He also recollected the first time he stole a kiss; they were outside in a grove picking berries in the moonlight. He felt the warmth of the moonlight as it glimmered over her face when his lips touched hers for the first time. After this, he could only conclude that his feelings were unmistakable in spite of the expanse of time since his beloved Isadora first awakened his emotions.

***

Jezalyn's cell phone rang, so she set down the page and ran into the bedroom to answer it. "Hello. Hi, Grandpa. How are you this morning?"

"I am good. I saw there was bad weather up that way last night. Are you alright up there?" he questioned. Jezalyn peered out the window and took in the picturesque scene once again. Her thoughts were interrupted by her grandpa's voice, "Hey! I said is everything okay up there?"

"Yes! Don't worry, Grandpa, I am fine. It snowed last night, and the ice covered trees greeted me with a bow, so I bowed right back."

"Oh. Well, do not get out on the road in these conditions," cautioned her grandfather as he always had, for he was the most protective guardian one had ever known.

Jezalyn thought, *He hears nothing about what interests me. He has a one-track mind that is always concerned with my safety. As much as I love him, I wish he would not worry so much and listen to me when I speak. I am an adult now,* and with that final thought, she responded with a sigh "I won't. School is closed, so I am staying in today."

"Good, I—"

The phone vibrated against her head, from a text message, drew her attention away from what her grandpa was telling her. She broke in and said, "Hey, grandpa don't worry I am staying in I promise, but I have to go. I am going downstairs to see if Ana has a candle I can borrow."

"Okay. Call me if you need something, or if you go somewhere."

"Okay, I will." Next, she said, "Bye, Grandpa," and hung up the phone as he returned her goodbye.

She quickly opened the message; it was from Blaise. "I tried to go back to sleep, but I couldn't. What you doing?"

She typed back, "Just talked to Grandpa and now about to read a book from the bookstore."

After a few minutes, she got another message that read, "Oh, ok—text me when you're done."

Torn between reading the journal and talking to Blaise, she decided it would be a good thing not to be readily available all the time, so she chose to read the book and responded back. "Ok, ttyl".

***

Larkin listened intently to Jezalyn's conversation. A smile broke out as she described the scene outside. His own thoughts took over and consumed his mind; *She sees the loveliness in things that most would only presume to be ordinary. I don't believe anyone else would have greeted the trees back either,* he thought. Then as if she had needed a defense for her way of thinking, Larkin continued to make a case in his head for her. *Besides, most people would walk by without ever observing any part of their surroundings. I myself see only slumped over trees where she sees them bowing gracefully toward her.* The wave of nostalgia returned as he thought about her perspective and presumable innocence. It was afterwards that he realized the old familiar sensation, almost painful, but pleasantly so were not his old feelings reemerging, but must belong if not to him then to Jezalyn. He assumed, *She must have been flooded with emotions, or was it affection, as she read my memoirs,* but before he could contemplate his new declaration, he heard her. *She is reading again. Wait—she must have flipped to the center. Oh no! She is about to read one of my secrets.*

Her voice rang in his head. . . *I have changed. . . I do not know how. Isadora said that the only way that someone could turn into a vampire is to be drained almost to the point of death at which point they must be replenished with her blood. I was killed trying to protect her from a witch hunter who was trying to capture and place her on trial. When I fell down, I saw my brother*

*pushing her into the forest. I awoke in a
shallow grave and no one was in sight.*

Larkin was not quite sure he wanted to know
Jezalyn's reaction, so he tried to block her thoughts but his
efforts were useless. *Vampire! Hmm, I wonder if it
represents the animalistic battle between the two brothers
for her love. On the other hand, could it represent the lust
that humans have; it consumes their very existence, thus
making them entwine and destined to become one.* He
listened as she abandoned the vampire analysis and fixated
on what she deemed the most heart-breaking portion of the
story. *Pushing her! She did not want to leave him,
especially since she had not turned him to be her
companion yet. I wonder if vampires get heartbroken—that
is a silly notion. I don't believe I would be able to watch the
love of my life die before my eyes. I would have struggled
to be removed too.*

***

Jezalyn was finishing her thoughts, when she
glanced over and noticed the time. *Where did the morning
go? I need to work on my homework, so I guess I will have
to wait until later to find out if he goes searching for her.*
She carefully gathered the papers up, deposited them back
in the box, and brought them into her bedroom where she
placed them onto her dresser. After setting the memoir
aside, Jezalyn grabbed her bag before returning to the
living room where she commenced to toil away on her
assignments.

***

As Jezalyn sat on her couch doing her homework, across
the world a man sat on a ten-foot throne shrouded deep
within the Carpathian Mountains near the crumbling ruins

of a stone grotto that overlooked a misty wooded valley. The medley of brooks, which sparkled as the water glided over and around old stone boulders, echoed through the valley. He found himself paralyzed with emotion and finally released a sinister snarl accompanied by a laugh as he forcefully proclaimed, "I have found you at last—I knew you weren't dead."

ᚲ ᚺ ᚪ ᛈ ᛏ ᛖ ᚱ 7: ᚈ ᚺ ᛖ ᛁ ᚾ ᛏ ᚱ ᛟ ᛞ ᚢ ᚲ ᛏ ᛁ ᛟ ᚾ

T HE FOLLOWING DAY Wyler awoke to emptiness and the sound of nothingness. His mind was usually engaged in the daily duties of being a keeper, shop owner, and husband. He frequently awoke with a busy mind that generally made lists for the day, but today there was nothing. Wyler's mind was not even plotting or scheming, considering yesterday's events. Feeling unburdened by his daily routines he reached over to grab Ana, but got nothing but pillow. A usually clear-headed Wyler felt out of sorts without Ana by his side. He got dressed and searched for her but only found Larkin in the kitchen fixing a cup of blood.

True to form and duty, Wyler offered to serve him. "Hey, Larkin. Let me help you with that."

"That's okay. I got it. I also fixed you a cup of tea," said Larkin as he extended the cup of tea toward Wyler.

He took the cup and said, "Thanks. Have you seen Ana?"

"She left for work already. She took her tea with her."

Ana's whereabouts caught Wyler by surprise, thus choking himself on a swallow of tea. After he caught his breath from all the coughing he exclaimed, "Work!" and thought, *It's unlike her not to wake me before leaving for work.*

Larkin pointed toward the refrigerator while he took a sip of blood. As the cup left his lips, he finally said, "She left a message for you. It's over there."

Without hesitation, Wyler reached around Larkin to pluck the folded note off the refrigerator after he sat his cup down on the counter. He instantly unfolded a piece of light pink stationery paper. Once he opened the paper, it revealed tiny pink flowers etched in a black border around Ana's beautiful handwriting. Wyler did not read the note aloud but merely smiled as he read the following words:

Good Morning My Love,

I hope you're not too disappointed at me for not waking you before I left. You were sleeping so peacefully.

The clinic called this morning. They were in desperate need for me to come in a couple hours early. Please don't worry. I promise I won't be doing any in home care unless the road conditions are completely safe.

Also with last night's storm, I might have to work a double. If so, I will abide this dismal time without you with daydreams until I can find myself back into your loving arms. I will miss you like the grass misses the dew in the late summer.

I will call you on my first break.
Until then —
I am forever yours,
Your loving bunny —

ANA

As Wyler closed the note, he jubilantly looked over at Larkin with a beaming grin and asked, "Did you figure out what to do with Jezalyn yet?"

Larkin cut his eyes upwards toward him and responded, "No."

Wyler reached for his cup of tea and said, "Jezalyn has to work today. I will ask her to make tea and while she is busy I will sneak upstairs and get your memoir back." All he heard was the sound of water as he thought, *Should I rephrase it as a question or just wait for a response?*

"No! Let her keep it," was the reply Larkin gave after he finished washing his favorite mug.

With a confused expression, Wyler stated, "I thought you wanted it back as soon as possible."

"I did, but it's a little too late now." Larkin explained to Wyler that Jezalyn had read the vampire parts, but he was still unsure if she thought his memoir was a work of fiction or nonfiction. Larkin conveyed the importance of his need to know how she perceived the writing, so he instructed Wyler to inquire about the memoir without directly inquiring about it. Larkin noticed a blank expression on Wyler's face, so he continued with examples as to how he could complete his task. He told him that the key was to create conversation, by asking her something as simple as, "Did you find the myth book useful; she returned your book so ask if she found anything else to read. Be creative if you have to."

Moving to the sink to wash is cup, Wyler said, "Okay. I scheduled her to work in half an hour. I will go ahead upstairs and prepare to open the store, after I clean my cup."

Larkin extended his hand to take the cup. "I will do it for you. Go ahead and open the shop."

Wyler gave him the cup and left the apartment. He had rounded the stockroom door when he caught a slight glimpse of a figure out of the corner of his eye. He immediately gasped as he reached for a handmade baseball bat.

The figure heard the gasp and immediately spoke out, "It's me."

Wyler inhaled deeply as his eyes fixed on Jezalyn's familiar face. Jezalyn had reported for duty before her scheduled time. He guessed she was eager to make a good impression on her first official day on the job. Loosening his grip on his wooden weapon, Wyler said, "I am sorry about that. You startled me for a second. I was not expecting you for a bit. If you ever need to defend yourself, you know where the bat is now. Just grab it."

"I didn't mean to startle you, I thought you might need some help this morning," taking note of where he placed the bat as she responded.

Wyler directed her to shadow him as he dictated the morning procedures for getting the shop ready to open. As they wandered around the shop he nervously thought, *Now would be a good time to ask about the memoir, but how. Maybe I will think of something. . .*

Jezalyn disrupted his thoughts, "I returned the book you loaned me the other day."

Wyler smiled and thought, *Yes, she is making this easy for me.*

Nervously flicking her nail, she asked, "Um, Wyler. How many books can I borrow at a time?"

Without hesitation he replied, "Two or three. Do you need some more for your report?"

"I was, um, wondering if you had a book on the War of the Roses."

"The War of the Roses!"

She fidgeted again as she replied, "Yeah, I read something that mentioned it, so I thought it would be interesting to learn a little more about it."

"Oh! Well, it is time to open. Go get the key out of the cash register and unlock the door. I will go in the back and see what I can find. It might take a minute. Can you man the front desk until I get back?" She nodded, and they strolled toward the register to retrieve the key. Once they reached the counter, she walked over to the register and he walked into the stockroom. He waited for her to start toward the door before he returned to the apartment to consult with Larkin.

Wyler entered the apartment and found Larkin at the kitchen table. "Larkin! I don't know what to do."

"I know; I heard her thoughts."

"What should I do? Give her a history book or go get your memoir?"

Larkin stood up. "No! Leave the memoir. Here is what we are going to do. You are going to go find a history book that mentions the War of the Roses. Tell her to take it upstairs so that it isn't lost or damaged. While she is upstairs, I am going to come up to the shop."

Wyler's mouth dropped open from shock, "You are going to what!?!"

Putting his hand on Wyler's shoulder, he repeated himself, "I am going upstairs to the shop." Then he continued, "You are going to introduce me to her as your particular friend or distant relative. I will be visiting and staying with you for awhile."

Still astounded at Larkin's plan, all Wyler could do was nod his head in compliance. Larkin gave him a gesture of dismissal, so he returned to the shop. Wyler promenaded over to a stack of books, pulled out a book about history, and did as Larkin directed. He returned to Jezalyn, handed her the book, and requested that she bring it upstairs for safekeeping. Jezalyn glowed with excitement as she returned to her apartment with the book.

While she was upstairs putting the book away, Larkin snuck upstairs and browsed the antique section. He instructed Wyler to do whatever it took to show her into the antiques where they would conveniently run into each other.

Although it was not Wyler's place to question Larkin, he felt as his Keeper that he needed to make sure Larkin was not making decisions that would endanger his safety. "Are you sure you want to do this? I really don't think this is a very good idea."

"Yes! Now go. She is on her way down."

Wyler obediently rushed to a cart that already had a few items on it and watched as Jezalyn walk up to him, "Thanks again, Wyler. I can't wait to read that book."

"You're welcome. Here come help me put some of the books out, so you will be aware where to find each genre."

"Okay," said Jezalyn following close behind stopping at a nearby shelf to put away a few books.

"Good, it looks like you are becoming familiar where each genre is located," said Wyler, after noticing Jezalyn took a few books off the cart and placed them in their proper places without being prompted.

"Almost," responded Jezalyn somewhat nervously. She did not want to give Wyler the impression that she was a slow learner, yet she comforted herself with his comment and the knowledge that it was still only her first day. She watched as Wyler unexpectedly broke his own rule and marched up to a customer. *What should I do? Should I follow him, but he said don't bother customers. Is this a test? I don't want to fail and get fired on my first day. Oh, but what if it was not a test and I was supposed to. . .* She fretted even as Wyler waving her over, *Oh no he looks concerned. Did I just fail?* Jezalyn pushed her thoughts to the back of her mind as she proceeded toward them. She was only several feet away when she saw the man whisper something to Wyler, who smiled. Her nerves eased as she neared them and Wyler's expression of concern still remained.

***

Wyler had walked over to Larkin, who was grinning. He turned to introduce them but noticed Jezalyn did not follow him. "Why did she not follow me? And what's up with the grin."

He let out a laugh and said, "She is following your directions not to bother customers."

"Oh," replied Wyler.

"Well don't just stand there. Wave her over."

Wyler waved her over without remembering to ask Larkin what introductory name he wanted.

Larkin leaned over and said, "Smile."

Wyler smiled, but it was too late to mention something to Larkin about it, because Jezalyn was within ear distance. He extended his arm toward Jezalyn and said, "This is Jezalyn. She is my new clerk and tenant." He swung it toward Larkin, "And this is. . ."

After a moment's pause, Larkin elbowed Wyler playfully and waved his hand in a friendly manner toward her, "Hi! My name is Larkin and as you can see my not so good friend over here has forgotten my name already."

Jezalyn slightly lifted her hand as she giggled about the comment. "Hi. It's nice to meet you."

Wyler tried to recover his blunder with a playful remark, "Oh, friend, I could never forget you. I was shocked to see you standing in the middle of my shop that's all. Jezalyn, he is going to be visiting with us for awhile."

"Oh."

Wyler turned to Larkin and said, "Would you like a tour of the shop?"

Before he could nod his head yes Jezalyn asked, "Do you need me to get his bags while you're showing him around?"

Without missing a beat or even a slight flinch as he spoke, Wyler quickly responded, "No! It would be ungentlemanly of me to let you carry in his bags. Could you show him around, while I grab them?" and without a response, he turned to ask Larkin where his bags were.

Larkin knew he had no bags, but responded in the same steady tone Wyler had. "Oh, they're right outside the door. I travel light, so I can get them later."

Jezalyn ogled him in alarm. "Aren't you scared someone will steal your stuff?" she asked.

Larkin cracked a smile and said, "Not really. This is a small town; nothing scandalous ever happens in a small town. Besides, there was a cop sitting next door."

Wyler observed them a moment before shaking his head in amazement at how well they were getting along. "Jezalyn, you show him the rest of the store and stockroom. I will get his things."

Wyler dashed off as she said flipping her hand out to the side, "Well, this is the antique section."

Larkin watched Wyler sprint toward the front door, so he pointed across the room to a small nook area and asked, "What is that over there?"

Jezalyn had never been to that section, so she responded, "I don't know. Let's go check it out." They passed by Wyler giving him an opportunity to grab Larkin's fictional bags and start toward the underground apartment.

By the time, they reached the stockroom entrance Wyler was waiting for them. "I placed your bags downstairs. What do you think about the shop?"

"It is quaint and organized."

Wyler laughed, "You might not want to go into the stockroom then." Turning toward his employee, he said, "Thank you, Jezalyn. Can you attend the shop alone while I show him where he will be staying?"

She nodded as the word "sure," escaped her throat as she took a seat on a little, wooden stool behind the counter.

They walked off side by side; Wyler slanted slightly close to Larkin and whispered, "I can't believe you made me do that. You know Ana's gonna flip when I tell her this."

He gave a chuckle as he responded, "Well, at least I haven't eaten her yet. Ana will be happy to hear that."

Chapter 8: Checking In

YLER WAS AT a loss to what he might tell Ana. He only knew he was happy she was not at home, because he knew she would be overly concerned about Larkin introducing himself to Jezalyn. As Wyler showed Larkin to the apartment all he could think was, *How do I tell her?* He mindlessly closed the door behind them as they entered. Wyler was so distracted that he had not noticed Larkin staring at him.

"Wyler." Larkin waited for him to respond, but he did not. "Wyler!"

Although Larkin's final exclamation caught his attention, Wyler responded lethargically and mechanically, "Hmm, Can I get you something, Larkin?"

"No, nothing. Stop obsessing—the situation is controllable."

"I know it is, I'm sure you'll figure out something with Jezalyn."

"Then what is bothering you?"

He took a deep breath before releasing his anxiety. "It's Ana. I don't know how to tell her about the new situation. She is already uneasy; for she is scared you'll choose to have her killed. They spent some time together the other day, and she seems to be quite fond of her. Anyway, the news of you introducing yourself to Jezalyn is only going to agitate her further."

"I wouldn't worry. She didn't have a problem with the Julius situation in the end."

The words, "I know" slipped out of Wyler's mouth as the phone began to ring.

Larkin, being closer, answered and held the receiver out to Wyler, while he mouth the words "it's her" with a rather smug smirk that he had not even tried to hide.

Gripping the phone tightly as he brought it to his ear, Wyler camouflaged his tension with a perky greeting. "Hi, Bunny. How is your day going?" As the conversation ensued, Larkin snapped his fingers to get Wyler's attention before pointing toward the door. Wyler shook his head and watched Larkin hurry out the door that led back to the shop.

Ana's voice broke his stare, "What are you and Larkin doing today?"

Unmasked anxiety entered his voice, "Oh, nothing."

Noticing her husband's nervous tone, she prodded, "That doesn't sound like nothing."

"Well, I think it would be better to discuss this when you come home."

"No! I want to discuss it now. Tell me what is going on over there." Wyler unfolded the morning's events to her trying to downplay Larkin's decision to introduce himself to Jezalyn. Before Wyler's wife could freak out, he quickly explained Jezalyn was under the impression that Larkin was an old friend who would be staying with them for awhile. Although she had quietly listened to her husband relate the incident, but when he paused for a moment, Ana's sense of calamity fade as a gritting response rang in his ear. "He did what? Why?"

"I don't know. I expressed our concern, but he told me not to worry; it was all under control. He must still be trying to decide what to do with her."

"That is why I called. I thought of a plan to get us out of this situation without Jezalyn having to die."

"You did!" exclaimed Wyler being caught off guard by his wife's proactive measures to keep Jezalyn out of harm's way.

"Don't say no until you hear me out."

"Okay. What is it?"

"What if we turn her into a Keeper? I think she could be helpful with Julius and we can go back to aiding only one vampire. And, the best part is she won't have to die. "

"I don't think that will work," replied Wyler.

"Why not? All we have to do is give her one of our cups of special tea," countered Ana.

"It's not that simple, my dear."

"Why not? All I had to do was drink! Didn't you?"

Wyler made no response as he pondered Ana's later question and the event that led to his present position as Larkin's Keeper:

Wyler's release from General Cornwallis was not the last time he would ever use his medical skills as he had hoped. Many battles ensued between patriot-loyalist mercenaries. He patched up the injured, regardless of distinction, for food and shelter before continuing southward. As he traveled closer to home, he encountered several brutal aftermaths. On one occasion, after stitching up bullet holes and bayonet injuries, he took lodging at a nearby abandoned house. He was exhausted from the sweltering heat, arduous amputations, and disheartening deaths. He did not notice the stench of blood that lingered on him as he curled up on an old porch swing that now sat in what once appeared to be a grand sitting room.

After a few hours, he awoke to find a tall figure lingering over him. He jumped back and exclaimed, "What do you want? Who are you?"

"A stray musket ball hit me. I can't reach it; it's lodged in-between my shoulders. I need you to remove it," requested the stranger.

Wyler had enough experience patching up soldiers to grant his request, so he grabbed his bag and silently walked into the kitchen. "Lie down," demanded the surgeon as he ran out the back to pump a pail of water. Without hesitation, the stranger did as he requested. Wyler returned to find him shirtless lying on his stomach. A short candle flickered in the dark reflecting a long image of a small knife and a pair of long tong-like tweezers moving towards the convalescent's back.

"You might want to bear down on something," insisted Wyler as he prepared to open the wound.

"Just get on with it," replied the patient without hesitation.

After making a larger incision directly over the hole where the bullet had entered, the stranger did not cry out. He only made a few grunting sounds as Wyler took his fingers and pulled against the sliced tissue to widen the hole. As he dug between his shoulder blades searching for the metal ball, Wyler thought, *I have never seen so much blood.* He poured some water onto his back so that he could get a better view to insert the tweezers and removed the bullet.

Once the bullet was removed, he placed an old dirty rag on the wound and threaded a needle. The rag was quickly saturated and Wyler was getting nervous that he might soon lose his patient from exsanguination. With his needle now threaded, he lifted the rag and blood gushed everywhere. He quickly clenched his teeth down on the threaded needle and gripped the separated skin closed with both hands.

The patient heard his surgeon's breaths become short and fast, so he spoke. "Calm down. Take a deep breath. You're almost done. You already got the ball out; I felt it leave my body. All you have to do is suture it up."

Through his clenched teeth Wyler muttered, "It's just so much blood. I can't see where to stitch it up." Wyler stood there as he thought, *I need another set of hands.* The patient tried to get up. "Don't move or you'll bleed to death!"

He laughed, but stood up any way. He stood with his back to Wyler, who still gripped the wound closed. "Listen, you will hand me a bowl of water and I will pour it down my back. Once the blood clears start stitching it closed."

"You pouring water would help, but I can't see to stitch from this angle."

The patient leaned forward, placed his elbows on the table, and said, "Can you see now?"

Wyler moved to the left side of the injured man and said, "Yes!" He handed the stranger a bowl to dip into the bucket of water, which now sat directly under the patient. "Quick, throw some water over your shoulder." It only took a few scoops of water gliding over his back to wash away enough blood to allow the procedure to continue. The stranger remained motionless as his bent torso dripped blood and water. As his surgeon stitched, he concentrated on the blood rolling around his ribs into the center of his chest before dripping into the almost empty pail of water.

Once his patient's wound was completely closed, he stepped back and wiped the sweat from his brow leaving a bloody mark against his forehead. Completely in awe of the strangers awareness, he stumbled back to take a seat on an old, flimsy three-legged chair. Exhaling deeply, Wyler said, "It's closed, but you lost a lot of blood. You should rest and pray that you make it through the night."

The unconcerned patient made no reference to the concerns, but instead gave a simple, "Thank you" as he put on his blood stained shirt.

"You-'re" he stuttered, trying to swallow hard so that he could finish his salutation, "welcome. Hand me a bowl of water; my mouth is dry."

The patient made a repugnant face and said, "I think some of my blood dripped in there."

He extended his hand, "I just need a sip. A little blood won't hurt."

The patient smiled at him brazenly, scooped the bowl into the water pail, and handed it over to him. He cradled the bowl with his blood-covered hands and gulped down the rose-tainted water. After several gulps, he inhaled deeply as he raised his head. "Thanks, so what is your name soldier?"

"Larkin Drythe; I am not a soldier."

He stood up and trudged off. "I'm Wyler," he uttered, heading back to his place of slumber.

***

After listening to a long pause, Ana finally said, "If it worked for us, then why would it not work for her?" Her question broke his daydreaming. And, in a somewhat inattentive moment Wyler asked his wife to repeat herself. With annoyance in her voice she granted his request, "I said, if the special tea worked for me, then why won't it work for her?"

"Becoming a Keeper has rules just as vampires do."

"What rules? All Larkin has to do is drink until the point of death and replenish the depleted body. It's kind of simple to turn someone into a vampire, much like drinking one of his special cups of tea. And, Jezalyn loves tea."

Trying to disguise his surprise at her over simplifying assumption, Wyler took a diplomatic approach when responding. "It's not that simple, my dear. Once, Larkin told me when a human is that close to the point of death their bodies release endorphins into the blood stream. He says most vampires can't give up the high that they get, so they don't or won't create."

With a sound of boredom she grumbled, "Whatever. What do vampire rules have to do with Keepers anyway?"

Wyler, being the original vampire keeper, had never actually had to discuss such topics as these, but since he was now sharing the honor he did what any loving husbands who was questioned. He took a firm yet gentle tone as he responded to her snarky remarks, "It is similar in the essence that vampires can't enter a dwelling unless invited or accepted in, and a human can't become a Keeper unless they accept the blood; it won't work if it's forced on them. Once the blood has been accepted, they are loyal for life."

"Okay, well. If we are loyal for life, no matter what—why do we drink that tea every day?" she retorted, not ready to consider her plan, for Jezalyn to become Julius' keeper, failed.

Becoming irritated at Ana, Wyler tried to restrain his annoyance, "Remember, I told you drinking what we call the special tea allows us to age slower; we only age a year for every ten that we drink it. Also, you can't drink pure vampire blood unless it's for the change or you will become ill, so we mix it with a liquid."

She gave a little giggle followed by a sigh, "I know. It's an attribute I wouldn't want to give up either."

"Do you understand why we can't trick her into drinking the tea?"

"Yes, but what would happen if I had given her the tea?"

Wyler's tone became serious, "If you tricked her, she would gain all the attributes of a Keeper, but none of the loyalty. She would never be loyal even if she wished to choose it for herself later. She would be more difficult to deal with then Julius."

"Oh! Good thing she was not awake this morning when I left," she said with relief in her voice.

With anger, he gripped the phone "You better never—"

Ana quickly interrupted him, "I was only joking, Darling. Please do not be cross with me. You know I would never do anything without talking to you about it first."

Wyler did not find it funny and said nothing.

"I am sorry, if I upset you. How is the rest of your day going? Did you get that little note I jotted down for you?"

His earlier countenance was replaced by a boyish smirk that slid across his face. "Yes, I did."

She waited a second for him to say more, but when he didn't she said, "And, what did you think?"

With all the affection of his heart, he said, "I am that grass anxiously awaiting the dew and you're the dew that rejuvenates my very soul. I would wither and die without you."

She tried to choke back a sigh, but could not. "Aw. I love you." He heard a smacking sound before she continued, "I wish I could come home to you now."

"Me too, Bunny. I have to go; I need to check on Larkin."

"Okay, but would you mention to Larkin about making her a Keeper?"

"Sure, Bunny. I will talk with you later."

"Okay, bye."

Chapter 9: To Be or Not to Be...

YLER LISTENED FOR the receiver to click before hanging up. His hand rested on the phone as his mind wandered back to the night he removed the musket ball from Larkin's back.

He awoke disorientated to the sound of shattering glass. The advanced years of war taught him the importance of quickly focusing to assess his surroundings for potential dangers. He did not jump up immediately, but quietly remained in the fetal position. He knew the first rule of survival was never to expose one's self unless you have a clear visual of your area. He had to first let his eyes adjust; it did not take long. Once adjusted he thought, *I can see everything so clearly. It must be a full moon out tonight, and the moonlight has flooded this dreary room.* Now that he could see, he found himself and his bag in an empty porcelain bathtub. He grabbed his medical bag took out his scalpel and a small shard of mirror. Holding the looking glass over the edge of the tub, Wyler observed that he was in a small-enclosed room. He was alone, so he took a deep breath and plotted out his next move. *How did I get up here?* Wyler silently question, for the last thing he could remember was falling back asleep on the old porch swing.

Suddenly, a loud thud from below startled Wyler. Moving quietly he tried to secure the door, but it would not lock. The thuds grew closer, and he froze as he could now hear the grunting of two men struggling. Thinking swiftly, he braced himself behind the door so that if it swung open he would be able to force it closed. Wyler tightly gripped his scalpel at the sound of accelerated footsteps. The door did not swing open as expected, but burst open like an explosion. Wyler watched wide-eyed as an individual erupted through the door and into the wall. There was a gaping hole where the assailant's body bounced before hitting the ground. Wyler was surprised to see that the man picking himself up out of the debris as if nothing had happened. The man spotted him and stared directly into his eyes. Wyler recognized his face at once, for it was the man he had patched up earlier that night.

Before Wyler could speak, he was gone. Wyler scanned the room but did not find him, *Where did he go? I didn't see him pass by me.* He moved to the tub, but found nothing. He heard a struggle downstairs; it sounded as if the house was coming down around him. Wyler debated on whether to try to run for safety or fight. He stepped to the window and saw several figures standing in the dim shade of the trees below; *It's not a full moon. How can I see so well?* Trying to comprehend the situation, Wyler heard several more thuds, before his former patient Larkin reappeared. Ducking down below the window seal, Wyler whispered, "They spotted me."

"I've taken care of all of them; it is safe to come out," reassured Larkin.

"No! There are two outside under the tree," replied Wyler.

"Are you sure?"

"Yes! They spotted me! I need a musket."

"A firearm won't help you now," said Larkin as he crouched down and closed his eyes.

"What is your name again?"

He answered, "Larkin" before making a shushing sound at him. After a few seconds, Larkin whispered, "You're right. There are two downstairs plus one on the roof."

Until his return, Larkin directed Wyler to remain quiet and out of sight. With a blank stare on his face, Wyler moved to the back of the porcelain tub and crouched down.

Wyler shifted from side to side as he debated on whether to help Larkin as the brawl below ensued. *If there are two he will need help. I must help him,* thought Wyler; although, he could not perceive why he felt the sudden urge to help, Wyler boldly charged out of the room. Before Wyler could reach the staircase, an adversary crashed through the ceiling landing on his feet directly in front of him. Wyler stumbled back in shock at the intruder's cat like reflexes.

Wyler's mysterious opponent moved one-step closer and said, "Your brother sends his regards."

"Brother! I don't have a brother," yelled a terrified Wyler.

"He is talking to me," Larkin said as he lunged forward gripping him from behind. Once he had him in a chokehold, Wyler's mysterious acquaintance's slammed their foe onto the floor with such force that they fell through to the first.

Wyler stood frozen for a minute as he gawked at the hole they created. Edging to the corner, he peered in to see if anyone survived. Neither was dead. He watched them fighting below as he pondered, *He moves like he was never injured.* Larkin was winning until the enemy swirled around him, grabbed his neck, and pounded his head into the wall several times. With Larkin's cheek pinned against the wall, the enemy pulled out a wooden dagger and plunged it into his back. With a slight, hesitation, Wyler pulled the scalpel out of his pocket, jumped down onto the enemy's back and slit his throat before he could snap Larkin's neck. Wyler stood stunned for a second as he watched the blood flow from his attacker's neck.

Wyler rushed as Larkin called to him "Hurry, remove the stake! He is not dead, yet."

He followed Larkin's directions, but alleged, "He looks pretty dead to me. I slit his throat from ear to ear." He reached up and pulled at the stake, but it wouldn't budge. He gripped it with both hands, but it still would not move. "I can't get it. It must be deep. If you remove it, you will likely bleed to death."

"Don't worry about that. Are there spikes at the end of the stake?"

"No."

"Okay. Go get your medical bag," demanded Larkin. "I am going to need you to sew me up again."

Without hesitation, Wyler ran up what was left of the tattered staircase. There were missing sections, holes, and boards that resembled splinters dangling from the railings. He had barely entered the bathroom, when he heard a loud growl. Grabbing his medical bag, Wyler ran back to the hole. Remembering Larkin's claim that the assailant was not dead, he took caution and stopped next to a hole. Peering down below, he could see Larkin still pinned against the wall as well as the attacker lying motionless on the floor.

Wyler's attention was drawn to Larkin, who was using his legs and forearms as leverage against the wall to push himself free. With every push, he let out a growl-like cry until he was free. Larkin held the center of his chest as he pulled the bloody stake out of the wall.

Wyler rubbed at his eyes for clarity when he observed the enemy, whose neck he had sliced open with his own hand, regain his footing. Instead of being completely paralyzed with fear, he immediately alerted Larkin. "Hey! Look out!"

The outburst caught the enemy's attention, which allowed Larkin enough time to thrust the stake into his rival's chest, grab his head, and twist until it snapped off letting his decapitated body fall to the floor.

Wyler jumped down to the first floor and stared at him in amazement. "How did you do that?"

"I am sure you have a lot of questions, and I will answer each one, but while you stitch me up."

Larkin removed his shirt and Wyler slinked over to him. There was blood oozing down both sides of his body. "I don't know where to start. I never stitched up a wound this large."

"Just stitch the outside closed to hold the blood in," Larkin instructed.

Wyler was skeptical as whether or not his new friend could actually survive such a trauma, but nevertheless he had been proven wrong about their now decapitated foe. Taking a deep breath, Wyler examined the wounds and determined it would be best to suture the wound closed while Larkin was standing. Perhaps, his patient might lose less blood, and if nothing else at least Wyler would be able to see where to stitch.

Larkin laughed, "Alright, so what is your question?"

He threaded his needle and said, "How did you pull his head off."

"I just twisted until it popped off, not to mention your fancy knife work helped."

"Technically, with all this blood loss you should be dead, but so should he," observed Wyler as he pointed to the headless body. "Why didn't he die after I slit his throat? And, why are you still alive?"

"I will tell you after you finish," replied an unemotional Larkin.

In a low mumble, he said, "This is not natural." Silence fell between them; and Wyler shook his head before blurting out, "No!"

"I want the answer to my question, or I won't stitch you up," demanded Wyler moving his hands away from the half sewn hole.

Larkin thought for a moment but knew he had to agree. He also knew it would take months to heal if he left his wound unstitched, thus leaving him vulnerable to future attacks. *He drank my blood, so he shouldn't refuse me. I will try once again, but this time more direct?* Larkin thought. He turned to Wyler and demanded, "No. You will stitch me up now, and I will tell you after." Larkin inhaled deeply causing blood to gush out.

Wyler pushed an old shirt at him and said, "Here hold this over that hole and turn around so I can stitch up your back." Larkin said nothing as he turned holding the shirt to his chest. With Larkin's back toward him, Wyler

thought, *Why did I agree against my own wishes?*
Mystified at his own behavior, he questioned Larkin as to
why he had not followed his own judgment. "Why do I feel
like I need to stitch you up right away? I was dead set
against helping you, if you had refused."

He stood there silently until he felt the needle pierce
his skin. Finally, Larkin answered, "You can't refuse me."

"Why not?" demanded his alarmed surgeon.

"Do you remember when you drank that cup of
water, after you removed the musket ball?"

"Yes."

"You drank a small dose of my blood, which made
you protective and loyal to me."

"What? Why? What are you? How long does it
last?" The questions rambled out of Wyler's mouth without
a pause.

Larkin did not make an interjection to his
blathering. Instead, he listened silently, and responded only
to the last. "Forever!" he said, before elaborating on such a
life changing effect, "You will always feel the need to be
loyal and protect me as long as you live."

Wyler took a deep breath as he tried to understand,
"What else happened to me when I drank that water?"

Feeling the tight pulling of his skin uniting, Larkin
explained that for a short period of time Wyler may
develop some of his supernatural attributes; such as, being
able to see clearer, hear sharper, or form better reflexes.
You might get one or all; it depends upon the benefactor."
Seeing Wyler's brow furrow with concern, Larkin added,

"The advantage of long term consumption will cause your rate of aging to slow down considerably."

It didn't take Wyler long to know which trait he had received, for now he could explain as to how he had seen figures standing by the tree. "They should have been masked by the darkness," mumbled Wyler.

A grim smile crossed Larkin's face, "Your abilities will weaken as the day wanes."

Wyler listened most astutely as Larkin assured him that the only way to retain his new features that he would need to drink of his blood daily. "Let me get this straight. By drinking your blood every day I will have better vision, reflexes, and age slower, but since I have already drunk it once I will be loyal to you even if I never drink it again," concluded his exasperated surgeon.

"Something like that," he confirmed, before offering Wyler a proposition. Larkin explained how Wyler's actions after drinking the blood tinted water interested him greatly, for he had noticed that Wyler went back to sleep with hardly any concern or interest of his well-being. Larkin confessed, "After drinking my blood, I thought perhaps you were immune. But, by the time I had considered that you hadn't drunk enough blood to bind you to me I heard them coming from afar. I could have left you, but I didn't because I knew if I had you would certainly meet death, so I stayed. Now, my duty to you is fulfilled, and I am glad I did not leave, since I want to retain your services as my Keeper."

"Keeper! What is that?" He said as he finished tying the knot on the last stitch. Wyler stood up to examine the injury he had sutured earlier that night. The lesion had vanished and all that remained were tiny pieces of thread. He gasped, "The other wound, it's healed."

"I heal quickly. Are you done back there?"

He mumbled, "Yes" and Larkin turned to face him. Even though the shirt Larkin held to his chest was blood soaked Wyler still told him, "Keep holding pressure against it, I need to rethread my needle."

"That headless enemy seemed to have some of the same attributes I currently have. Was he a Keeper?"

"No."

"Okay, move the shirt. Is he like you?"

"Kind of."

Wyler thought to himself, *Kind of. What does that mean? Why is he always so vague with me?* Blood spurted out onto the floor as he continued to close the hole in Larkin's chest, and he thought, *Oh, this is a lot of blood. I wonder why he isn't dead yet.* Wyler took a deep breath and slowly exhaled before he asked, "I am getting close to being finished. Will you tell me now how you are still alive after this significant loss of blood?" and thought, *Not to mention the type of wound he sustained.*

Knowing that Wyler could not refuse to continue suturing him up, he told all. "The reason we didn't die from life-threatening injuries is because we are already dead."

"Already dead! What does that mean? What are you?"

"We are Vampires. Well I am, and he was. Our blood helps us heal the most critical injuries."

"Is that why when I slashed his throat open it didn't kill him?"

"Yes. We are extremely difficult to kill. The heart must be removed and incinerated or we will regenerate."

Staring at their headless attacker, Wyler screeched, "Wait! Are you saying that thing is still alive?"

"Beheading is the most serious injury that we cannot revive from immediately, but if someone came along and reattached the head, then yes he would in time revive."

"How could that be?"

"You see how you are stitching me closed right now?" Wyler shook his head yes, so Larkin continued, "If we leave that body untouched and someone comes along, finds it, stitches it back together, feeds it, or buries it, then the body will rest underground until it is completely restored. Once regenerated, he will revive and come after us again."

"Can you kill them by burning the body without decapitating them?"

"Yes, as long as you get the heart. If you merely set one on fire without incineration, the body will slowly heal until they rejuvenate back to normal. The best way to ensure that they are turned to ash is to making sure they are immobile so that they can't find a means of putting themselves out."

"Why are you telling me all of this?"

"Because you asked, and I want you to be my Keeper. Do you accept?"

"Do I have a choice?"

"Yes. Although you will feel loyal to me for life, I will not force you to do my will." For some reason, Larkin felt Wyler was not like anyone he had retained before. Generally, if they accept the blood then they will be faithfully forever; however, Wyler's initial resistance was different, so Larkin asked Wyler to make a true commitment, one of his own free will.

"I owe you my life, so I will not refuse." Wyler omitted to Larkin that he was on his way home to nothing but his father's old medical office. He had no one else, so he welcomed Larkin's invitation, not to mention he found himself fascinated with this anomaly.

"You owe me nothing. Do not consent out of duty."

"I do not only accept out of duty, but out of honor." Without waiting for a response, Wyler said, "All done. How do you feel?"

"Like I am no longer a fountain. Thank you. Now I need to replenish myself. I stuffed two humans in the closet during the attack. Go see if one of them survived. If they did, bring one to me."

"I thought they were all vampires."

"No, they usually send human scouts in as traps. We are more vulnerable when we feed."

"Feed?"

"As vampires, we drink human blood." Fear swept over Wyler as he turned to follow Larkin's command. Larkin caught sight of the fear and added, "Don't worry; your blood is safe."

The fear eased away, and he immediately opened the closet. They were unconscious, so he felt for a pulse. He found a pulse on the more stocky man, but not on the other. He reached to grab the one he knew was alive but noticed as he pulled him up that the chest slowly moved up and down on the other, so he grabbed him instead. He pulled him across the floor over to Larkin who propped himself against the wall for leverage, "Here–, this one is almost…"

The dead body fell to the floor before Wyler could finish his sentence, ". . . gone." Unsure of what to do next Wyler said, "Do you want me to bring you the other one?"

"No. He was enough for now. We need to gather these bodies first."

Wyler stood there not knowing what to say or do, so he recounted the night's events. He stared down as Larkin removed the heart from the decapitated body, and recollected some of the conversation that ensued between him and the vampire. *He said kind of like me. He never said how they were different. He just said they were vampires.*

Larkin returned, "I gathered all the pumpers and placed them in the bathtub upstairs. Do you have a light?"

Wyler grabbed his bag and rummaged through it pulling out all the medical supplies as he searched for a flint. "Earlier you said that man was kind of like you. How is he different from you?" He found the flint and steel and said as he extended it toward him, "Is there more than one kind of vampire?"

Larkin grabbed the match from Wyler. "I am growing bored with these questions; I will tell you another day. You have nothing but time now."

After setting the organs on fire, it was Larkin's turn to inquire about his new Keeper, "So you don't have a brother?"

"No. I am an only sibling, and my father perished during the Battle of Charlottesville." He thought for a moment, *My attacker said something about a brother,* and asked Larkin, "Why is your brother trying to kill you?"

Larkin never took his eyes off of the flame. He only replied, emotionless, "That's an ever longer story."

CHAPTER 10: A MOMENT OF WEAKNESS

LEAVING WYLER ALONE to deal with his worrisome wife, Larkin returned upstairs to find Jezalyn sitting where they left her. Her hair cupped her diamond shaped face as she tilted her head to the side to inspect underneath the counter. She reached in and retrieved a laptop with small red heart stickers. Hiding out of view, Larkin listened to her thoughts, *This is pretty; it must be Ana's. I am sure she wouldn't mind if I borrowed it a sec to check my grades.* He watched her fidget as she navigated through the internet. As she slowly scrolled down the page, he could see the muscles in her arms tense up and release as she softly laughed, "It's an A!" If he wanted to talk to her without the presence of Wyler, he needed to approach her soon. Larkin lightly tiptoed up behind her as if to steal a kiss and in her ear he whispered, "Hey, what you have there?" Startled, she sprung forward up off the stool causing the computer to slide across the counter. Their hands scrambled to grasp the laptop; luckily, they caught it before it slipped off the edge. After her panic subsided, she glanced down and saw that not only did she catch the computer, but she had also caught Larkin. She stood there for a moment frozen with her hand over his. She got a chill and instantly an "Oh, sorry!" escaped out of her mouth as she released him.

"It's okay. I didn't mean to scare you. I am glad your laptop didn't break."

"Me too. Especially since it's not mine." Larkin let out a slight laugh, and Jezalyn thought, *I hope he doesn't tell Wyler I almost dropped it.*

She still felt a little awkward, so she tried to change the subject and ease the tension. She flashed him a smile and teased, "Wow! You must have been outside quite a while for your fingers to still be cold."

He quickly made an excuse as to why his hands were cold. "I lost my gloves, so it will probably take them a while to warm up."

"Oh. I think I saw a pair under the counter earlier." She bent over tilting her head to the side once again. He watched as her hair slipped down and dangled in her face. She brushed it back with one hand exposing her fair slender neck as she retrieved the gloves with the other. The gloves she found were light pink with tiny white checks. She handed them over to him with a giggle, "I hope you like pink." He took them from her and unrolled them. They were not gloves but mittens, but he tried them on anyway.

After squeezing his fingers into the narrow holes, he lifted his hands, "What do you think?"

Softly giggling, she observed, "I think you need another three inches."

He laughed and said, "To be sure you are correct." He pulled his hands out of the mittens, rolled them back together, and tossed them back under the counter. "I hope I didn't stretch them out, but if I did, I guess Ana could always use them as booties." Another soft giggle escaped her supple strawberry lips. He could not help but notice them, since he could practically taste the strawberry lip balm from the smell. The transformation from human to vampire heightened his senses. Now he barely had to inhale to smell something halfway across the room. He could also see sharper, hear from greater distances, and move faster.

Larkin grabbed the computer, swung it around, and opened it. "Let's see what was amusing you when I walked up."

"It was my grades. I got an A on my rough draft I submitted the other night."

"Looks like you also have a few comments. Did you read them yet?" he said while flipping the computer back around to face her.

"No! There are comments? You must have surprised me before I could see them." She pulled the computer close and began to read. *Your insight into the Medusa myth, in regards to the relationship between Medusa and Athena, is a good topic to explore. You have enough factual material; now try to add more depth to your paper.* Fear swept over her and Larkin watched and listened to her continue, *It feels like you just scratched the surface of their relationship. I would like to see it developed a little further by making a claim or claims and then supporting them. Here are some questions that might help you. Do you think that Medusa and Athena were natural enemies? Do you think that Medusa's punishment was fitting? Should she have had to bear any punishment? Why or why not? I think you have a good start here, but if you have any questions or concerns, do not hesitate to contact me for further guidance through the internal course email.*

Even though Larkin already knew the content of her comments, he tried to ask with some excitement, "Well, what does it say?"

Without a word, she flipped the computer around toward him with a hesitant motion. "You can read it if you want," she finally stated as he pulled the laptop closer. She watched in silence as he read.

He lifted his head only after allowing enough time to pass so that Jezalyn would assume he read the comments before he offered his assistance. "I love mythology," he confessed. "I'll read your paper and give some pointers if you'd like."

"Yeah, that would be great! When do you think you could look at it?" asked Jezalyn

"Any time is good. I could do it now if you had it."

Without a word, Jezalyn took hold of the computer and retrieved her email that retained the attached document. She opened the report, got up, and offered Larkin her seat. She became flustered at the thought of him reading her report. *What if he thinks I am stupid? I should have never accepted.* She bit her lip as Larkin sat down. *I should go make some tea. It would not only help calm me, but keep me busy while he reads.* She waited a few minutes before she decided, *Yep that's what I am going to do.* She informed Larkin of her plan to make tea and offered to make him a cup as well. "It might help you warm up some," she said.

With a smile Larkin responded, "Yes, I would love a cup. Add two sugars please."

She nodded her head and mumbled, "Just like Wyler. It should be easy to remember," as she pranced out of the room.

Waiting for the water to boil, Jezalyn grabbed two cups and reached for the sugar. After scooping out a teaspoon, she thought *Huh, two cubes just like Wyler.* After a few more seconds of pondering, she realized Wyler and Larkin had a few things in common. Not only did they both want two sugars in their tea, but they also were nice and helpful. Searching for more comparisons, Jezalyn thought about how loving Wyler was toward Ana, which made her wonder about Larkin. *Well, he is cuter then Wyler, but looks don't really matter. Yet, there is no way he single; he's too hot not to have someone special. I bet she is tall, beautiful, and mean. The cruel ones always get the good men.* Her attention was swiftly diverted to the rattling electric tea kettle letting her know that it was ready to be depleted. Soon, Jezalyn returned to the front counter with two cups of tea where she sat one down next to him.

"Thank you" said Larkin, as she wandered off in the direction of the mythology section.

Lost in thought she did not hear him thank her. *I guess I should find some books to help me scratch more than the surface,* she quipped, letting out a sigh. Now at the mythology section, she browsed books by their indexes to determine the usefulness each book held toward her report. About a quarter of the way down almost below eye level, she pulled a large Greek mythology book off of the shelf. *Surely, there must be something helpful in a book this large,* she thought, but before she could scan the index, she peered through the hole and saw Larkin. She observed that he had dark chocolate hair that parted from left to right and stopped at the collar of his shirt; she watched as he used his right hand to sweep back the fallen strands out of his face. Jezalyn couldn't take her eyes off his tousled locks as she thought, *it looks nice and clean, yet it has an unkempt bouncy wildness to it.*

Larkin knew her eyes were upon him, so he could not smile at her little assessment nor would he dare glance up and risk ending it either. After he reawaked as an immortal, Larkin had a mind of a seventy-eight year old with the body and face of a twenty-four year old. It didn't take Larkin long to discover the power of a boyish face with a knowledgeable mind, but he wondered how Jezalyn would feel about his youthfulness with a now five plus century wit. Larkin pondered if he would be able to challenge her yet conceal his extensive wisdom, but then, he quickly shook his head. *What am I thinking? That is what I have Julius for – he may only have a mind of a sixty year old, but he has the cleverness of ancient. Now, if he just had the maturity of an ancient*, thought Larkin as he took another sip of his tea.

Luckily, while Jezalyn was in the stockroom making the tea, Larkin had already read her report and added helpful statements here and there. When she returned with the tea, he pretended to read so that she would not wonder at his quickness of being finished. He barely glanced up as he took a sip of his tea.

Jezalyn watched as Larkin drank his tea. His skin was currently a wan ivory that she attributed to him wandering about in the cold. Mesmerized by his youthful appearance, she noticed his defined jaw line, and thought, *I bet he would have been mistaken as the son of a Greek god, with structural features like that, or at least as a hero.* She watched him raise his head in contemplation and found herself thinking, *Perhaps like Hercules or Perseus.*

Larkin tried not to flinch, because he did not want to interrupt her assessment of him. Bewilderment quickly consumed Larkin as he speculated over his interest in her perception of him. *What am I doing? Why am I holding any regard in her opinion of me? She is a nonessential, disposable being that should not hold an inkling of fascination for me.* He paused, cut his eyes in her direction, and thought, *She must die. I will tell Wyler my decision when he returns.*

Jezalyn ducked into the stacks; *did he see me? I hope he didn't catch me staring*, thought Jezalyn as she debated whether to keep or replace the book. She decided to keep the book as an effort to help minimize the fidgeting that would occur in case he actually had caught her staring at him. She put on a smile and cheerily waltzed toward the counter, book in tow, "Did you finish? What do you think?" Their eyes met, and his once gentle baby-blue eyes sharpened to a slant. Without warning, he lunged over the counter hurling his body onto hers. She instinctively struggled against him, but relented when she felt a sharp stinging sensation on her neck.

CHAPTER 11: A DOMESTIC DISTURBANCE

RED AND BLUE lights flickered against the wall as Jezalyn sat on a stretcher with a compress firmly secured against her neck. Two officers in black stood in front of her. She heard the older man say, "Go talk to the store owner while I talk to the victim." The officer nodded his head, took out a little dark green leather notebook, and strolled over to Wyler.

"Hey, Wyler, how's your shop doing now that y'all are settled?"

"I still have a lot of inventory to put out, but business has picked up."

"That's good to hear. Well, I have to ask you a few questions."

"Okay."

"So, what happened here?" asked the officer ready to take Wyler's statement.

He gazed at Jezalyn's neck before answering the question. "I am not sure. I wasn't up here when it occurred. I was downstairs."

"Okay, so you didn't see anything."

"No."

"Did you hear anything?"

"I heard a loud thud, so I ran upstairs."

"What did you see after coming upstairs?"

"I saw Jezalyn on the floor and Larkin was bent over her. . ." Wyler was finishing his statement with Rex Wheeler, the local deputy, when he overheard Jezalyn giving her statement to Lloyd Ellison, Transylvania's detective and chief of police. The town truly only needed one authority, but Lloyd appointed Rex to be his deputy after Lloyd fell violently ill. The town would not hear of Lloyd's removal, and Lloyd was too kindhearted to get rid of Rex, so now both enforced the law. This incident was the most action either of them had seen in this small town of less than a thousand in over a decade. Unlike most towns, Transylvania did not have petty crimes, much less attempted murder.

Wyler heard Jezalyn report, "He jumped over the counter and flung me onto the floor."

"And what happened next?"

She slowly placed her hand up to her injured neck and said, "Then. . . I felt a sharp piercing pain in my neck."

"I see. Is that all?"

"Yes, that's all I remember; I must have fainted from the assault. When I awoke, Wyler was holding my neck."

Deputy Wheeler returned interrupting the interview and said, "Hey, Cap, you got a moment?" He glanced back at Jezalyn and said, "Let Ray, the paramedic, check you out. I'll be right back." She shrugged her shoulders with a little nod as the paramedic approached her and removed the bandage that Wyler placed on her neck.

While the authorities were huddled in a corner and Jezalyn got her wounds treated, Wyler eased back over to Larkin. "What are we going to do?"

Without even a cursory glance he said, "Nothing. You told your side. I will tell mine, if asked."

"But what are you going to say?"

"I will tell them what happened."

"You can't! How are you. . ." he finished the rest of his thought in his head, *going to explain her neck?*

He turned to Wyler, looked into his eyes, and replied, "Stop worrying. It's covered."

Wyler watched Deputy Wheeler walk outside as Chief Ellison return to Ray and Jezalyn. Wyler had his suspicions that Larkin had bit her, but was not sure why. He thought, *If he wanted to change her or kill her, he would have told me first. Maybe he just wanted a little taste. No, that can't be it. He would never compromise. . . so why then?* He finally said, "Okay, but at least tell me what happened up here."

Larkin said nothing as he watched Lloyd talk to Ray. They were speaking low out of Jezalyn and Wyler's earshot, but not his. He listened to Ray give an inconclusive report as to the cause of how she sustained her injuries.

"Larkin!"

"Later," whispered Larkin, never taking his eyes of the chief as he approached them.

A moment later, the chief stood confidently in front of them. "So you are the owner correct?" he said as he pointed at Wyler. Without waiting for a response, he redirected his finger toward Larkin, "And you're the one who flung himself on top of Ms. Williford?"

The latter responded, "Yes."

"According to Ms. Williford, you jumped over the counter and tackled her. Is that correct?"

"Yes. It is."

"Well, I must say she is a lucky girl to still be alive."

"Yes, but she still got injured," sighed Larkin compassionately, trying to hide the contempt he held for her. "If only—"

Not being able to hold back any longer, Wyler interrupted, "Wait a second, could someone please tell me what is going on around here?"

Although Larkin knew the whole story, he could not relate it without bringing up further questions, so he said, "I am not exactly sure myself."

Chief Ellison gave them a puzzled look and said, "Oh! I am sorry I thought Rex had filled you in. Come with me." They sauntered over to the front near the door where Jezalyn sat on the stretcher all bandaged up.

The paramedic remarked, "She doesn't actually need to go to the hospital; it's only a mild flesh wound. I gave her a sedative to help her relax. I must say whoever bandaged her before I got here did a good job. The injury had already begun to clot by the time I came on the scene." With no further injury to attend to, he announced his departure. "Well, I have to get going; my wife called, and she thinks one of the girls twisted an ankle." Turning directly to the Ellison, he said, "By the way, Chief, my wife said for me to invite you to Sunday dinner."

The chief raised his hand and with a smile said, "Thanks, Ray. Tell Olive and the girls that I said hi, and I would love to come over for Sunday dinner."

Ray waved his hand backward as he exited the bookstore with the stretcher, "Sure will, Lloyd. See ya Sunday."

Now that Ray was gone, Chief Ellison's expression turned serious. "I usually don't tell anyone the particulars of an ongoing investigation, but I think I have this one pretty much wrapped up, so I will tell y'all what we are going to do about this situation."

Jezalyn stood quietly with a red spotted bandage where blood had seeped through in certain spots on her neck and thought, *What happened? It all happened so fast. Does he know Larkin attacked me?* She scowled at Larkin, *Of course he knows. I am being ridiculous. I told him Larkin jumped over the counter and attacked me, but why would he attack me? And why has he not been arrested yet?* She took a deep breath trying to calm down as she contemplated his motive for attacking her.

Everyone else stared at Lloyd waiting for him to go on, but he did not. He simply peered out of the window until Wyler finally broke the silence and said, "I still don't know what is going on." He thought to himself, *Please don't say you are going to have to take Larkin in.*

He slowly turned around toward them. "Here is what happened and what is going to happen," he said as all eyes were upon him. Even Jezalyn had abandoned her pondering to listen, but another thought instinctively crossed her mind, *I hope he arrests Larkin so that he won't be able to try attacking me again.*

Lloyd asked, "Do you know the Petersons?"

All except for Wyler shook their heads no. Wyler said, "Don't the Petersons own the general store?"

"Yes, and since it will be local news instead of standard gossip tomorrow morning, I might as well go ahead and mention that Mr. Peterson was having an affair with Greta from over at the post office."

"Oh, I hadn't heard about that," said Wyler as the others attentively listened to the conversation.

The chief continued, "I received a dispatch of domestic dispute. My deputy was the first on scene; he heard it from his parked car at the tire shop next door. It seems Mrs. Peterson found out about her husband and Greta. Distraught by her husband's actions, she grabbed one of the store's pistols, loaded it, and unloaded a few rounds at her husband. She claims she only intended to scare him."

Wyler directly responded, "Was anyone hurt over there?"

"No. When we arrived, she was sitting in the middle of the floor crying and holding the gun with a box of shells in her lap."

"Where was her husband?" asked a shocked Wyler.

"He was lying face down on the floor in the office. He said he was too trapped to do anything else."

"Oh, that's good if no one got hurt," remarked Jezalyn.

"Well, I wouldn't say no one," replied the officer.

She eyed him peculiarly, "What do you mean?"

"You got hurt, didn't you?"

She glanced over at Larkin for a moment, swallowed hard, and took a step closer to Chief Ellison out of Larkin's direct line of view as she said, "Yes, but I don't see how that has anything to do with Larkin attacking me."

Larkin barely glanced in her direction as she continued, "I thought you were here to arrest him."

"No, my dear. I will not be arresting anyone in this shop today," replied Chief Ellison, letting his hands rest on his gun and handcuff holsters.

She hesitated but feared for her own safety, so she retorted with one hand on her hip, "And why not?"

Seeing she was not understanding the gravity of the situation, he motioned to Larkin and said, "Could I have the honor of telling her or would you like to?"

Wyler now extremely anxious over the situation said, "I wish someone would tell me already."

Larkin said nothing. He put his hand on Wyler's shoulder as a signal to relax as he gave the chief a little shrug and gestured for him to continue. Chief Ellison loved to tell a good story, and this occasion afforded him practice for later, so he continued, "When Mrs. Peterson began shooting at her husband next door, she didn't quite try to kill him. She just shot aimlessly around the store trying to scare him, and several of the bullets penetrated the walls. Your neck injury is from one of the bullets that breached the wall." They turned to look, all except Larkin whose eyes remained fixed on Chief Ellison.

"You see, my dear, Larkin is not your attacker; he is your savior."

She instantly stared at Larkin; her green eyes enlarged and brightened from the events, and said, "I am so sorry. How could I ever think you would attack me after all your help? Please forgive me." She ran up and latched onto him giving him the tightest squeeze she could muster up, all the while she thought, *Why am I so relieved he did not attack me? And why am I holding onto him so hard?* Larkin laughed inside as he listened to her apology until she immediately released him with her last thought. He was amused when she felt guilty about accusing him of harming her, but his entertainment faded when she realized she was clinging to him like her savior.

Wyler observed a minute smile cross Larkin's face that quickly subsided when she pulled away. Wyler turned to the Chief of Police and said, "So, what is going to happen to Mrs. Peterson?"

"We have arrested her on several charges, including domestic assault and felony reckless conduct, but I suppose we will have to add assault and battery if Jezalyn wants to file a report on her."

"A report!"

"Yes, and everyone will be expected to appear in court, so don't leave town," the chief ordered.

Before Wyler's alarm had the chance to overtake his emotions, Jezalyn quickly said, "I don't want to press charges." More than one was intrigued by her declaration.

"You may not have a choice, if her bullet grazed your neck," said Chief Ellison.

Jezalyn hesitated before she responded, "I am not sure the bullet even grazed my neck. I could have been injured when Larkin knocked me down."

"Are you sure you hurt yourself while he was trying to protect you?" Chief Ellison knew he was trying to trap her into saying the bullet had actually hit her. He knew if she did not claim the injury as Mrs. Peterson's fault, he could not add the third charge.

"Yes, I am sure; it's more likely that the zipper or a button from his leather jacket caused it."

He produced a card with his name and phone number. "Here, take this. Sleep on it. If you change your mind and want to file, give me a call."

"Okay," she replied taking his card and slipping it into her back pocket.

He turned to leave, and with one foot out the door, he glanced back at Larkin and said, "I have one last question. How did you know to duck and cover?"

"I heard the first shot; it was low and kind of muffled. I was not sure where it came from, so I jumped over the counter to protect Jezalyn. It was an instinctual reflex. I didn't intend to hurt her. I hope she doesn't hold it against me," he added gazing into her eyes.

"No, I certainly do not," blurted out Jezalyn.

Lloyd peered back out into the parking lot, "Well, it looks like my deputy has Mrs. Peterson in custody. Y'all have a good day," trailed out of his mouth as the door closed behind him.

Jezalyn quickly studied Larkin's face to determine if Larkin was angry with her. "I am so sorry for accusing you of attacking me."

With a smirk he responded, "It's fine. I would have thought the same thing in your position."

Wyler interrupted, "How is your neck? Do you really think it was from Larkin and not a bullet?"

She fidgeted with her fingers as she said, "I am not sure; it all happened so fast." Growing silent to reflect, Jezalyn decided, *it was probably the bullet because I felt a warm stinging sensation before I fainted.* After a short pause, she proclaimed, "I owe you my life."

Larkin said, "You owe me nothing." Finally turning to Wyler, he offered in a friendly tone as he tried to disguise his authority over Wyler. "Maybe closing for the day would be a good idea. What do you think?"

Picking up on, Larkin's masked command, "I think we should. I don't want people in here nosing around, moving things here and there, gossiping and trying to find out what happened." He glanced over at Jezalyn and said, "Considering the circumstances, you can have the rest of the day off, too."

Giving him a warm smile, she said, "Thanks, Wyler, my neck is throbbing."

Trying to break the ominous tension, Wyler tried to make a light hearted joke. "Perhaps tomorrow will be a better day. You might even make it the entire day without shedding a drop of blood, but then again there are always paper cuts," he said with a chuckle.

She glared at him and joined in on the joke, even if it was at her own expense. "A little more sweat and a little less blood could do the trick," she said. Larkin and Wyler laughed as she giggled before she continued, "Yeah. I give the phrase 'sweat and blood' a whole new meaning, huh?" They watched as she placed her hand against her neck. Jezalyn informed them, "I'll be upstairs; I'm going to go lay down for awhile."

She was almost to the stairs when she heard Larkin's voice, "Hey, by the way, I finished making comments on your report."

"Oh, thanks. I am grateful for your help, and I don't want to be rude, but I will have to go over it later. I think that pill the EMT gave me is making me sleepy."

"It's okay. I just wanted you to know I was done in case you wanted to work on it later."

"Thanks," she said as she walked up the stairs to her apartment. He watched her frolic away before asking Wyler to make a fresh cup of tea.

"Okay, but let's go downstairs so that we can talk."

Not a word passed between them as they descended to the underground apartment; however, Larkin's mind was not so quiet. *Ugh—almost!? Mrs. Peterson would have all the blame and my Keepers wouldn't have to cover up anything. She would be dead; I would be free from her thoughts and emotions. The incident was a perfect way to get rid of her, if only I hadn't miscalculated. By being passive, I've let time deteriorate my abilities.*

They had reached the kitchen. Wyler moved directly as instructed; he put the water on to boil. Larkin quietly sat down on the couch.

"Larkin?"

"Yes."

"Did you really save Jezalyn?"

"I thought we just decided I did."

Tired of receiving the runaround Wyler abruptly responded, "You are avoiding the question. Did you bite Jezalyn?"

Irritated at the insinuation, he snapped, "No! And do not question me again."

Finding his place, Wyler apologized, "I am sorry. I don't want us to end up in another Julius situation."

Larkin, with a calmer voice, said, "I know you are worried, but that was six decades ago and this time is different."

"I hope so; I don't think I can protect three vampires," he said with a sigh. In light of the situation, Wyler took a deep breath and revealed his wife's plan to make Jezalyn a Keeper.

Without so much as a glance in Wyler's direction, Larkin firmly stated, "You know it doesn't work like that. You can't go around making whoever you want a Keeper. Not only does she have to accept the blood, but she has to be chosen."

Conceding that his master was correct, he tried another route to get rid of Jezalyn. "What if we introduced her to Julius? No one can resist his charms; she might choose to accept the role."

Larkin grew agitated inside, but did not exactly know why. He told Wyler no without revealing any of his inner turmoil. "I don't think that's a good idea. You know how Julius is; he is difficult to keep out of trouble." Besides, he already decided the best course of action. Now, all he needed was to be present when the next opportunity for disposal presented itself.

Wyler now believed, after recalling Larkin's smiling face as Jezalyn gave him an appreciative hug that Larkin had an ulterior motive for deciding against the plan. Although it was true, Julius was difficult to keep safe since he was always bucking against the order of things. Not wanting to press his luck, Wyler made one final remark on the subject. "Okay, think about it though. You may want to try it as a last resort," before he changed the conversation back to Jezalyn's reaction to pressing charges on Mrs. Peterson.

"Yes, it somewhat caught me by surprise even though I was reading her thoughts."

"Is she in denial, or does she really think your jacket could have done it?"

"She knows it was a bullet."

"So, why did she lie?"

"She had several reasons."

He sat there waiting for Larkin to elaborate, but all he heard was the sound of the kettle hissing and shrilling over the small stovetop flame. He got up directly, turned off the stove, grabbed two cups, and added a tea bag and two cubes of sugar to each cup. "Like what?" he asked Larkin as he poured the boiling water into the cups.

"Mrs. Peterson already had two charges, and Jezalyn didn't want to add a third."

Wyler handed Larkin a cup before taking a seat next to him. Wyler contemplated as to whether Jezalyn had truly not pressed charges out of pity. He recalled how insistent she was to have Larkin arrested when she thought it was him who attacked her. Finally, Wyler mumbled, "She didn't look sure it was the bullet anyway."

Although Wyler's response was not intended conversation, Larkin had heard and made a response. "No, it was the bullet. Not only did I hear it flutter by, but I can still feel the burning sensation where the metal grazed her neck," he responded before taking a sip of his tea.

"I am thinking maybe she does not know. I am sure she has never been shot before," replied Wyler.

"No. I read her mind, she knows. She noticed the word 'if' the cop used. She realized that he wasn't sure as to what caused the injury, so she made up an excuse so that she would not have to press charges."

"But why? She was ready to send you to jail when she thought you attacked her."

"Yes, but if she had said it was a bullet that injured her, she would have to go to court. If that happened, she would have to explain what happened here today to her overly anxious grandfather, and he would make her return home. I am sure she doesn't want to be forced back home. I bet that is why she would rather report an accident over an incident any day."

He halted, with a note of intense uncertainty on his face, as he remembered Ana describing Jezalyn's motives for accepting a position an hour away from college. From this recollection, Wyler concluded that Larkin's assessment that Jezalyn's family, being overly concerned, was the driving force behind her reaction and decision not to press charges. "Ana did say her grandfather was extremely protective," Wyler finally spoke out.

"Well, either way she is more perceptive than you thought. I know you think her somewhat daft when it comes to awareness, but be careful what you and Ana say around her from now on. She knew Chief Ellison could not prove she was actually hit by the bullet from his word choice," warned Larkin bring the tea cup to his lips but never taking a sip. Instead, he waited for Wyler to finish his tea before requesting its removal. "I don't want this after all," he said, and handed the cup to Wyler to put in the sink.

"Do you need some blood?"

He made no response as he got up and lay down on the floor, propping his feet on the couch. After closing his eyes, he finally said, "No. I am going to meditate awhile. That stupid paramedic gave Jezalyn a sedative, and now I'm starting to feel sluggish."

"Are you sure? A little blood might help."

Larkin lay on his back unresponsive and thought to himself, *She is about to read my memoir again. I will quench my thirst soon, so it doesn't matter if she figures out vampires aren't illusionary.*

Wyler quietly finished rinsing the dishes; he knew from previous experiences that he would not get another response from Larkin for awhile. Then a rather arbitrary thought came to him, *Did Larkin refuse blood because he already had some?* He found the thought of Larkin drinking Jezalyn's blood plausible, so he quietly slipped out of the shop door locking it behind him. Once in the street, he mumbled under his breath, "I must find Ana."

CHAPTER 12: IT IS COLD OUTSIDE, IN

S WYLER LEFT the bookstore, Jezalyn hung up her phone. She had tried to call Blaise, but only got his voicemail. She left a message that said, *Hey, it's me. I fell and scraped my neck at work today. You know clumsy ole' me. Anyway, I am feeling tired, so I'm gonna lay down for a while. I'll call you when I get up. Okay, talk to you later.* After leaving the message, she retrieved Larkin's memoir. Now all snuggled up under the covers, she continued to read somewhere near where she left off.

1545, April

I searched for Isadora and Theron for nearly a year, but found no trace of their existence. If they were still alive, they had become efficient at covering their tracks. I returned home once again to try to feel Theron's presence, but I felt nothing. I concluded, if I could no longer telepathically connect with my brother, then he must have perished as well. It was with that thought that I heard someone sneaking up through the wilderness that had once been our garden. I could not see who was approaching through the boarded up windows, so I had to rely on other instincts. The scent in the air was a mixture of lye soap, cologne, and death, which was unmistakable since I had once lived with it. He has found me!

Theron had returned, and I embraced him and told him that I had been searching for them, but he pulled away when I asked if Isadora was secure. He looked at me, and with a hint of pain in his eyes, he choked out, "Isadora struggled to leave you behind; as a result, we were captured."

"Captured!"

"She did not struggle against them. She kept screaming, 'Is he dead!?!' I confirmed her assumption since our telepathic connection was. . ."

"I know. I can't feel or hear you any more either. The transformation must have severed it."

The pain in his eyes now turned to anger. "Transformation! Isadora lied. She changed you didn't she?"

"Calm down, Theron. She did not change me. I don't know what happened. I just woke up like this."

"Don't lie to me, brother. You can't just wake up a vampire."

"I am being truthful with you. To my knowledge she did not change me."

"To your knowledge? That sounds more like an omission than a denial."

"No. I am saying if she did change me, she did it without me knowing. Where is Isadora? You can ask her for yourself."

Pain returned to Theron's eyes, "She is dead!"

Without a thought I lunged forward lifted him above my head and shook him. "Dead!" and with that word, my grief overcame my anger and I instantly released my grip on my brother. "Theron, she can't be dead; You're still alive."

***

Larkin listened to the words that once pierced his heart with tears in his eyes. For a moment he forgot he was bonded to Jezalyn until he heard her thought, *That is so sad. She cannot be dead. They loved each other too much.*

***

"I told you we were captured, but I didn't tell you we were tested." He removed his left glove and held out his hand revealing a scarred impression, §, "They branded our palms and split us up. I was frantic with worry. The next morning they checked to see if the imprint remained. I knew her hand would heal, but I could do nothing to help her. They proclaimed her a witch and instantly burned her at the stake."

I watched my brother lightly brush his finger over the scar as he said, "I am only alive because this brand remained." My anguish about Isadora's death was intense, and at that moment, I was glad to have our brotherly bond severed so that

Theron would not have to endure my pain.
If our brotherly telepathic connection had
remained after my change, I do not think
he would have survived.

***

Jezalyn stopped reading not because she was
uninterested, but because she was crying so hard she could
no longer make out the words. She placed the book aside
and grabbed a tissue. "I can't believe she died," said
Jezalyn as she lay back down on the bed.

***

Larkin felt Jezalyn's sorrow and could not believe
that anyone could feel that kind of heartache over a
stranger. He felt vibrations in his chest as she cried
uncontrollably. He finally heard a thought, *Why can't I
stop?* A few minutes later it was accompanied by, *It's just a
story! Take a deep breath.* He finally felt the vibrations in
his chest fade away as she drifted off to sleep. Larkin did
not drift off to sleep along with her. Instead, his mind
wandered back to that first encounter as a vampire with his
brother, for that was when Larkin discovered he had lost
his beloved Isadora forever.

It was in the year 1545, almost a year after he
turned, that Larkin's brother told him Isadora had not
survived the mob attack. Larkin felt like he had fallen into
an abyss of despair. He unwillingly fought the urge to cease
to exist; like any other creature, vampires also have an
overwhelming urge to self-preserve. Larkin's animalistic
intellect would not allow himself to find comfort in a
reckless termination, and now he found himself in an
eternity of discontented hell.

The reflection moved beyond his recollection of Isadora's demise to Theron, who asked, "What happened to you? What does it feel like—to be a vampire?"

Larkin's explanation began from the moment he had reawaken, "I climbed out of a shallow grave only to find no one in sight. It was late and the breeze felt like a bitter frost that rapped against me."

"Cold! It was in the late spring when we got attacked."

"Yes, I know. I was unsure as to why I was cold; everything was hazy. I stumbled around for a while searching for shelter, but the cold was harsh and I found it difficult to proceed, so I huddled underneath a nearby tree. It was there that I realized what I had become."

Theron did not respond to Larkin's last statement. He paused and with an attentive ear waited for his bother to continue.

After a moment, Larkin went on. "I remembered that we were fleeing the village, but the Myron brothers cut us off at the pass. We killed one, and I fought off the other so that you could escort Isadora to safety, but once you reached the edge of the woods, their father ambushed me with his pitchfork."

Watching Larkin rub his stomach Theron asked, "Did it leave a scar?"

Larkin raised his shirt, "No, but when I recollected that I was run through with a pitch fork I checked and found three holes the size of a grape."

"A grape? Are you sure you are remembering correctly?"

"Yes, brother. Do you recall when Isadora pierced her palm with that rose shaped glass perfume stopper?"

"Yes. The hole shrank until it was gone."

"Precisely! It was the combination of remembering my fatal wound and Isadora's healing power, alongside my enhanced vision and hearing that led me to conclude that I was no longer human."

"Enhanced?" he asked with a puzzled look on his face. Trying to hold back his sudden anger, Theron questioned, "Isadora has healing power? Did she plan the change?"

Larkin gave a simple shake of the head and continued on with the account of his transformation. "I knew it was a light breeze because the leaves barely moved. However, it sounded and felt like it was rushing through me. I felt cold from within, so cold that it gave a new connotation to the phrase chilled to the bone."

"So that's why you felt cold, because your senses were enhanced."

"No. Not really," he said. "It had to do more with. . ." he hesitated and stopped.

Theron overly jealous toward his vampire brother blurted out, "With what?"

Larkin peered past him as he recollected, "The night was rapidly approaching dawn, so I ran for cover remembering that Isadora once told me that the sun and fire were a vampire's only true rival. Luckily, I came upon a graveyard because the sun was about ready for battle, so I ran toward the entrance of the closest tomb. I was only a few yards from safety when the sun beamed down on me, but I did not stop running. I entered the tomb and did a quick check. I was surprised to discover the sun did not affect me like Isadora said it would."

Theron in a fit of anger charged at his brother yelling, "I knew it! Admit it! It was planned."

He flung his attacker to the ground knocking the wind out of him with as much effort as it would take to raise one finger. "No! I told you. It wasn't planned. You have to believe me. Have I ever lied to you before?" He reached one hand out to his brother who was on the floor holding his lower neck gasping for air, "I am sorry, Brother. I was only trying to divert you. I forget my ability sometimes."

Theron's breathing had returned to normal as he took his hand. "If it was not planned, then why did she tell you what it would be like to turn?"

"She told me because I asked."

"I asked too, but she never revealed the information about the sun."

"Maybe she didn't find it important since we were only Keepers."

"She found it important enough to inform you."

"No," I asked. "Once in the garden, I was holding my spectacles by my side. A beam reflected off the lens creating a small fire. Immediately, I stomped out the fire. Isadora picked up a half-burnt leaf and twirled it about. She blew on the leaf and watched the red line eat away at the leaf until it disappeared. It was after that she told me the leaf was like a vampire caught in the sun."

Theron was about to doubt his response, but he was not sure how his brother would react to being questioned again. He waited to see if his brother would continue, and he did. "Finally, Isadora let the charred stem fall to the ground, so I questioned her logic. 'If the sun disintegrates vampires like it did that leaf, then how it was that she was able to sit in the midst of the day and be fine.' She did not know how or why she was immune to the death rays, for it was rare and almost unheard of." He paused a second and added, "She was not like other vampires."

Noticing his brother's hesitation, Theron insisted that Larkin was not being completely truthful.

He cut his eyes at him and sharply responded, "I'm not lying. I remembered that she told me if I were to change I would be incinerated by the sun."

"And?" said Theron, urging his brother to continue.

"And—that's not what happened. Instead of burning me to a crisp, the sun warmed me." He lightly rubbing his arm, "I could feel the heat."

"Well, at least you weren't cold any longer," Theron said with a roll of the eyes. He was becoming increasingly irritated with the whole conversation. His brother had what he had longed for since his introduction to Isadora. Theron spitefully thought, *First he won her heart, and now he has her eternal gift.*

He only smiled at Theron's sarcasm. "The sun did warm the skin, but I still shivered from within. It was not until the grave keeper came by that I was able to become completely warm." Theron was still lost in his own thought and did not actually hear what his brother said. Instead, he glowered at him and demanded, "Change me!"

***

Larkin's memory was interrupted as the weariness of Jezalyn's sedative took hold on not only her, but also him.

***

While Jezalyn and Larkin were under a drug-induced slumber, Wyler was at the clinic searching for Ana. He entered the building and stopped the first staff person he saw. After reading the name tag he said, "Ms. Sara, I am looking for my wife Ana. Could you point me in the correct direction?"

"I am sorry, sir. She left out on a call about ten minutes ago."

Wyler had decided to wait for his wife until the nurse told him that she would not be back for several hours. Wyler smiled warmly and said, "I see. Thank you."

He had already turned to leave when he heard Ms. Sara call after him, "I will tell her you came by."

He made a full stop, turned, and said, "Tell her nothing serious is the matter, and that I popped by because I never heard back from her." He knew he had to leave a flippant message for Ana, in light of the situation, so she would not drive frantically home.

Wyler wandered away, and after a while he found himself standing in front of Julius's place. Julius lived in a modest house Larkin had built for him. The dwelling was simple in design as not to draw attention from the neighbors. He had double pane windows with UV ray protection on both sides installed. This protection only allowed Julius to view the sun for the first and last minutes of the day without harm. The door opened before Wyler could knock, and he stepped in.

"Good afternoon," said Wyler as the second door shut behind him closing out any possibility of light.

"Wyler?" he mocked, taking a sturdy stance next to his fireplace.

"I only stopped by to see if you have everything you need?"

"You know I do. You were just here a few days ago."

The word "right," escaped from his lips coupled by a distant gaze.

"Why are you really here?" demanded Julius, who always liked getting right to the point of things.

Wyler took a deep breath. "It is Larkin."

"Is he in trouble?"

"In a sense," said Wyler, and then he relayed the whole story of Jezalyn and Larkin's incident. He began from the moment Larkin consumed her blood until the most recent event where he claimed to have saved her life.

"I am sure it is nothing."

"I am not. I've been with him for decades; something is different this time. He is not being truthful about what happened."

"What do you think is different?"

"I don't know. Maybe she did get hurt—or maybe he indulged."

Julius chuckled to himself before he replied, "That's not exactly a crime."

"He did it upstairs in the shop; anyone could have seen him."

"The windows!"

"I know; it's careless and unlike Larkin. He won't talk to me, but I know he is hiding something. I need you to drop by and talk to him about it."

"What makes you think he will tell me?"

"I don't, but I do know you can use your gift to confirm or deny my assumption."

"I'll think about it."

Wyler nodded as he took a seat on the sofa.

Knowing Wyler wanted an immediate response Julius said, "Later! It's dinner time." Flashing a venomous smile, he said, "You're welcome to stay. Blonde is on the menu tonight, but I have red if you prefer."

CHAPTER 13: Julius Visits Larkin

LARKIN AWOKE TO a figure hovering over him in a crouched position. His hazy eyes were unable to distinguish the features, so he closed them again. Although his sight was unreliable his other senses were unaffected, Larkin immediately knew he was in the presence of another vampire.

"Julius," he said trying to hide a playful grin.

"Larkin," he said followed by a sarcastic tone, "let me guess, fell off the couch drunk on amber."

Larkin chuckled and thought, *Wyler.* He did not move; he only responded, "This visit is unexpected. To what do I owe the pleasure?"

"Since when do I need an invitation or reason?"

"You misunderstand me; I only assumed you were coerced here." Then he said in a rather authoritative tone, "Wyler, bring our friend something to eat."

Before Wyler could respond Julius said, "No, thanks. I have already had dinner, but I would love some dessert."

Larkin did not respond. He simply lay on the floor listening to Wyler, "What do you have in mind? I- I mean Wyler will get you whatever you need."

Without an acknowledgement or cursory glance toward Wyler, Julius said, "I think something exotic," as he held out his hand toward Larkin.

Larkin took his hand as he mumbled the word exotic under his breath, and then he turned to Wyler and said, "Never mind. We will be going out."

Wyler nodded his head and walked away. Without another word, Larkin and Julius proceeded to enter the underground cellar that emerged a few blocks either up or down town depending on which route they took. Julius silently followed Larkin as they took the path that would lead them to the edge of Transylvania just near the town's clever tribute to fiction, the bat water tower. The well-concealed exit was overgrown with wild grass and untamed shrubberies making it hard for the public to discover. When they reached the exit, they listened for a moment for the sound of human voices, but all they heard was the wind as it rattled by. Larkin pushed against the stone covering so that they could exit the tunnel, and after emerging Larkin glared at Julius and said, "What's this really about?"

"Dessert."

"I think I'll pass."

"Then why did you come?" asked Julius.

"I thought you needed to talk. You know as well as I that there is nothing exotic in this town except Mr. Peterson's striptease."

Julius shook his head and said with a hint of laughter, "The things humans will do for pleasure."

Larkin, intrigued at Julius's amusement, continued, "Mrs. Peterson found out about her husband's affair with Greta."

Julius scoffed, "I bet she cried."

"Yes, but while holding a gun."

Julius could not hold his laughter in as he replied, "So I heard."

Larkin tried to use Julius's sense of humor to extract his true agenda, so he teased, "You hear a lot for someone residing in another town. What else did you happen upon?"

He stopped laughing and with a fixed stare, he offered, "Join me for dessert, and I will tell you."

Larkin knew it was a long shot but well worth the try. He also knew he would not get anything else out of Julius without giving something back.

Using his supernatural senses, Julius perceived that Larkin was not ready to hear what he had to say. Instead, Julius thought he would avert the topic until the right moment presented itself.

Although Larkin had consented to have dessert with him, he did so with one condition. "Okay, but it's my choice," said Larkin.

Julius conceded with a smirk and followed him as they strolled through the woods back toward town. They chose the same old path that Mr. Peterson took every time he met up with Greta for their secret rendezvous, which were excessive as of late. They walked down the recently worn path in silence. They were both quietly formulating a strategy to manipulate the other into exposing the motive for their vagueness.

When they reached the back of Peterson's General Store, Julius asked, "So… what will it be tonight? I hope something a little exotic."

"You will see. Stay here and keep a look out. There have been many people around since the incident. I'll be back in a moment."

Larkin ducked in the store as a smile crossed Julius's face. He was not smiling at Larkin's attempts to keep their delectable dessert a secret. It was the thought of Mrs. Peterson with tears streaming down her face, holding a gun, and shooting rapidly throughout the store with no aim, all the while cursing at her cheating husband that had him smiling. He simply shook his head at his final thought: *Humans are so dramatic. It's like going to a show every day.*

"Let's go," said Larkin reemerging from the shop.

As they edged their way around the building, Larkin presented Julius with an ice cream cone.

They reached Main Street undetected before Julius blurted out in a questioning tone, "Ice cream?"

"Yes, ice cream. What's the matter? You said you wanted something exotic."

"Are you confused? There is nothing exotic about an ice cream cone."

Larkin took a bite. And, with a devilish grin said, "Nothing. . . except only a vampire would be cold blooded enough to eat ice cream in the dead of snow."

"Now that you put it that way, I guess the circumstance makes it a little exotic. Nice choice."

"Okay, we got some dessert. No more games. What did you hear?"

Still predicting an unfavorable reaction from Larkin's bodily expressions, Julius tried to prolong the conversation, "Nothing much. Do you want another?"

With a fiery gaze, Larkin placed one hand roughly on his shoulder, and said, "No more stalling! And do not lie to me either. I made you, so I know you have an ulterior motive for being here."

They turned down an alley just off of Main Street as Julius took the last bite of his ice cream cone. "I hear you have a guest."

Larkin slowed his step as he responded, "Wyler rented out your old apartment to his new clerk, but I suspect you already knew that. What else did Wyler tell you?"

Julius sensed the time was now. If he prolonged the topic any further, Larkin might become enraged and uncontrollable. Although there was no one else in the ally, there were still several individuals scuttling about on Main Street. Julius did not particularly care if a scene occurred. He knew Larkin would despise himself if such an event took place in public, so Julius opened his discussion with basic facts until they had strutted far enough down the alley to be isolated from society.

After he was done, Julius turned to Larkin and said, "Does Wyler have a reason to be concerned?"

Trying not to reveal too much, he responded, "I didn't know he was troubled. Ana's usually the worrywart."

"You know very well he is only concerned that you are hiding something from him about her."

Larkin slowed his step again as he responded, "Who? Ana! Why would I hide something about her?"

Now halted, they turned face to face as Julius responded, "These games are unnecessary between us. You know very well that Wyler thinks you attacked Jezalyn."

"Oh, that. I thought I made myself clear. I will have another talk with him," responded Larkin nonchalantly.

"Stop avoiding the implication. Did you attack her?"

"You're the one who has been evading the topic all night not me. And to answer your question, no."

"So you maintain you saved her?"

"Yes."

"Okay," said Julius as they both commenced their stroll down the alley, "but one more thing."

"What is it now?"

Julius could tell Larkin's tone had changed, but it did not stop him from pursuing his questioning, "Did you drink from her?"

Larkin's look of annoyance had left him. Instead, it was replaced with exasperation as he stated, "I already told you. I did not attack her."

Julius sensed Larkin was hiding something as he thought about Larkin's last response, *I did not ask if he attacked her again, I asked if he fed off of her, and yet he is still defending himself. I will have to push him if I want to discover the truth.*

Julius took several large steps, turned, and stopped in front of Larkin so that they would be face to face once again. Without hesitation, he brushed his tongue over his left fang and asked, "Is she tasty," trying to extract the information out of Larkin by provoking him.

Larkin lunged forward at him, but Julius's reflexes were swift. They found themselves squared off against each other's shoulders.

Larkin roared, "Just leave it alone!"

"Stop avoiding! Tell me what really happened."

Larkin released his forceful grip, leaned forward, twisted to the right, and Julius sailed past him into the brick wall. Julius retaliated by lunging forward at Larkin's midsection, leaving the crumbled bricks behind him. The force of the impact caused them both to crash through the metal siding of a storage unit. Once they scrambled back to their feet, Larkin saw a piece of torn metal protruding out from Julius's left shoulder. Larkin quickly moved forward to remove the piece of metal, but when he got close enough Julius lunged at him. Larkin broke free, pushed himself back, and said, "Alright, that's enough. Look at your shoulder."

Julius's only response was, "You're going to have to kill me because I won't stop until you tell me the truth."

Larkin smiled. He had always loved Julius's intensity, which is one of the reasons he converted him;

however, intriguing as Julius was, Larkin hated it when Julius used his keen ability of perception against him. Letting the smile fade a bit, Larkin said, "I hate when you use your innate abilities against me. How long have you known I was hiding something?"

He laughed and said, "Ever since you proclaimed my visit to be unexpected and coerced."

Julius scanned the storage unit before sitting down on the edge of an old couch surrounded by boxes. Larkin walked over and directed, "Close your eyes. I will remove it swiftly."

He put his hand up, "No. It is too deep. If it's removed now, I will leave a blood trail back to the shop. Just leave it for Wyler."

"Are you sure?"

Pain crossed his face as he placed his hand under the metal shard for support and said, "Yes. Now tell me what really happened between you and Jezalyn."

Larkin ripped through several boxes and pulled out a red and green Christmas throw. "Okay, but let's get home first. If the chief catches us here, we'll be visiting Mrs. Peterson," he said as he wrapped the throw around Julius's shoulders to hide the wound.

They peered around the jagged, metal edge of the building and saw no one in the alley, so they stepped out and started their journey back toward the water tower. Julius expanded on Larkin's detainment comment with haughty amusement, "If we get hauled in, would you do a rendition of Mrs. Peterson crying?"

Larkin perceived his riddled sarcasm and said with a deep breath, "Yes, I attacked her."

Julius released a short chuckle and said, "Wyler was correct."

Julius slouched over as Larkin supported him so that the shard of metal would not be visible. Although Larkin could not see Julius's face, Larkin knew that he released a sinister smile as he pronounced Wyler's earlier assumptions accurate.

"Not exactly, I. . ." He slowed his step and clarified, "I did, but I didn't. Not the way Wyler is thinking. I am sure Wyler told you about the bloody tea incident."

"He did. He also thinks you may be too attached since you haven't decided whether to eradicate or release her yet."

"I had found her somewhat interesting; she likes Mythology."

"Fascinating," Julius replied, filling his voice with sarcasm.

"Never mind. Anyway, I finally decided to get rid of her, so I was waiting for Wyler to come back upstairs so that I could tell him. But then I heard Mrs. Peterson cursing and screaming. I also heard the gun cock back and two shots, but the bullets only lodged in the wall."

Hearing that the bullets had not penetrated the wall, Julius was ready to make a declaration. "So you did cause the wound," proclaimed Julius, who tried to marvel in his conclusions, but could not since the metal implement caused him too much discomfort. It was something of an irritation, for every little wriggle sent an intense pang down his arm.

"No, it was a bullet. She was in front of me when I heard the bullet break through the wall. I jumped over the counter and lunged myself toward her."

"Wyler did say you saved Jezalyn from a stray bullet," said Julius thinking out loud. He was trying to work out the facts, yet he was becoming increasingly bored with the situation.

Larkin hung his head, "I did not save her. I pushed her. . ."

Julius let out a chuckle accompanied by the word, "Really? So you're a villainous hero?"

"Sure, if that's what you call it." Julius stared intensely at Larkin until he continued, "Okay! Okay! When I heard the bullets penetrated through the wall, all I could think was this would be the perfect chance to get rid of her."

"Your rendition of this little escapade is a few details shy of a narrative," he said, after listening to Larkin contradict the previous details.

Perplexed, Larkin responded, "What do you mean?"

"It's sounding more like a fable than reality. The bullets either did or didn't penetrate the wall, which is it?" Julius questioned.

Feeling he needed to defend himself, Larkin quickly gave justification to his story to refute Julius's underlying claim that what he was reporting to him was the truth.

"Both, some did and some didn't. I pushed her into one that did, and it clipped her neck," Larkin explained.

Julius laughed again and said, "And?"

Feeling his taunt, Larkin shot back "That's it."

"That's not it because if you wanted her dead, she would be dead."

Larkin shook his head and said, "It was an unfortunate turn of events," and afterward mumbled, "if it had been only a few more inches. . ."

"I am sure it was not by pure misfortune that the bullet only grazed her," and with that remark they reached the entrance near the water tower.

Larkin said, "Here let me help you down."

With a devilish grin he replied, "Right after you tell the truth about why she is still alive."

"It was a bad calculation that's all. Come, so Wyler can stitch you up."

Julius let out an ominous grunt and said, "Our precision is our specialty. Save us both energy and come out with it, or Wyler will be pulling this metal shard out of your skull."

Julius tossed the throw off and gripped the shard, but before he could tug, Larkin said, "Stop! The blood." Julius made no response as he gave Larkin an unwavering glare and gripped the metal tighter causing his hand to slice open and blood droplets to fall to the ground. As the blood droplets hit the ground, a light pounding rang in their ears, which inevitably forced the truth from Larkin's lips. Larkin watched as the blood hit the ground and felt no reaction to

Julius's nonverbal threat to expose their underground tunnel. However, his failure to kill Jezalyn was weighing on him and he needed someone to confide in. Julius was the closest thing to a blood family member Larkin had left, so he glanced up at Julius and with a sigh said, "Don't be so dramatic, Julius."

"Huh, only humans are dramatic. I am simply passionate."

Larkin bent down to pick up the bloody throw that had once been covering Julius's wound, and finally admitted, "I don't know why she is alive. She was already bleeding, and all I had to do was suck, but for some reason when it came time I choked." True, the bullet had displayed a wound that would have cloaked his entry. True, when it came time to press his lips against her neck he was unable to follow through. False, he had not known why he did not follow through, for when he peered into his victims face he saw Isadora's eyes. Taking a deep breath, without acknowledging his companion, Larkin self-justified his weakness, "I think I have been stagnant way too long."

"Thank you. Was that so hard to admit?"

"The decision to kill or not to kill—no. The recognition that I buckled under pressure—yes."

They entered the entrance to the underground tunnel. As Larkin closed and hinged the exit shut, Julius for a brief moment unguarded his selfish whims and casually told his maker, "You know - you don't have to do it right now. If her thoughts start to madden you, you sedate yourself while she is awake." Noticing no response to his suggestion, Julius reverted back to his old behavior and added, "Besides, you can always waste away with your meditation at any point of the day."

Larkin understood his wisecrack as it was meant to aide him in a plan to keep his sanity, for he could see having a reverse schedule was a good plan since Jezalyn did not dream, so he acknowledged Julius's final suggestion with a nodding glance. They were almost back to the apartment when Julius made another joking remark about their evening. "You know ice-cream is always a good date desert, but you might want to think about spending the whole dollar and order the malt if you want another date."

Larkin replied, "Perhaps, but you never seem to acquire a second date."

Julius let out a robust laugh that melted away any evident tension, and they both joked and laughed hysterically until they reached Wyler. Their laughter caught Wyler's attention, so he was ready and waiting to attend to them at the entrance.

"What happened?" said Wyler as he saw the blood soaked Christmas throw in Larkin's hands.

"We had a little misunderstanding."

"Where!?! With whom? How long is the blood trail? Is it something or someone?"

As Larkin moved past Wyler, Julius came into view and replied, "No. It was with each other, and we were careful with the blood."

They entered the kitchen where Wyler kept his old black medical bag.

"Here bite down on this," said Wyler as he handed him one of Ana's wooden spoons.

"I won't need this. Just pull it out."

With the spoon still out toward him, Wyler said, "Indulge me. The object is embed deep, so it may take a few tugs."

Larkin made a fire in the old wood heater as Julius clamped his teeth down on the spoon. Julius rolled the wood back in forth between his teeth before uttering; "Get on with it."

Larkin watched as Wyler examined closely around the impaled object. Then with a slight twist of the wrist, Larkin flung the throw into the fire and watched it burn as he tried to determine beyond Julius's muffled groans if Jezalyn had been awakened.

ChAPCER 14: CEA FOR Chree

TWILIGHT WAS FLEETING when Wyler finished patching up Julius's wound. The clouds radiated a reddish-burnt orange that faded into a shade of creamy tangerine; the sun was coming, and Julius was running out of time. Unlike his creator, he could not venture out into the sunlight. There had always been two lines of vampires: ones who could and ones who could not endure the sun. Luckily for the human world, the majority of vampires suffered the same limitations as Julius.

As Wyler put away his surgical tools, Larkin tossed something to Julius and said, "The sun is about to peek."

Julius snagged the cloth with a firm grip before letting it dangle. A light shake of the material revealed that Larkin had flung him a black single pocket tee. "Since it looks like I'll be staying here awhile," he paused and gave a mischievous grin, "what do you have on tap?"

Larkin moved to the refrigerator and said, "Let's see." He carelessly opened the door. "We have aged and aged. What would you prefer?"

"I think I will take the second aged," replied Julius with a more serious edge than it deserved.

"Very well, I will take the first." Larkin popped the two bags of blood into the microwave and pulled two cups from the cupboard.

Wyler peered back in astonishment at their mutual changes in temperament. Just a short while ago, they had tried to kill each other; but now, they stood almost side by side as they passed light bantering back and forth, while having an early morning snack, as if nothing had ever occurred. Wyler mumbled, "Uh! I need a cup of tea." He moved to put the kettle on but stopped short when he remembered all of the sugar was upstairs.

With the wound pretty much patched up, Wyler said, "If you don't need anything else, I'll be upstairs making a cup of tea."

After quickly surveying Wyler's handy work, Julius waved a dismissal the way one would wave off the nuisance of a fly. Trying to alleviate any hard feelings for such an ungrateful brush off, Larkin stepped forward. "It looks like the bleeding has almost stopped. Go ahead and make your tea. I'll come up to the shop after I get Julius all settled in."

It had never been Wyler's idea to be a Keeper, and he especially never expected to fulfill the role for two once he had accepted. He had always found his duties to preserve Larkin doable although sometimes challenging, for he liked things a particular way, yet he never placed himself into harm's way. However, once Julius entered the family, life as a Keeper for Wyler had become taxing. It was rare that Julius showed Wyler any appreciation, and only adhered under the direction of Larkin. Although there were many reasons for Wyler to despise Julius, he did not. He would simply fold to the will of both Larkin and Julius. Ana, however, faulted Julius for all his bad behavior, but if not for any reason alone, Julius's lack of regard for her husband was enough to make Ana despise him for all eternity. Therefore, when Julius coolly called out, "Thanks for the help." Wyler did not notice Julius's dispassionate gratitude; he had one target in mind. Instead, Wyler proceeded to the stockroom. He always needed a cup of tea after stitching up one of the vampires. Their recent medical needs, as well as Jezalyn's, had brought back memories of the war, and a cup of tea always soothed him from the discombobulating sentiments.

When the door shut, Wyler left the thought of blood, needles, and thread behind. He meditated on his soon to be hot cup of tea. He thought about the aroma, the smooth blend, and the way it would flow warmly down his throat. His anticipation was so great it almost seemed as if he could smell the tea brewing. He weaved around a few piles of books and finally made it to the kitchen area where he saw Jezalyn sitting at a small table holding a little green and white teacup.

"Good morning, Wyler." she said, taking a sip of her tea. "I made a pot of tea. Hope you don't mind."

Startled at the sight of her, Wyler responded, "Oh, no. Not at all, I just came up to make a cup myself."

Jezalyn gestured toward the kettle while holding the cup with both hands, "I think there is enough water left for another cup."

Wyler nodded and moved toward the kettle, "How is your neck?"

She lightly cupped her hand over the wound, "It's a little sore. Thanks again for taking care of me."

"You're welcome," said Wyler as he turned and leaned against the counter, "so are you feeling up to working today."

She gave a sweet smile as she responded, "I took an ibuprofen this morning, so I'm good to go. Besides, it's not as if today's events will be a matinee of yesterdays. I am determined to make it through one day of work without so much as a paper cut."

Wyler only stared not knowing how to respond, but all the while he was laughing within. A paper cut was the least of his worries; he just stitched up a large gaping hole in Julius's chest, which had to have left a trail of blood. Pouring himself a cup of tea, Wyler contemplated how and when he would be able to clean up the careless mess of his vampire rulers.

There was an instance of silence, before they heard the chiming tolls of an old grandfather clock marking the hour. Wyler smiled and said, "I guess we should get set up."

"Okay. I'll clean up my mess and be out in a jiff."

Wyler nodded his head and walked toward the entrance that led into the shop. When he exited the entranceway, Wyler saw Larkin pop up from behind the counter.

Stunned to see him behind the counter, Wyler said with some surprise, "Larkin! What are you doing?"

Grinning at Wyler's alarmed face, he coolly responded, "I see my presence is startling even after I told you I would be right up."

"No. I'm fine," he told Larkin, moving closer to the counter. "Jezalyn is in the back. She will be out in a moment."

"I know. I can hear her. She is humming a little ditty to herself, and now she's thinking, *One more saucer and I will be done. No, wait, maybe I should ask Wyler if he wants me to clean his cup, too.*"

Wyler stared at him with almost a blank expression as he mumbled, "What? Why would she. . ."

Larkin ducked behind the side of the counter as Jezalyn appeared, "Hey, Wyler."

"Yes?"

"Would you like me to wash your cup before I drain the dish water?" she asked sweetly.

Interested as to the reasoning why Larkin hid, Wyler took a big gulp of his tea and handed the cup to Jezalyn. The tea being quite warm burned into the pit of his stomach, but it was worth it he thought so long as it gave him a couple more minutes alone with Larkin.

Accepting his empty cup and his thank you, Jezalyn bounced back into the stockroom. Her departure brought the arrival of Larkin into his view, for he reemerged and said, "See, I told you."

Uninterested in his lighthearted banter, Wyler ignored the tease and asked, "Why did you hide?"

"Me? Hide? I did not hide."

"Yes, you did. One minute you're standing right there, and the next you are crouching down out of sight moments before she came in."

"My pants leg was twisted, and I simply bent down to straighten it out. Besides, what reason would I have to hide?" he said, still evading Wyler and his suspicious questioning.

"I don't know; that's what I am trying to find out."

Larkin smiled and said, "She is letting the water out of the sink. Maybe I should go see if she will make another pot."

Wyler suspiciously thought Larkin was not ready to see Jezalyn yet, so he decided to test out his theory. *If I tell him to go see if she will make another pot of tea and he recants the idea, then I will know he was definitely avoiding her.*

"That's a good idea. I could go for another cup of tea, and while you're gone I'll open the shop," responded Wyler putting Larkin to the test.

Larkin did not show one hint of reluctance as he turned to prance out of the shop. Wyler lingered a moment as he reflected on the outcome. *This just reminds me why I never play poker with him anymore,* and with that thought, he turned, moved toward the door, flipped over the open sign, and unlocked the door, but before he could fully open the blinds covering the windows, he heard the door open. Wyler turned to find a woman with tight blonde curls standing in front of a man with a rather large video camera. Wyler knew who she was before she even opened her mouth. Her name was Mary Sherwood, a reporter for Channel 3 News and Transylvania's Watchman.

"Excuse me," said the woman. "I am Mary Sherwood from Channel 3. I am looking for Jezalyn Williford and," she glanced down at the notepad, "you must be Larkin. How does it feel to be a hero?"

Wyler held up his hand, "You are mistaken. I am Wyler and this is my shop."

"Oh, I am sorry," she said and continued to point a microphone toward Wyler. "Mr. Wyler, how do you feel about the events that unfolded in your shop yesterday? Were you afraid for your life?"

With almost no emotion Wyler responded, "There was no incident in my shop yesterday. I think you are inquiring about the incident that took place at Transylvania General Store. You should check with Mr. Peterson next door."

"I did, but I got a tip that someone at your shop was injured, so I am here to acquire an interview with either Jezalyn or her rescuer. Aka, knight in shining armor," she said with a little wink. "Do you know how I can get in touch with them?"

Wyler looked at her with masked frustration, "Sorry, but no. I am trying to run a business, so I must ask you to leave."

"And a nice shop it is. I'll poke around a bit before I go," she said, not waiting for a response as she scurried over to the closest bookshelf.

Wyler moving to her agreed, but not without one condition, "Sure, but you'll have to leave the cameras behind."

With some irritation, she whipped around and said, "Wait for me outside, Paul." She winked at him as they both turned; Paul left the store and Mary faced Wyler once again. She gave Wyler a smiling nod and walked over to the next bookshelf and scanned the collection, but that was not all she was scanning. She slowly made her way to the end of the shelf. Once at the end of it, she squatted down to take a book from the bottom shelf on the pretext of probing. Every once in a while Mary abandoned the bookshelf to examine the wall adjacent to the general store. She moved up several bookshelves before Wyler caught on to her scheme, and before he could scamper over to her, Mary had already discovered a bullet hole. As he approached, she pushed her little notepad back in her pocket.

He hovered over her. Not wanting to be thrown out before making it to the next shelf, she held up a worn pocket-size red velvet book. Its condition was somewhat good; it only had a few bald spots for its age.

"How much is this?"

With a blunt tone Wyler responded, "Fifty-two dollars."

Mary swallowed hard, but did not let it show. She thought twelve dollars was more than sufficient for any used book. She debated in her mind over it and eventually decided, *Sometimes you have to pay for the scoop, but this time It's a small fortune.*

She handed Wyler the book and said, "I will take it."

"Alright, the register is this way," he said as he hesitantly scuttled off with Mary trailing behind.

Mary lagged behind letting some space gap between them. Instead of following Wyler to the register, she ducked off behind another bookshelf, but this time she did not linger. She rushed directly to the wall and examined it. There were two more bullet holes. One hole looked clean as if the bullet had passed straight through, while the sheetrock around the other had pothole type indentions like the shell had been dug out.

Wyler had reached the register alone. Angrily he charged back through the store and once he spotted Mary, he advanced upon her rapidly. "You are trying my patience; I told you there is no story here. I think it's time you left."

Mary was stunned at his tone, but did not waver. "If there's not a story here then how do you explain those," she said as she pointed to the bullet holes.

"That is the results of having artwork brandished throughout the store. No more inquires. Now purchase your book or leave."

She had agreed to purchase the book so that she could get a closer look at the back of the store even if it would be from a distance. This time Wyler walked beside her, so she would not be able disappear again. As he was checking her out, Ana appeared next to him. She had just arrived home from her double shift. Mary took one glance at her and eagerly proclaimed, "You must be Jezalyn. Do you feel Mrs. Peterson should be charged with your attempted murder?"

Ana peered at her with some confusion, "Who are you?"

Mary tried to respond, "I am. . . ," but Wyler cut her off.

Wyler's anger was now borderline fury, which was unmistakable in his tone, "This is my wife, Ana." He shoved the book across the counter and with a point of his finger he demanded, "Get out of my shop!"

Mary grabbed her book and said as she retreated, "If there was no story then you wouldn't be so defensive."

Wyler followed her to the door, and before she left he said, "If you call someone liking to not have their privacy invaded a story, then sure there is a story."

As he slammed the door and locked it, he heard her say, "I won't consider this story over until I get my interviews. Paul! Get the gear out we're setting up camp."

Ana glanced at Wyler alarmingly. "What's happening around here? And why is a reporter snooping around?"

"Mrs. Peterson found out about Mr. Peterson's affair with Greta. Her reaction caused quite a scandal," he explained. Wyler tried to relate the event, but Ana held up her hand to stop him.

"Wait! I am too tired to hear all of the details; I need a nap. Come down and tell me later."

"Okay, Bunny. But, before you go down. I should warn you Julius is stuck here until dusk."

"What? Why is he here?"

"He and Larkin had words," replied Wyler as an exhausted expression crossed his face.

She shook her head and thought, *Not again. Last time we were cleaning up blood for days.* "Did you finish cleaning up behind their temper tantrum?"

"Yes," he said. He had cleaned up downstairs while he waited to see if Julius's wound was appropriately closed. However, he still had the tunnel to deal with, yet he didn't want to worry his tired wife with that so he simply stated, "Yes," with a grand smile hoping it was believable enough for her to go rest as she had planned.

Thanks to the fatigue, it did not matter if Ana believed him or not, she closed her burning eyes and through her loving smile she kissed her husband's cheek.

Upon withdrawal she said, "Well, the details on that occurrence can also wait. I am going to bed."

Wyler returned her little token and watched her depart. Several minutes later Larkin and Jezalyn finally reemerged. "We got your cup of tea," announced Jezalyn. Trying to justify the presentation of a new dish, Jezalyn added, "Sorry it's in a new cup. I had just finished washing our cups when you sent Larkin to tell me to brew another pot. And, it took so long, because I misjudged the amount of water it would take to make tea for three, so I had to make two pots."

Wyler took the cup and said, "That's fine. It was better that the both of you were still in the back. A nosey reporter came around wanting to interview the two of you about yesterday."

Anxiety crept over Jezalyn's face at the thought of having to recount the events. And, Larkin felt Jezalyn's uneasiness, yet waited until her facial expression gave it away before he asked, "Are you feeling alright Jezalyn?"

"Yeah, I am fine. I just don't want to give any interviews," said Jezalyn, trying not fidget.

Wyler placed his hand on her shoulder. "You don't have to do anything you don't want to do. Maybe you should take a few days off until it blows over."

Her expression did not brighten, "Thanks, Wyler that is a nice offer, but I can't afford to be off work that long."

"Oh no, my dear, consider this paid personal leave," he said. "I'm leaving town to acquire a few pieces for my personal collection, so we'll be closed anyway."

Jezalyn's gloom subsided and she thanked Wyler for upcoming vacation. He only smiled as he thought, *that was easy. Now if I can only smooth over things downstairs with such ease.* Wyler knew, even in his wife's state, that fatigue would not stop her from speaking her mind when it came to capricious Julius.

ᏟᎻᎪᑭͲᎬᏒ 15: Ͳhe ᏟᎪᏞᏞ

EVERAL HOURS LATER, the reporter was still camped outside Wyler's Rare Bookstore. She stood in front of the general store where she gave a live report on the altercation that took place the previous day.

She began with her usual good evening satire before plunging into her report:

Yesterday. Here in this small town of Transylvania, Louisiana, a domestic disturbance took place, which ended in tears and gunfire, when a woman discovered her husband was having an adulterous affair. It was about noon yesterday when police officers responded to a 911 call that reported gunshots fired inside this local general store. The police arrived on the scene to find Mr. and Mrs. Peterson, the owners, at the end of their domestic dispute. Mrs. Peterson sat slumped over in the middle of the floor crying with a gun in her lap while her husband hid locked away in the back office. The husband was not injured, but it has been reported by a reliable source that Mrs. Peterson fired erratically throughout the store leaving a wide trail of bullets. Some bullets merely lodged in the wall while others punctured through into the nearby bookstore.

One source disclosed to Channel 3, 'One of the stray bullets penetrated through the wall hitting a young female employee in the neck.' The source went on to state, 'The victim would be in critical condition if not dead had it not been for the heroic actions of one man who pushed her out of the way just in the nick of time.'

All requests for an interview with the injured and heroic party have been denied, but it has been this reporter's goal to not rest until an official interview has been conducted. Until next time, this is Mary Sherwood reporting for Channel 3 news in the once quiet town of Transylvania. Now back to you at the studio, Mark.

***

Wyler, who stood next to the television, violently pushed the off button, "Well that's just great! Now what are we going to do about this?"

Larkin said nothing as he sat on the couch with a cold, but rather fresh cup of blood that Julius brought back from his hunt. Julius, however, gave his input. "We have three options that I can see: The first two are to either grant her the interview or ignore her. She will either get tired of waiting, or she will get what she came for and leave."

"I think it is best to wait her out," said Wyler, not mentioning that Julius had only revealed two of his three choices. He knew Julius well enough to guess the third, so he kept quiet. Yet, he was not the only one. Larkin sat only sipping his beverage as he listened to each view.

"I would let them do the interview so that she will leave. Or maybe you would rather draw the issue out so that the reporter can give free press and advertisement for the shop," quipped Julius.

Wyler did not fall into Julius's taunt, "No, it is not up to me. Jezalyn told me she doesn't want to do the interview."

A long pause of silence fell across the room. Larkin knew that Julius was contemplating over the reasons why Jezalyn did not want to give an interview. He also did not want the conversation to turn on her, which could lead to exposure of his previous behavior, so Larkin finally spoke, "You said three options?"

"Yes. I did," said Julius with a mischievous grin, for it was his personal preference. After quickly running his tongue over his left fang, Julius added, "I could always make her my next snack." He immediately saw alarm cross Wyler's face, but it quickly faded. The short lived alarm did not giving Julius enough satisfaction, so he did what he usually did best and joshed, "I like option three; it's fool proof," and with a mischievous wink, he added, "everyone wins."

Wyler had always been good at concealing his emotions, although tonight was an exception. However, he held them much better than his wife, Ana, who awoke from her nap after working a double shift to get a drink of water and overheard Julius's plan to release the reporter of her present duties. Ana, hair bedraggled, stormed up to Julius, put her finger in his face, and said, "How can you say option three is the best idea; the only one winning will be you. Killing that reporter will cause only more chaos and suspicion. They will send another reporter to take her place, except the new reporter will not only be trying to acquire interviews but also discover what happened to the last reporter."

Ana was not his Keeper and nor did she pretend to be, which was the only thing that Julius respected about her. So when she had these types of outburst on him, which was rare, he ignored them; perhaps more so because he liked the banter her imprudent behavior caused. "She will not be discovered nor will her disappearance be in any way connected to the shop, so it sounds like to me the problem is solved. Now kindly remove your finger," said Julius with a complacent smile on his face.

Wyler pulled Ana back several steps, for he and Ana were not Julius's official Keeper, yet Wyler served Julius at the simple request of Larkin. And even at that Larkin had not pressed it upon him. Wyler accepted the tedious challenge, because no matter which request small or large he felt obliged to follow through; and he did so even with advance knowledge of Julius bad natured temper. Thus once his wife was out of Julius's direct arm reach, Wyler cautiously told Julius, "No, not problem solved. You can't solve everything with death."

He moved a few steps closer to Ana and said, "You sure about that?"

Ignoring the smooth gestures of her husband, this time she did not back away. The tension mounted between the two as they both stood there squared off; both too unrelenting to back down from one another. Finally, Larkin broke the tension and uncomfortable silence, "You are both right. We don't need to increase suspicion around us, and the best way to get the reporter to leave is to do the interview."

Wyler felt some relief as Julius's attention to his wife dwindled but not enough, so he interjected further possible issues, "How are we going to do that? Jezalyn said she wasn't going to do the interview."

Ana immediately offered to talk to Jezalyn about giving the interview, but Larkin said, "No. Leave it to me. I think we will have a better chance at getting her to do the interview if I speak with her."

Wyler broke in; panicked and uneasy, "How are you going to do that? She barely knows you."

Julius, hoping to stir the excitement further, electively inserted himself into the conversation, "She barely knows any of you, so why does it matter who talks to her."

Larkin had not perceived him to be on his side, for he understood the hidden meaning that lay beneath the comment, especially when Julius continued with a chuckle, "Besides, she is more likely to open up to her hero than anyone else." He expected his comment to create some type of tension between them, but it hadn't. Wyler nodded his head in agreement. He felt that perhaps Jezalyn would open up to him, since after all he had saved her life.

Larkin made no emotional response to the statements set before him. Instead, he announced that a plan would soon be devised and all should go to bed so that he could think. Of course, Wyler proposed to stay up and help come up with an effective plan or scenarios for tomorrow. He ended his offer with an unsuccessful attempt at hiding a yawn.

Ana smiling gingerly at her husband, kissed his cheek and said, "Honey, I think Larkin has this under control now, so come to bed." Giving a goodnight nod, Wyler took his wife's hand to leave the room. As they proceeded to leave, Ana glowered at Julius, who moved to take a seat next to Larkin, and said, "I suspect you are staying the night again."

"Why, thank you for the invite. I think I will stay," he said, with as much of a charmingly punch as possible. It was not her intention for him to stay or to invite him to stay. She was trying to use subtle sarcasm, as she had done in the past, to ward off his presence. However, tonight it did not work. The only possible response left for her to give him was goodnight, which she did with a dreadfully heated expression upon her face.

As Julius took a seat next to Larkin in the emptied living room, he could not help but make one final crack about Ana. "I wouldn't want to offend her by taking off after tonight's little heated discussion. Besides, I am not abandoning plan three until after the lovely Mary Sherwood has left the premises. She looks exceptionally tasty," he said with a mischievous chuckle.

Larkin gave into Julius's playful behavior and replied, "Do what you will for the night, but don't touch the reporter until it's a last resort. If it does lead to that, save me a small treat." When he finished he let his head fall backwards with closed eyes.

Larkin was deep either in thought or in meditation, but Julius did not care which. He himself was cleverly devising his own plan. Earlier, he had inadvertently called into question Larkin's motive for being the one to talk Jezalyn into giving an interview, but all the while giving Larkin a reason to spend more time with Jezalyn. Julius found Larkin's intrigue with Jezalyn fascinating; it was a bond he had never expected his maker to experience again.

He perceived there was something more going on than what Larkin claimed. Maybe Larkin did not even realize it himself yet, but either way, Julius was determined to see the outcome of his maker's new found attachment to the end.

***

The following morning Jezalyn awoke to her phone ringing. It was her grandfather. He did not give her a salutary greeting. But instead he immediately rambled off part of his newspaper to her. "Yesterday's altercation at Transylvania's general store was tragic, but did not end in tragedy. Mrs. Peterson was shooting off several rounds at her husband when a stray bullet inadvertently hit an innocent bystander after puncturing the wall of Wyler's Rare Bookstore. The identity of the employee has not been released, but reports say, 'Although she did not escape unscathed she is alive and well due to the heroic act of one kind gentleman.'"

When he finished reading, he made no further inquiries; instead, he sat silently waiting for a response. Jezalyn knew her grandfather all too well. She would not be able to brush the report off without any details, so with a deep breath she responded to his silent inquiry. "That report is not entirely true. Yes. There were gunshots next door, but I wasn't shot. "

"The report claims a female was injured, if not you then who?"

"Well, I did sustain a minor scratch on my neck, but it was only a graze."

"I figured as much. Pack your bags you are coming home immediately."

"No, grandpa! I don't want to come home; it's—"

He cut her short, not allowing her to finish her line of reasoning, "Oh, Yes ma'am you are. I will not have you living and working in a dangerous place."

As the word "place" left his tongue she responded, "But Grandpa, this isn't a dangerous town; the people here say that this was the first time something like this has occurred in over fifty years."

"You're not making a strong case for yourself, young lady, and it sounds like a history of violence to me."

"A fifty year history, so the next occurrence should not be scheduled to happen in a long while. I'll be dead by then," she said, trying to build an argument for saving her independence.

"Poor choice of words, my dear, and none the less it is history. It is not a given that it will strike every fifty years; it could be in a few days or months. The future is unpredictable, my dear, so go on and start packing, and call me when you're on your way," he demanded in a composed manner.

Jezalyn's frustration showed in her pink face. She was getting nowhere, so she took several deep breaths, letting the color restore in her face before trying a more subtle approach. "Grandpa, listen. I know the report scared you, and I should have called right away. It's just that I did not want to alarm you. The bullet barely nicked me."

"Only because someone pushed you out of its way. I am sure next time you will not be so lucky," he said with a stern voice.

"Yes, but, Grandpa, please," she pleaded. She stated her love for the shop, the job, the cheap rent, and the easy commute. She also tried to argue the point of an independent life in Transylvania as the best opportunity to gain responsible life skills. Jezalyn finished up her appeal with the fact that her boss was really, really nice. And to prove it she told her grandfather that Wyler had given her a few days off, with pay, until the reporters cleared out so that she could rest and concentrate on school. "Please, Grandpa. I want to stay," she whined.

"I am sorry but no. You must come home now. I feel that Transylvania is not safe for you."

She was silent as she thought of another defense for staying, for it had not taken long for Jezalyn to realize that her plea was more similar to a sixteen year old begging for a later curfew than one of an independent college student. Although both her reasoning and heartfelt plea had failed leaving her with only one option left, directness. "Grandpa, I love you but no, I am not leaving. I want to be independent and out on my own. I am almost nineteen years old now. Please stop treating me like a child. I will not pack up and leave because some stupid wife got mad at her cheating husband. I am in no danger here, so I am staying with or without your consent." When she concluded, her breast heaved and she was gasping for air. Jezalyn had spoken as fervently as possible trying to make her grandfather understand how important it was for her to remain away from home.

Her grandfather showed no signs of relenting, and he merely responded, "I have to go. There is someone at the door, but this conversation is far from over."

Before she could make a rebuttal to his last response, she heard the line go dead. Then in a fit of annoyance, at her grandfather and the situation that she now found herself in, she forcefully flung her phone onto the bed.

Chapter 16: A Party of Callers

*W*HILE JEZALYN WAS upstairs getting ready after her meltdown with her grandfather, Wyler was in the shop with Larkin trying to get him to divulge his plan. "Did you figure out what you are going to do to get Jezalyn to agree to give an interview yet?"

Nodding his head, Larkin said, "I'm going to suggest that we do the interview together. I'll promise to do most of the talking so that all she'll have to do is stand there."

"Sounds logical, but what if she still doesn't want to give it?" he questioned. Wyler silently pointed to the onlookers gathered about; they were nosey spectators who arrived at the shop after hearing Mary's embellished storylines. After a brief silence, Wyler suggested, "Maybe you could sneak her out of the shop for fresh air for awhile and propose the plan. You could use the sneaking around and isolation as another reason for her to do the interview."

"That could probably work," replied an unconfident Larkin, for his first thought of being secluded with Jezalyn was not one of persuasion, but one of liberation. He secretly thought to himself that now could be the time to get rid of her. Although he had altered his schedule to decrease the constant chatter in his head, Larkin did not feel in control. He soon realized that his altered schedule was an inconvenience that he was not willing to maintain until she met her maker. Larkin let his mind race with possible scenarios to return his world to normalcy.

Nevertheless, one detail remained. "How do you expect to get out of this shop without everyone seeing the two of you?" questioned Julius, bringing Larkin back into reality.

Before a plan could be devised to get Jezalyn out of the shop, she was already downstairs upon them. She was somewhat shocked to find them in the shop so early in the morning. She had thought she would be able to sneak away unnoticed for awhile to clear her head. After the initial surprise of seeing them, she forced a small smile and said, "Good morning. I was just about to go out for a walk."

Wyler shook his head and pointed to the crowd of people as he had done moments before, "I am not so sure if a walk is such a good idea this morning. It looks like last night's news report has the whole town gawking outside."

Jezalyn rubbed her temple and let her finger glide down the left side of her face with some pressure.

Larkin saw his opening and he took it, "I was about to try to sneak away myself. Would you like to get away with me for awhile if I can get us past all these people?"

She was totally against the idea, but her need to escape this reality was greater than the awkwardness of running off with a stranger, so she agreed with a simple nod of her head.

Wyler looked at them and said, "Wait here a minute; I will be right back." A few minutes later, he reemerged with Ana who was dragging her coat behind her as her husband pulled her by one hand toward them. He reached out his hand and said, "Jezalyn give me your keys."

She pulled them from her pocket and promptly handed them to him, which in turn he passed over to Ana.

"Here is the plan. Ana, you are going to take Jezalyn's car and they are going to take yours. A few minutes before Ana leaves to go to work, I am going to open the store. Everyone will swarm in, and during all the confusion you'll bolt for the cars and leave unnoticed."

Wyler laid the plan out in a fast ramble leaving his wife and Jezalyn clueless.

Perplexed, Ana asked, "What?"

Jezalyn adding her own confusion asked, "What about the reporter?"

Wyler looked at them and responded in small phrase like steps. "I am going to open the store. People will come in. You all will be able to leave undetected. The reporter won't be able to pick anyone out from the confusion, but if she notices the cars are gone, she will be more likely to follow Jezalyn's and not Ana's."

"Oh, I see why we switched now," said Jezalyn, and they all nodded in agreement as Wyler pronounced it the best plan for the time being. Larkin put on a jacket and gloves before taking Jezalyn's hand. He could feel her heart beat as it pulsated fast through her hand to his. Larkin found himself wondering if it was him or the adrenaline pumping through Jezalyn's body raising her heart rate as they prepared for their attempted escape.

Wyler glanced around, pulled a book off of the shelf, and handed it to Jezalyn. "Here, take this; it might help you blend in once I open the doors," he said.

They glanced over each other once more as Larkin asked, Jezalyn and Ana, "You ready?" With a nod of their heads, Wyler opened the doors.

They hung back a bit as everyone flooded into the shop. Some ran to the walls to check for bullet holes while others went directly to the shelves out of curiosity. Jezalyn mumbled, "Wow! It kind of reminds me of the day after Thanksgiving sale."

Ana gave a little chuckle and said, "Let's go before we get noticed."

They made a break for it. The onlookers were too preoccupied with their own agenda's to notice them, so they made it safely into the vehicles undetected. But as predicted, the reporter waited only a few seconds before she followed Jezalyn's car as it pulled out of the parking lot.

Larkin drove a good distance down the road making sure they got away before he asked, "So, where would you like to go?"

She shrugged her shoulders a little, "I don't know. Somewhere quiet where I can get some fresh air would be nice."

He maneuvered the car to turn northeast toward the neighboring town of Epps. As Larkin drove them toward a peaceful location, he realized that there was not the typical uncomfortable tension present like there should be for two people who barely knew each other; instead, they sat there quietly listening to the radio as if they had been long time friends. Every once in a while she would softly sing a few lyrics to a song that she seemed to genuinely like until they pulled off onto a small dirt road. He slowly brought the car to a halt about a mile or so down the one-lane dirt road.

Larkin got out of the car, and Jezalyn followed, "Where are we?"

"You will see," he said and held his hand out to her.

She timidly took his hand as he guided her across the road. Once on the other side of the ditch, they strolled side by side in what seemed to be the deep woods. After wandering what seemed to be about ten or fifteen minutes, Jezalyn noticed the trees, looked dead from the cold winter's frost, split to form what appeared to be a small lane. The tree branches above their heads crossed over the path and tangled into one another. Her literary perspective quickly took over, and she now found herself analyzing the imagery that stood before her. Jezalyn immediately thought, *Not even a path could split the course of nature. The tree branches resembled arms reaching out to embrace that which the path has split.* A branch snapped beneath her foot, and her reflections faded. Jezalyn stumbled about for another five minutes before her mind drifted to the wonder of what the path would look like in the spring or summer when everything was not dead. She thought to herself, *Would the trees still appear sad as if they were reaching out to a lost loved one, or would they look as if they were embraced in merriment of wonders?*

Soon the path led to a clearing with a little, old wooden picnic table positioned to the far left of a pond the size of a lake. Larkin directed Jezalyn to the table and took a seat while she stood peering out at the water that was an ugly brownish color. They had not said more than a few words since they left the bookstore; it was Larkin who finally broke the silence.

"It is prettier here in the spring," he said from his observation of her previous thoughts. "The trees are full of life, flowers bloom everywhere, and the pond is usually full of lily pads and frogs."

"I was thinking earlier that it would be nice to see the lane in full bloom this spring. Perhaps if you are still in town, we can return in the spring. Everything looks so dead and drab right now. The only thing to enjoy is the peace of mind you get from the quiet, well, bedsides the leaves rustling about from the squirrels." She put a small smile on her face as she took a seat next to him. They had not been stationary for long before they decided to stroll down to the little dock to get a better view of the dirty water. Larkin encouraged the stroll; it would be his chance to get rid of her, for he had decided her fate would be accidental drowning.

"Look," he said, leaning his torso over the edge of the pier wall that came about waist high, as he pointed into the water. Responding to his demand, Jezalyn mimicked his body position a few feet away.

"Wow! I am surprised you can see the bottom with water this brown," she said with a giggle.

Without a smile he replied, "You're missing it, look again."

"Okay," she said as she peered deep into the water before finally saying, "Not much here, but moss and a few cans."

"No - not the trash. You're still gazing beyond the water."

She stood there staring for a long while thinking, *Beyond the water. What does that mean? There is nothing here. Maybe if I just stare at it for a while he will drop the subject.*

Finally she saw it; beautiful circles and swirls in different shades of white and gray. She stared for a moment longer before she realized that she was no longer looking through the water but gazing into the water.

She motioned to Larkin, "Look!"

Larkin moved closer and Jezalyn pointed, "Look beyond your reflection but not to the bottom."

Larkin placed his hand on her back as he peered over, putting himself in a good position to push her over, so he smiled and said, "It's beautiful is it not?"

Turning to him, she smiled. "Yes, it is. I wonder how it does that?"

Caught up in their conversation, Larkin delayed his plan to drown her. "It's the sky. The sun pushes through layers of clouds and into the water where its reflection is captured within the depths."

"I take back what I said about this place only being a good place to find peace of mind during the winter," she said with a chuckle. "And, it looks like they do too," added Jezalyn pointing to two men, across the lake, pushing an aluminum boat into the water. She saw a small camper behind them, so she concluded that the camper's side of the pond must be a recreation area.

"There's beauty within the cold if you only search for it," he said, taking no notice of the men, as he turned and saunter back to the table.

She followed him but did not respond. Instead, she observed the way he moved. Jezalyn contemplated on his lighthearted steps and relaxed movements, which seemed to portray to her that he lived in a carefree world. She soon found herself envious and before long the stressful events of her life returned to mind and with them, the recollection of the argument she had with her grandfather earlier that morning.

They sat there in silence. Jezalyn probed her mind for a feasible solution to the situation with her grandfather while Larkin intrusively listened to her internal arguments against her grandfather. She was so deep in thought, she did not hear the first time he mentioned lunch. It was only after he made a remark about a bear and her stomach did she respond. A nervous laugh escaped her mouth as she clutched her belly, "Lunch! Yeah, let's get. . ." then the smile faded, "but let's not go back to the shop just yet."

Since drowning was no longer a possibility to Larkin's situation, he decided to use her response as a segue to mention the interview, "Okay, but I should warn you that the reporter will be waiting when we get back."

Jezalyn shrugged her shoulders, "Maybe she'll give up and leave."

"I wouldn't count on it; she is a reporter. They don't leave until they get their story, and unfortunately, it is us."

She did not respond, but she did not need to in order for the conversation to move forward since he could read her thoughts, so he continued on the subject, "May I make a suggestion?"

"Sure," she said as she stared into his hypnotic, powder blue eyes.

"I think we should make a deal with her. Tell her we will grant one interview together if she promises to leave us alone."

Bewilderment crossed Jezalyn's face. "I can't," she said.

"Are you sure? The situation can't get much worse than it is, could it?"

She mumbled under her breath, "Tell that to my grandfather."

Larkin observed her and pretended not to understand the context of her response, "What do you mean?"

Taking a deep breath Jezalyn explained, "He feels Transylvania is too dangerous and demands that I come home, but I want to stay. What if she interviews us and makes it sound worse than it is. He will surely make me return home."

He smiled and responded, "Let me think for a minute; in the meantime let's get lunch. I know the perfect place."

***

When they reached the town of Epps, she was not shocked, but it was to her surprise that he parked in front of the local church. They crossed the grassy lawn to a white gazebo, and he left her sitting there surrounded by unpruned shrubs and once fragrant rosebushes. She scarcely had time to observe her surroundings before Larkin returned with two corndogs, two sodas, and a basket of fries.

"Lunch is served," he said as he pushed the food toward her and took a swig of his soda.

She laughed and handed him a corndog.

He pushed it back toward her. "I got those for you. I am still full from breakfast." Then, before she could respond, he produced the book Wyler handed her before they left the shop and sat it down next to her.

"Wyler's book," grumbled Jezalyn covering her mouth while chomping down on her lunch.

"I thought you might want to read, while I devise a plan to get rid of the reporter."

Jezalyn thought, *hopefully his plan will also be a way to combat my grandfather*, as she took another bite of her corndog. Her thoughts made her feel unsettled, and she did not finish her lunch; instead, she picked up the book, slipped off her shoes exposing her fluffy winter socks, sat cross-legged, and began to read.

She was trying to re-read page two when Larkin decided enough time had passed to inform her of his pre-developed plan to get rid of the reporter. Jezalyn wanted to be reluctant to his idea, but for some reason she felt obliged to say yes since it seemed to be the most logical defense against her grandfather. After agreeing on a plan, she gazed down and pretended to read. Occasionally they glanced at each other inconspicuously, each trying to study one another. She caught him glancing at her once, but any suspicion of interest was deflected when he immediately announced it was time to get going so that they could put their plan into action.

Jezalyn reached for her half-eaten lunch, "Do you see a trash can?"

"Here let me," said Larkin as he pointed to a trashcan down by the edge of the road.

"Thanks, I'll meet you at the car," she said while slipping her shoes back on.

He was already half way back from the trashcan when she lost her balance and stumbled down the gazebo steps. She tried to catch herself on the railing; it broke her fall, but did not save her from stumbling into the corner of a thorny hedge. When he reached her, she was sitting on the bottom step trying to untangle a brier from around her ankle.

"Wait! It will rip your clothes if you keep pulling at it like that."

Her cheeks flushed with red embarrassment at the thought of him seeing her fall. He moved close and pulled at her clothes lightly until the brier released her. A quick once over of her leg revealed several small scratches but nothing severe.

"I guess I forgot to mention that I am a klutz," said Jezalyn trying to sooth her embarrassed ego.

"Rose bushes transform into thorn thickets in the winter making them a deadly opponent, but I think you got the better of it," he said with a playful grin. "Here let me help you up."

She placed one hand on the step to push herself up as he took the other, and once she was up a pain shot down her left hand. Jezalyn raised her hand and exposed a large thorn about half an inch wide sticking out of her hand. The blood had already pooled around the thorn by the time she had picked it out.

"It's like a battlefield out here," Larkin joked as he pulled her to the car and gave her a napkin.

After remembering Wyler's book policy, Jezalyn fidgeted with concern over the whereabouts of the novel she was reading and exclaimed, "The book! It's still in the gazebo."

"I'll get it. You stay here and apply pressure." A few seconds later, he returned with the book in hand, "You still bleeding?" She pulled the tissue away to reveal a small red puncture. He impulsively grabbed her hand gave it a small kiss and said, "Feel better."

She lightly slid her hand out of his with a smile and nodded. He returned her smile as they backed up to head out of town.

However, the events under the gazebo did not go unnoticed. While Jezalyn and Larkin were discreetly checking each other out, a tall dark-haired man was doing the same to them. Once they left, he approached the gazebo, retrieved the bloodstained thorn and stuck it in his mouth. He released a sinister snarl accompanied by a hideous laugh as he forcefully spit out the now unstained thorn.

CnApceR 17: Cne LAsc CAlleR

EZALYN AND LARKIN arrived at the bookstore, and to their surprise all that remained were Mary and her camera crew. Larkin left Jezalyn in the car, and she watched as he darted over and spoke to the reporter. After a short while, he returned to the vehicle, and Mary followed. They set up the camera and angled it to capture the bookstore as well as the general store in the background. Mary conducted the interview, and Jezalyn barely said anything; she mostly smiled and nodded a few times in agreement with Larkin's responses. He kept things straight forward with little to no details. After the interview, they excused themselves and walked into the bookstore. Jezalyn stopped and turned toward Larkin with a concerned look on her face.

"Do you think that worked?" Jezalyn asked Larkin.

Larkin left her standing in the middle of the store as he returned to the window and peered out. "I think it did; they are packing up to leave. We will know for sure tonight when Mary does her evening report."

Unexpectedly, an unfamiliar voice rang in Larkin's ears, "Thank God!" followed by a startling gasp that expelled from Jezalyn's throat; it sounded like a shortness of breath that one gets from being unexpectedly detained. Coinciding with the gasp, Larkin felt the fear that filled Jezalyn's body. He swiftly turned in a protective manner, but found her sense of fear had quickly faded to an overwhelming sense of security that stopped Larkin in his tracks. Larkin watched as a man, about five-eleven, with blonde hair, and in athletic clothing, spun Jezalyn around. The unknown man stopped swirling her about and planted a rather fiery kiss upon her lips as she wrapped her arms around his athletically built body. Larkin, in a daze of what he was witnessing, tried not to take note of the expression on her face, but he was unable to stop himself from studying them. He had never seen two people so relaxed in the presence of one another; nevertheless, he recalled the comfortable, pleasant drive that he had experienced with Jezalyn.

He thought, *How can she be as comfortable with me as she is with him? Perhaps, he is family and she is happy to see him. . . But no, if he was family the kiss would not have been so, so. . .*

Larkin, still frozen in the moment, soon realized Jezalyn did not just look happy; she was radiant. Her smile was big and bright. Her eyes more than sparkled; the tiny yellow flecks in them glimmered, and her face was almost unrecognizable. Before the presence of this mystery man, her face had a sort of pasty hue as a result of being out in the cold January weather; even so, Larkin had always considered her to be pretty from the moment his eyes had set on her. However, her once fair skin now flushed with color revealing a beauty that he presumed was unmistakable to everyone in the room. He collected his thoughts, mustered all his might, and stepped toward them.

Jezalyn caught a glimpse of Larkin's approach out of the corner of her eye. "Oh, hi, Larkin," Jezalyn said as her cozy posture turned awkward and her already flushed face blushed brighter. With her hand still against Blaise's chest, Jezalyn did not meet Larkin's eye as she said, "This is Blaise," and with a slight point in Larkin's direction, she continued the introduction, "Blaise, this is Larkin."

From her thoughts Larkin had determined that Blaise was her boyfriend; however, he was not quite sure how she actually felt. He sensed a flutter in her stomach, yet it was unclear if the reaction was her love for Blaise or her nervousness over Larkin's presence. His evaluation was useless, for he only had a few seconds to take in his surroundings. Larkin did not even remove his glove as Blaise extended his hand. As they shook hands in a welcoming manner, they were both too busy sizing up each other to notice Ana had walked in.

Ana lifted the keys; they jingled a little, as she said, "Hey, Jezalyn! I filled her up for you."

Her voice interrupted the uncomfortable silence that progressed between the men as they tried to assess one another. Both wished the interruption could have been delayed another minute or so as they searched for any sign of immediate threat or future danger. Jezalyn, however, found Ana's entrance most welcoming. She sensed the tension between the men and wondered if they were reacting to her anxiousness. She did not know why she felt so edgy. It was not as if she did anything wrong by spending the day with a friend, but still she remembered the kiss Larkin planted on her palm, and her stomach wrenched. The jingling keys, now dangling in front of her face, interrupted Jezalyn's thoughts.

Jezalyn clenched the keys with a tight fist and said, "Thanks, Ana, but you didn't have to."

"I know, but I figured you might need some gas for school in the morning."

"School," she said and the word trailed off at Wyler's approach. He silently crept up behind Ana grabbing her around the waist, she let out the same gasp Jezalyn had before, and she tensed her body in a defensive manner. Wyler twisted her around to face him and all the tension faded away as she fell relaxed into his arms. The hugging and kissing felt a little like déjà vu to Larkin, so he didn't wait for them to release before he quickly excused himself from the group.

"It was nice to meet you," said Larkin as he slightly tipped his head forward. In an earlier period, it would have conveyed to the other to have a good day, but Larkin did not bow a good day to Blaise. The slight tip of his head was directed at Jezalyn.

"Nice to have met you, too," responded Blaise as he wrapped his arm around Jezalyn's waist when he saw Larkin's eyes fixed on her.

"Thanks again for today. I think I would have gone crazy," said Jezalyn, in response to Larkin's nod.

Without another nod or word, Larkin walked away. Jezalyn and Ana found his abrupt removal significant in altering the atmosphere. Blaise was no longer assessing anyone, and with Larkin's presence removed from the group, Blaise's hardened features softened to allow his charm and fluidity to prevail. Jezalyn's posture was visibly at ease as she introduced Blaise to Ana and Wyler.

"So, how did you meet Jezalyn?" asked Ana.

Blaise laughed, "Well, I saved her from a faulty heel."

Ana's face showed slight confusion at his response, and Jezalyn lightly swatted at his arm and said, "He saved me from complete embarrassment. I wasn't paying attention when I stepped off the elevator, and I tripped." Jezalyn caressed Blaise's arm with affection as she continued, "And that's when he saved me from a clumsy stumble."

"Oh, how romantic," was Ana's reaction to the story. Ana always found introductions dreamy, especially if it led to any romantic connection.

Wyler pulled Ana close, "Let's give them some privacy. She only got here a few minutes ago."

"It was nice to meet you," said Ana, who gently took Wyler's hand into hers. They dashed off toward their loft all the while glancing flirtatiously back and forth. Once Wyler and Ana were out of Jezalyn's sight, she hugged Blaise and lifted up her head in wait of a tender kiss.

After kissing her affectionately, Blaise wrapped his arms around her and asked, "Are you alright?"

"Yes, I am fine."

"Are you sure? I saw the news and when I didn't get you on the phone I got worried, so I called your grandpa. He told me you got shot!"

"I was not shot," Jezalyn replied somewhat agitated.

Pointing to the bandage on her neck, Blaise responded, "Oh really, that's not what it looks like."

"My neck was more like grazed. Larkin's jacket zipper scraped my neck when he tried to save me from the sounds of gunshots. Wait, you talked to my grandpa?" said Jezalyn as she backed out of Blaise's arms.

"I did. He's extremely concerned about—"

Cutting him off, she said, "I know. . . he thinks it's dangerous," as she rolled her eyes.

"I told him I would check on things since I was coming down for a visit."

"You what? Do you agree with him?"

"I think. . . if you're in danger. . . then yes, I do think you should leave."

"There isn't any danger. Besides, I am not leaving anyway. I'm staying!"

"I think getting shot says that you are."

"I wasn't shot! I just told you Larkin's zipper got caught on my neck and it took a chunk of skin with it once it dislodged."

"Okay, Babe," said Blaise placing both of his hands on her shoulders, "please, don't get mad. I was worried about you, and I am sure your grandpa is also."

"I know. I am sorry I got so upset, but it's just that grandpa is so relentless and won't listen to reason. I don't want to go home; it's time for me to be independent."

Blaise, not finding any clear danger around, tried to win himself some brownie points, by aligning himself on her side. "Don't worry, Babe. I will tell him that you are perfectly safe here."

"Like that will matter," she said under her breath.

"I'll call him later and tell him I checked out the place, and I feel like you are perfectly safe staying here."

Jezalyn moved closer and gave him a peck on the cheek. "Thanks, so how long are you able to stay?"

Blaise frowned and said, "Not too long. I have to get back, so I can get in bed early for soccer practice. Before I go, I have time for a short walk."

As Blaise and Jezalyn took a stroll through town, Larkin was downstairs confiding in his friend Julius.

"I don't see how I could have missed the fact that she has a boyfriend," said Larkin.

"Perhaps, he is a she and that is why you did not sense anything," teased Julius.

"If you're not going to be serious, then don't bother," snapped Larkin. "I almost drowned her at the lake today. If campers hadn't been so close, we would have a serious problem right now."

Throwing his hands up Julius responded, "Alright, no need to get testy. Did you think, perhaps, the reason you did not observe anything between them is because she does not have true feelings for him?"

"No. Maybe, but I definitely sensed something today while they were hugging and kissing. I don't know maybe I am losing my edge," Larkin finally confessed.

Julius shook his head. "I think you overlooked her lover because you are more interested in her than you let on, and that's why you can't tell. Maybe your judgment is clouded," said Julius trying to be blatantly honest.

"No, I don't think so. My judgment is intact. I think you were correct about her feelings not being strong enough toward him for me to pick up on."

"Alright," said Julius, "but if I am correct, then what did you feel today?"

"The feelings were unclear, but I did feel a spark of something," said Larkin, as he stared mindlessly at the wall.

Julius was always the type to poke the sleeping bear, so he could not hold back his last response, "Or, it could be your own feelings that are making things unclear."

Larkin snapped his gaze toward Julius and said, "Don't start a quarrel with me. I'll rip your head off and then hers to prove a point."

With the sun still awake, Julius backed down from what could have been an entertaining squabble or clash; it was all the same to him. Besides, Ana just glided in all sprightly as if she was walking on air, so he told Larkin, "No need to get violent. I only wanted you to consider all the variables. Plus, I like when you agree that I am right."

Larkin, still somewhat ruffled, did not respond so Julius redirected his attentions toward an easier target. "Hello, Ana. How was your day?"

The mere sight of Julius made Ana want to cringe, but she held back her loathing out of respect for Wyler and Larkin. "Amazing," she said sharply.

"How about making me a drink? Something young if you got it."

"Don't be silly. You've made our home yours for the last few nights, so feel free to help yourself."

"Why thank you, but I wouldn't want to be rude and decline your lovely hospitality or hosting duties," said Julius choking back his amusement.

Ana turned and marched back in the kitchen. In less than a couple of minutes Julius had unnerved her, and now she looked as if she had just stumbled over hot coals. Her face was flushed with anger, and her feet tread lightly so that she did not spark anymore bickering with Julius.

Ana handed him the cup, and as she trekked away she said, "We only had aged," with a self-gratifying grin.

***

The sun was going down, so Blaise walked Jezalyn back to the bookstore entrance. Jezalyn pointed out the rays of pink and purple that flowed through the night, and as she tilted her head up to observe the sky, Blaise placed his hands firmly on her cheeks, leaned in, and kissed her lips. Jezalyn kissed him back and after a moment they parted ways.

Jezalyn locked the door behind her, and Blaise retreated to his truck where he took out his phone and dialed. As the phone rang, he nervously glanced around. He was checking to make sure he was alone so that his conversation could not be overheard.

"Hello," said a strong voiced man on the other end.

"It's me; I am checking in," said Blaise as he shivered from a gust of wind. It had been warmer in the day, but now as dusk approached the temperature dropped. He thought with his shiver, *the cold always approaches with darkness*.

A deep voice questioned, "Where are you?"

"Still in Transylvania."

"Did you check on the girl?"

"Yes. She is fine."

"Is there any cause for an abrupt removal?"

"No, it is my recommendation that she will not leave willingly or quietly, and we should monitor the situation from afar. In addition, someone needs to speak with her guardian."

"Don't worry about the guardian; just keep a watchful eye on her."

"Understood," said Blaise before the line went dead.

Blaise closed his phone, looked up at Jezalyn's window, observed the surroundings, and drove out of town.

***

Upstairs Jezalyn was getting ready to watch the six o'clock news when she heard a knock at the door. She cheerfully swung opened the door. A surprised expression cross her face. "Oh! Hey, Larkin. What's up?"

"Just came to see if you wanted to come down and watch Mary's news report tonight."

"Um, thanks, but I am all set up here. Do you want to come in and watch it with me?" she asked.

"Sure," said Larkin stepping around her and taking a seat on the couch. This had not gone as he had planned, yet it would work. After a close examination of his conversation with Julius, Larkin decided it would be best to test the validity of his claims. Surely he himself could not feel the way Julius had claimed, for Larkin attributed all the emotional entanglements to be those of Jezalyn's and none of his own. However, it had dawned on him that he had indeed felt something when she had read his memoir, yet he questioned if those were his feelings or hers. So, without a clear stance to conclude on, Larkin found himself upstairs trying to spend time with her so that he could prove to himself that Julius was wrong.

"Can I get you something to drink?" asked Jezalyn shutting the door behind them.

"No, thank you," said Larkin, as he pointing at the television and added, "Quick. It's about to come on."

Jezalyn flung her hand down and said, "Nah, I am sure they won't put us on first. I am going to grab a drink out of the kitchen. Are you sure you don't want anything?"

"I am sure. Thanks anyway."

While Jezalyn was in the kitchen, the evening news came on with the opening statement: "Since we received an overwhelming number of inquiries about the story of Mrs. Peterson's victim and her hero, it's going to be our breaking story tonight."

Larkin called to Jezalyn, "Hurry! It's on."

"Already?" yelled back Jezalyn.

"Yes!"

Jezalyn, empty soda can in hand, ran into the living room. Her socks slid across the slippery wooden floor as she made her mad dash to the television. She was less than five feet away when she lost her balance and glided across the living room floor falling into Larkin's lap. They gazed into each other's eyes as he caught her.

"You okay?" Larkin softly asked.

Still sitting in his lap, she nodded, "I'm sorry the floor gets slippery sometimes." Her gaze was swiftly drawn away as she heard the sound of Larkin's voice coming from the opposite direction.

"Look!" said Jezalyn pointing toward the television, "We're on t.v."

The report had begun and Larkin was answering a question about how Jezalyn's injury occurred. *Well her injury was a result of my zipper catching her neck, not a bullet.* (Jezalyn took note of herself standing behind Larkin and nodding in agreement.) Mary directed another question to Larkin: *how exactly is your zipper responsible for the injury that Jezalyn sustained during the shooting?* With the microphone pointed toward Larkin's face, he said, *When I heard the shot, I jumped over the counter to cover her and that's when my zipper rubbed harshly against her neck.* (Jezalyn watched herself nodding again in agreement with Larkin.) Mary returned the microphone back in her direction, B*ullet or no bullet, you are a true hero for your courage and bravery to protect her.* Larkin gave a bold smile and said, *Thank you.* Turning away from Larkin and Jezalyn, Mary gazed directly into the camera and wrapped up the story: *Well folks, there you have it, mystery solved. Mrs. Peterson's only victim was drywall, but a true hero has emerged in my book. Up next: vandalism resulting in the demolishing of a storage unit, and stay tuned for the weather.*

Jezalyn, not aware she was still sitting in Larkin's lap, released a sigh of relief and blurted out, "Thank God that's over!"

"I told you it would work. You just have to make the story uninteresting, and they will not want to pursue it or you," said Larkin, as he let his hand rest on the top of her leg.

The sudden weight of the placement of his hand brought her back to reality. She glanced tenderly into his eyes. "Oh, I am sorry about falling on you," said Jezalyn as she promptly got up still holding the empty can of soda in her hand.

"It's okay, no harm done. Well, I guess I should be going," replied Larkin.

"Oh, okay," said Jezalyn as she leisurely trailed to the door and opened it.

Now was the time for him to test his plan, so he took a deep breath to endure his serenity. Larkin moved toward her slouching down as if he was going to kiss her, but instead, he comforted her. "I don't think you have to worry about any more reporters."

Her body became tense at the closeness of his body next to hers, so she nervously replied, "And it's all because of your quick thinking. Thank you!"

"You're welcome," said Larkin, leaning in slightly further wrapping one arm around her awarding her, with a friendly hug.

Jezalyn made no vocal response, but simply embraced him back. Larkin could hear the pounding of her heart as it raced faster and faster the longer they stood their locked into each other's arms. "Goodnight," said Larkin as he released her and instantly raced down the stairs without another glance or word. She closed and locked the door behind him falling backwards on the door taken back by her altered emotions. She questioned herself about the significance of his hand on her leg and the length of the hug. She nervously thought, *Was I flirting with him or was he flirting with me?* Either way, she knew there was some flirting going on and found herself somewhat shocked at her own reaction to the situation considering her relationship with Blaise. She abruptly clasped her hand to her mouth feeling somewhat guilty. Jezalyn thought, *Oh my God, Blaise!*

Chapter 18: A Romantic Feeling

EVERAL WEEKS HAD passed and everything was back to normal. Jezalyn's grandfather was talking to her again, and she was punctual to work and school. There were no more reporters or onlookers questioning the mishap that took place between the Petersons. Jezalyn also found herself spending all of her free time with either Blaise or Larkin. She cherished each one; they were so similar, yet so unalike. They both had a strong protective nature that initially drew her close to them, but as time progressed, each individual's charm kept her interested.

Blaise was athletic and passionate about every activity or discussion they shared. He spoke to her with such intensity on matters that had little or no value, but the ambiance between them made everything count. He had only wished the passion would lead to the bedroom, but he respected her wishes to wait until she was ready. Jezalyn was not being completely truthful when she told Blaise she wanted to wait until they knew each other better. She was sheltered by her grandfather from being able to receive more intimate affections from boys and was truly not ready; however, the presence of Larkin's attentions and her feelings toward him made her not quite sure Blaise was the one she needed to be cozying up with.

However, Jezalyn also found Larkin romantic and adoring. His affections were unmarked, yet clear. She knew he doted on her with every poem, picnic, or stroll they took. She pretended the vibe between the two was that of old friends, yet she felt drawn to him and perhaps more so than to Blaise. Jezalyn found herself in a dilemma that most pretty girls found themselves in when they allowed themselves to be courted by two handsome men, but her response was to ignore the situation and carry on with each until a deciding factor came forth causing her to choose one over the other.

**

A few more weeks passed as they had before; it was February, and the weather was substantially colder. Only one event disrupted the fluidity of her days. It was Valentine's Day tomorrow, and both men had already requested her presence: one for lunch and the other for the evening. She had rearranged her schedule so that she could accommodate all of her activities. She requested the day off with Wyler so that she could spend some time with Larkin, and later that night she would go out to dinner with Blaise after class.

**

Jezalyn lay awake in bed; it was Monday, Valentine's Day. A day most females longed for every year. They adored being fussed over and pampered by their boyfriends, companions, husbands, or significant others. She lay snuggled in her bed deep in thought because this year promised a true romantic date, which was something she had never had the good fortune to experience. However, she would soon find this Valentine's Day to be filled with challenges that presented a combination of mixed emotions and uncertainty in her life. Nothing could prepare Jezalyn for the frantic day that lay in wait.

Jezalyn had planned to be off from the shop today, but Ana had an emergency with her job and Wyler was off scouring for antiques, so Jezalyn felt obliged to help Ana out of a tough spot and opened the store for her. Jezalyn was dusting the books, when Larkin snuck up behind her.

"Hey. You ready to go?" said Larkin. He knew she had to work, but continued with the plan so that it did not seem as if he stood Jezalyn up.

"Oh," she said with a deep breath. "I am sorry. I can't leave now. I have to cover for Ana; she had some sort of work emergency."

"I see," said Larkin.

Jezalyn gazed at him a moment before she said, "Wyler is supposed to be back about lunch time. When he returns, we can go. Besides, what are we doing today?"

Larkin held up a finger that silently said Nah-ah-ah and with a subdued smile he said, "It's a surprise."

"Okay," said Jezalyn with pondering eyes.

Larkin's immediate reaction to her occupied expression was to recoil. He thought, *Perhaps she isn't interested in receiving a surprise from me.* However, he quickly realized her eyes were not avoidant of their conversation, but attentively rested on a customer, a heavyset male who appeared to be in his late forties, approaching them. It was also Jezalyn's irritation, at the thought of the customer's interruption of their conversation, that convinced him to continue with his Valentine's Day plan. Larkin of course delighted in this reaction, for he was now an emotional junky. After feeling empty inside for so long, Larkin now welcomed the flood of emotions that he felt when he was with Jezalyn. Being unsure if these feelings were hers, his, or both of theirs made no matter to Larkin, since he was just happy to feel something similar to what he once felt with beloved Isadora. His new craving outweighed the irritation of her ramblings. Plus, he had taken Julius' advice and changed his resting schedule so that he could minimize the blathering.

After a while, Larkin found her thoughts barely bearable. Therefore, in lieu of an upcoming romantic event that he was sure would produce intense emotions, Larkin sent Wyler out under the ruse of antique collecting. He requested that Wyler drive into Monroe and rent a canoe and pick up other various items. A few items included on his list were a blanket, a bottle of wine, and a single blue orchid. It had not taken Wyler long to conclude that he was gathering items for a romantic Valentine's Day row, which put him on edge.

"Excuse me," said the man holding out a piece of paper. The customer's interruption forced Jezalyn and Larkin's distracted thoughts to converge upon him.

"Do you have any of these?" continued the man.

Jezalyn reached for the slip of paper and Larkin turned to her and said, "I will be back later."

She nodded to Larkin as she glanced over the paper. Larkin lingered a moment somewhat mesmerized as Jezalyn slightly cocked her head to the left running her thin fingers through her wavy hair as she pondered the location of her customer's request. Larkin returned downstairs only after she turned away to guide her customer to a nearby bookshelf.

***

It was shortly after one when Wyler returned, but he had not returned alone. Blaise appeared by the door as he struggled to open it without dropping his bags. Blaise offered to take a few bags, but Wyler, being the gentleman that he was, declined his offer and instead accepted the door being held for him. They exchanged small talk as they meandered to the back of the store until Jezalyn had spotted them. Out of shock, she ran up and wrapped her arms around Blaise.

Realizing she was still at work and in the presence of Wyler, Jezalyn quickly released Blaise and gave him a playful pat on the chest as she backed away. "What are you doing here?" Jezalyn questioned, but before he could answer, she asked another. "I thought you were picking me up after class, weren't you?" she said with a concerned face.

"Can't I just surprise you?" asked Blaise as Wyler slipped into the back and down to the underground apartment where Larkin was waiting.

"Well, of course," she said with a flirty smile. "I just didn't expect to see you until our romantic date."

He made a little frown and spoke lightly as he responded to her assumption, "Yeah, about that. There's been a change in plans. My hard drive crashed, and I need to work late tonight rewriting my chem. paper."

"Are you canceling?" she interrupted with a tremble in her voice and a tremulous expression.

Blaise noticed Jezalyn's eyes had turned glassy, and he immediately moved to comfort her. "No, Babe. I thought it would be better to deliver the news in person and ask if you will still be my Valentine. Also, I hoped you would consent to a romantic luncheon in the place of tonight's diner?"

She moved close and said, "I would be delighted to be your luncheon Valentine."

They stared at each other a moment followed by a burst of laughter. Once they composed themselves Jezalyn said, "Wait right here while I change, I'll be right back."

Blaise nodded with a smile, wandered over to a bookshelf, and glanced disinterestedly over the titles while he waited for Jezalyn to return.

Meanwhile, downstairs, Wyler was apologizing for the delay on completing the Valentine's Day errand and informing Larkin of their impending company.

"I know," Larkin replied. "She is upstairs getting ready to leave."

"If she is leaving with Blaise, then what am I to do with all this stuff?" said Wyler, pointing toward the bags.

"Finish setting everything up," Larkin commanded as he pulled the blue orchid out of the bag and placed it in the freezer.

Without thinking Wyler automatically questioned Larkin as if he was speaking to his wife, "But, what's the point if she will not even be here. Doesn't she have class tonight?"

Without hesitation Larkin responded, "I think Ana would love a moonlit Valentine's Day row with wine and poetry."

"Really!" exclaimed Wyler before trying to gracefully accept, "Are you sure? You could save this outing for another day."

"No! I have my own change of plans."

"Thank you, I am sure Ana will enjoy it," said Wyler, and with that response, Larkin walked over to the couch, sat down, and concentrated on Jezalyn's thoughts. She pondered over the style of earrings she would wear with her emerald dress.

Hmm… diamonds or pearls.

Classy,

Sophisticated,

Classy,

Sophisticated,

Classy,

Sophisticated,

Oh, just pick already! Jezalyn told herself. After settling on a pair of earrings, she let herself speculate as to what Blaise might have planned.

I wonder if he is taking me to Olive Garden with their to die for salad and bread or the Seaside Cafe with their seafood gumbo and crab cakes. No, wait! I bet he will bring me to the Lakefront Grill. They have the yummiest barbeque shrimp and one of the best homemade cheesecakes in the town. (Larkin heard a little giggle.) *They serve lunch on a deck overlooking the bayou. Oh how romantic it would be, holding hands and feeding each other cheesecake as we peer out over the bayou.*

Larkin tried to soak in the thrill of her giddy rendition of the perspective date. He felt the excitement was mixed with pain, so he found himself wondering if he was off base in her attraction to him. He could no longer lie to himself about his feeling for her, and it was those feeling that were the root of his uncertainty. Since he could not tell the difference anymore between his emotions and hers, it was hard to determine the validity of her attraction to him. Moreover, as he listened to Jezalyn ramble on in excitement about her date with Blaise, Larkin found himself quite agitated with the idea. Before he could deliberate on his feelings, he heard Jezalyn speak his name, "Larkin!"

Oh no, what am I going to do? I told him that I would go with him when Wyler came back. I wonder what he wanted to show me. How do I tell him I can't go? —I know, I'll write a letter, I am sure he will understand. Larkin probably just wanted to show me a new creek or field. He is always finding little quaint places.

Larkin closed his eyes and sat in silence as he listened to Jezalyn compose his brush off note.

Larkin—no, Dear Larkin. Yeah, I that sounds better. I know our outing got postponed already once today, and I am sorry to say something else has come up. I hope you are not too put out with your surprise. Perhaps you could show me tomorrow; from my guess, it is a new romantic spot for us. NO. . . I can't say that. . . . there, that should do it.

Larkin opened his eyes, "Wyler."

"Yes," said Wyler as he walked over to him.

"Perhaps you should close the store early today."

"Really? Wouldn't that seem odd to the town?"

"Who cares? Tape a sign to the door: Closed Early for Valentine's Day."

"Okay. I will go set up my date for Ana tonight. Do you need anything before I go?"

"Yes, make me a drink and make it AB negative," said Larkin.

Wyler only looked at him because he knew from experience that it was best not to question him when he was in that type of mood. Larkin only asked for AB negative when he was either severely depressed or angry. Wyler, not wanting to find out which emotion Larkin was feeling, lingered only a moment before scurrying away without a word to fulfill Larkin's request.

***

Back upstairs in the shop, Blaise was patiently waiting for Jezalyn. The quaintness of the store had slowly moved him toward the front where he had a clear view of the town. Blaise watched as an old hearse passed by; it had been the only traffic in town since he arrived, but nonetheless the sighting made him feel anxious as if something peculiar was going on.

"You ready to go?" called Jezalyn.

Blaise spun around to see Jezalyn wearing an emerald dress with a shawl draped around her shoulders. "Wow, you look beautiful," he said, noticing the sparkle of her diamond earring as it caught the sunlight peering through the window.

She smiled and kissed his check, "Thanks."

With one hand on her back, he navigated her out of the door and into the driver's seat of her car. He bent down, kissed her again, shut the door, and skipped off to his own vehicle.

"Wait," said Jezalyn, "where are we going?"

"Oh, just follow me" he responded and hastened to his truck.

As they drove away, Larkin went upstairs to retrieve the letter Jezalyn had left for him on the register.

CHAPTER 19: He LOVES ME, He LOVES ME NOT

Dear Larkin,

    I know our outing was postponed once already today, and I am sorry to say something else has come up, so I will have to wait another day to discover your lovely surprise. I hope you are not too disappointed at the postponement. I will ponder the surprise until tomorrow.

             Jezalyn

***

Blaise and Jezalyn arrived at a park nearby her school. The cold had kept most people in, but she could see a few people sitting around enjoying the scenery of the park. Jezalyn was surprised they had stopped at the park when a restaurant was supposed to be the destination in her mind. However, she quickly thought, *Maybe we parking here so that we can ride to the restaurant together*, but that assumption was rapidly fading as Blaise took her hand and led her down to two bikes propped up against a nearby tree.

Blaise waved his hand over the bikes and said, "I thought a bike ride would be a good way to work up an appetite. What do you say?"

Not knowing what to say she simply smiled and nodded. Jezalyn hiked up her dress and folded it over in her lap, so it wouldn't tangle in the wheel or drag the ground. They rode side by side until he took a narrow trail off the path. She hated that she felt a little let down by the expectations she had placed on the date. She found herself freezing from being inappropriately clothed for such an activity. Her mind wandered to Larkin and the surprise she had forfeited so that she could freeze on an ordinary bike ride. A sudden stop brought her back to reality. She surveyed the view that lay before them; it was a little brook. They dismounted their bikes and strolled along the leafy bank. She listened to leaves crunch and sticks pop under her feet and thought, *Thank goodness! My frozen legs are finally covered. Next time I am wearing tights.*

"Here we are," exclaimed Blaise with a large smile on his face.

"Where are we?" asked Jezalyn with a confused, yet irritated expression.

He guided her over to a table where his friend stood guard next to a prearranged picnic.

"Oh, a picnic. How sweet," she said and rushed toward the table pulling him behind.

The friend held her seat out for her and placed a napkin in her lap.

"Thank you," said Jezalyn as Blaise took his seat across from her.

Blaise smile and said, "Thank you for keeping an eye on everything, Chris, I got it from here."

Chris smiled and replied, "Have a nice time," and scuttled off.

"Would you like some champagne, madam?" asked Blaise with snicker.

"You know I can't drink that," she replied looking at him eerily, for not only was she underage she still had to drive an hour home.

"Ah, my dear," he said with a cheesy grin, "that's why I have a chilled, sparkling grape juice. I purchased the white, because the red packs quite a punch, and I wouldn't want you to get a DUI riding back to the car," chuckled Blaise, completely amused with himself.

Jezalyn giggled at his little anecdote. "I would love a glass," she replied lifting her plastic champagne glass out toward him.

Jezalyn was used to this type of date since Larkin frequently planned similar activities, and yet she was still somewhat impressed. It was the most romantic thing she had ever seen Blaise pull together. After the date ended, he kissed her tenderly and said goodnight although the sun was still out. Even though it was not quite evening, time had passed hastily, and Jezalyn now found she only had thirty minutes to get to class.

"I have to go, Babe, or I'll be late for class."

"Okay, I know it wasn't as romantic as an evening date, but I hope you still had a good time."

"I understand; I know how important your paper is." Jezalyn pulled him through the window of her car and kissed him again. "Stop worrying about all that. I loved it."

Although her mouth had said, "I understand," her heart secretly had not. Even though she received flowers, chocolates, and even little stuffed animals in the past, it was now as an independent woman that she was supposed to attend her first romantic Valentine's date. She had always envisioned red tablecloths, candles, flowers, and music. Her mind inadvertently wandered back toward Larkin.

She had her car in reverse when Blaise regained her attention. She watched him run toward her with both arms flung above his head, so she stopped instantly in the middle of the road.

She rolled down her window. "Hey, you forget something?" she said with a giggle.

Blaise said, "I sure did," as he leaned into the window of her car and whispered something in her ear. He gave her a huge smile and slowly backed away. Now in shock, Jezalyn replied by simply blowing him a kiss before driving away with an enormous grin on her face.

"I'll call you tomorrow," called out Blaise as he watched her speed away. Insecurity swept over him and he soon regretted telling her not to respond. He hoped she was speeding to class and not away from him.

Jezalyn parked and gathered her things for class with only a few minutes to spare. She found herself in amazement, and she repeated what he whispered in her ear to herself as if trying to memorize or convince herself of what had taken place. Blaise had whispered, *I know it's kind of soon, and I don't expect a response form you yet, but I wanted you to know —I love you.*

She thought, *He said he loves me, and I said nothing. How could I have not said anything? What is wrong with me?* During class, Jezalyn replayed the scene repeatedly in her mind, but still could not come up with a conclusion on why she had only responded with a peck on the cheek. The event had enveloped her and she had not even noticed class had been released until she saw people packing up to leave. Now that class had let out, Jezalyn decided to check in with Blaise and respond to his declaration, but his phone went directly to voicemail. She immediately assumed Blaise had not answered his phone because he was busily writing his paper. Closing her phone, Jezalyn hopped into her car and drove directly to Blaise's apartment with a love struck grin on her face. *He is going to be so excited to see me,* thought Jezalyn.

She had intended to surprise him, but found herself surprised instead when she discovered his car was not parked in the driveway. She got out and banged on the door until Chris, the man from the park, answered.

Jezalyn smiled at the friendly face and asked, "Is Blaise here?"

"No, isn't he with you?"

"No. I just got out of class," she said as her body shifted uneasily to the news of him missing. "I left him at the park. He said he was coming home to write his chemistry paper."

"He did come home, but left a while ago."

Jezalyn bit her bottom lip as she questioned, "Do you know where he went?"

"Um, Yeah. He said he was going to stay at your place again."

"My place! Okay thank you," She replied mechanically. On her way back to the car, Jezalyn mumbled the word, "Again?" Jezalyn cranked up the car and turned on heat; even though, she was shivering not from the cold, but from the anger.

He lied to me. He is not at home writing his paper, and he is certainly not staying at my house with me. He has never stayed the night with me. That son of a bitch! I bet he is cheating on me.

Jezalyn drove home angry and hurt trying not to cry at the dilemma that had recently developed in her relationship. She questioned his newly professed love against the horrific lie she had uncovered. She could think of no reason other than another woman for Blaise having told such a lie to her and his roommate. Her thoughts wondered to what a date with Larkin might be like. She shook her head and thought, *I am being silly; his surprise almost certainly was not a date. He probably found something beautiful in nature that he wanted to share.* Her thoughts continued as she parked outside Wyler's rare bookstore, *Besides, why would he plan a romantic evening for me when he knows that I am dating Blaise. Well, was dating Blaise.*

Jezalyn's phone rang as she climbed the stairs to her apartment, it was Blaise and she was too angry to answer. It was only an hour ago, she was ready to tell him that she, in fact, cared for him too, but now she felt more as if she loathed him for lying to not only his roommate, but also to her. Now inside the apartment, Jezalyn threw the phone onto the couch and thought as she dropped the rest of her stuff onto the floor, *If he had lied about sleeping at my house had he also lied about the chemistry paper and needing to re-schedule his date perhaps to go out with someone else?* Jezalyn cringed at the thought and the tears flowed down her face. There was a sudden knock at the door, and she hopelessly tried to pull herself together. The door opened and Larkin stood before her holding a large box with a few bags on his arms.

"Are you alright?" asked Larkin.

"Yeah, I am fine. I have something in my eye. Come in and make yourself comfortable while I go get it out."

"Take your time," replied Larkin as he walked past her placing the box on the coffee table.

"What's in the box?" asked Jezalyn as she hurried into the bathroom.

"It's a surprise, but if you want to change into something more comfortable, go ahead," called back Larkin.

Jezalyn washed her face and peered into the mirror, but after seeing her red-splotched face, she started crying again. She desperately tried to recompose herself and once composed Jezalyn rewashed her face this time disregarding the mirror.

She peeked out into the hall but saw nothing, so she called out to Larkin, "You okay in there?"

A faint, "Yes," entered her ears, and she found herself wondering what Larkin was doing.

"Okay, give me a moment to get changed," she said as she fluttered into her bedroom to change; she wanted to feel sexy after what she had just been through with Blaise.

"Sure thing," mumbled a busy Larkin.

***

Thirty minutes had past, and Jezalyn had finally emerged from her room wearing a short shimmering red dress; it was a mesh sequin material with a satin lining. She accented it with a pair of black high heels that embellished a candy apple sole. The short dress showed off her long, lean legs as she turned the corner into the kitchen. She found Larkin standing next to the table holding a chair out for her to take a seat. He had covered the table with a crimson cloth, and as she moved closer, she could see an ivory candle burning in between two covered plates.

"This looks beautiful," said Jezalyn as she took her seat and felt Larkin gently nudge her chair closer to the table.

Larkin sat in the chair across from Jezalyn. She watched as he bent over, and all of a sudden, music flowed through the air. Jezalyn let out a little giggle as she recognized the song; *Take My Breath Away*, from the movie Top Gun.

Larkin smiled gingerly and pulled the lid off the top of her plate to reveal two large grilled cheese sandwiches cutout in the shape of hearts slightly overlapping next to a bowl of tomato soup with the words 'Be Mine' spelled out in fresh basil. Jezalyn's eyes lingered on the words a moment before they disappeared from the stirring of her spoon.

Larkin did not wait for her to respond, because he in no way wanted to make her uncomfortable, so instead he asked, "Shall it be milk or orange juice tonight?" as he pointed at the two cartons sitting at the edge of the table.

"I think I'll have milk. No, wait, orange juice," said Jezalyn.

"You could have a glass of both," Larkin joked.

The awkwardness she felt when she gazed into the soup had soon faded away, as they ate and chatted like two old friends. They were halfway through their dinner when she recognized an Aerosmith song. She sang along with it as she gobbled down some more of her grilled cheese. Larkin watched her with a smirk on his face as she hummed thru the next few lyrics before attempting to converse. Larkin, amused at her ease and comfort with him, interrupted her bliss and asked, "That was good, are you finished?"

"Yes, I am. It was really good. Thank you," she said muffled through her napkin as she placed it over her mouth to chew down the last bite.

Larkin smiled, "I'll get this cleaned up for you."

"Oh, no leave it. I will pack it up and bring it down to you tomorrow."

"Alright," said Larkin. "How about a dance before I go," hearing the song, *Everything I do (I do for you)* by Bryan Adams on the radio.

"Sure," said Jezalyn. They moved to the middle of the living room and before they commenced to dancing he produced a single blue orchid. He placed it in her honey colored hair, and as they danced Jezalyn thanked him again, "You know, you really made my night."

"Happy to hear it," he said pulling her closer. He led her through a few fancy turns that resembled something like a waltz. When the song neared the end, he sweetly whispered in her ear, "Thank you for the dance, goodnight" and kissed her appropriately on the cheek.

Jezalyn's face grew flushed, and Larkin soon realized that he had embarrassed her, so he quickly moved for the door. However, it was not embarrassment Jezalyn was feeling, but something she had never felt so strongly before, so she stood there silently staring at him in her own bewilderment.

She watched as the door closed behind him. Jezalyn lunged forward, flung open the door, and grabbed his hand. Although she had stopped him, she still found herself speechless. He gazed at her as she moved closer to him. With her hand still on his, her heart raced as the inches between them disappeared. Larkin could no longer restrain himself from clasping her around the waist with his free arm. Without any more encouragement, he kissed her with such passion that she did not want him to let go. It was when he pulled away that she spontaneously and uncontrollably whispered in his ear, "I think I'm falling in love with you."

He planted another fiery kiss upon her lips and guided her backward into her loft.

CHAPTER 20: CHE MORNING AFTER

JEZALYN LAY AWAKE in bed; it was now Tuesday, no longer Valentine's Day. This year Jezalyn was somewhat glad the day was over as she lay nestled in her bed deep in thought. There had been two declarations of love made yesterday, one she received and one she gave. As she deliberated on her Valentine's Day events, her phone rang; it was Blaise, and she answered the phone with an icy hello.

"Hey," Blaise replied upbeat trying to compensate for her coolness.

Jezalyn sat there silently not because she didn't know what to say or ask, but because she no longer felt she had the right to question him after what she had done herself last night.

After hearing her pause, he continued, "Chris told me you came by looking for me last night."

Blaise heard an "Um-hmm" escape Jezalyn's voice.

He attributed her shortness to unhappiness with him, so he reminded her of his prompt response to her late night visit; "When I heard you had dropped by, I tried to call you a back. When I got no answer, I got a little worried. . ."

Jezalyn, no longer being able to hold in her hurt and anger, cut him off, "Really? Were you worried that I found about your late night rendezvous?"

Blaise responded coolly, "You mean my date with the campus library to finish my chemistry paper."

Jezalyn sat up in the bed as her temper grew at his response, but she kept her voice calm not wanting him to suspect the level of her anger just yet. "Oh, so that's where you were last night?"

"Yep, I was there until about three this morning," responded Blaise cheerily.

"Really, it just so happens that I drove by the library on my way out last night and you were not there, either! What lie are you going to give me now?" Jezalyn blurted out heatedly.

Blaise sat there silently for a moment as he tried to deliberate on the turn in conversation, but that silence only prompted Jezalyn to respond with more conviction.

"Who is she?"

"Who is who?" Blaise angrily shot back at her.

"Oh, don't deny it. Your roommate told me last night you were staying the night with me —again! You have never spent the night with me once, so it can't be that you stayed with me again." Thus without a slight pause or chance for Blaise to come up with a more suitable explanation, Jezalyn continued, "So, I ask again. Who is the girl you are staying over with?"

"There is no girl," blurted out Blaise, realizing the conversation was leading into an area where he knew he could not explain himself.

Jezalyn fired back, "If there isn't someone else, then why are you lying to him and me about where you were?"

There was only silence; Blaise made no response, not even an overwhelmed sigh. His only thought was, *If I tell her the truth, there certainly won't be a chance for us.*

Jezalyn sat there for a moment waiting for him to respond, but when he did not, she took a deep breath and said, "Fine. I am sorry, but I can't be with a cheating liar."

Blaise made one last remark, although now he was too angry to try to pacifying her, "I swear, Babe, there is only you."

"Just tell me where you were last night, and preferably the truth," she demanded.

"This is bullshit! I'll talk to you later," said Blaise as the phone went dead.

Even though there was not enough time for Jezalyn to respond, she instantly decided that his avoidance and anger on the subject proved his guilt. She found herself half at ease at Blaise's reaction since she herself was just as wrong as he. Jezalyn was glad she did not have to divulge to Blaise that she let Larkin stay the night. Although he would immediately suspect they had slept together, he would not have been entirely wrong. It was true Jezalyn had spent the night nestled safely in Larkin's arms until the break of dawn, but it would have been Blaise's assumption that she had given Larkin the intimate caresses that he had longed for, which would have been incorrect. Jezalyn smiled, as she thought about Larkin and the night they had spent together.

She thought about how Larkin had questioned her, once they came up for air, about her relationship with Blaise. She could not believe it; Larkin was questioning her motives as she had done earlier, but this time it was toward her own declaration, not Blaise's. Jezalyn had decided right away that she would tell him everything. She told him about the Valentine's Day date at the park, Blaise's pledge of love, and her thoughts of his betrayal and lies. However, she did not tell Larkin the part about the date not living up to her expectations, or how she once wished she were on a date with him instead. She expected herself to cry as she related the story to him, but she did not and that left her somewhat puzzled and justified in her current feelings.

Jezalyn smiled again to herself as she remembered relating to Larkin how her feelings for him came about:

I know that, to you, it must look like I am only responding to Blaise's unfaithfulness, but tonight you made me realize he was not the disloyal one. I must have been slowly slipping from my relationship with him as I unsuspectingly found myself thinking of you. As I danced with you tonight, while you were spinning me to and fro. Then, she recalled a little laughter broke out between them. *I felt a sensation in the pit of my stomach that I had never felt before, and all I knew was that I couldn't let you walk out that door.*

A sudden pulsation interrupted her thoughts, she gazed down at her hand and without a moment's thought clicked the end button on her phone. Less than a minute later the phone rang again, and she repeated the same function as before, except this time after pressing the end button, she threw the phone onto the bed and pranced into the kitchen to retrieve some left over orange juice. She unconsciously smiled as she took a sip staring somewhat lost in thought out of the window. Jezalyn cheerily returned to her bedroom, juice still in hand, letting thoughts of Larkin run wildly through her mind. She picked up her phone, but before she made a call, she noticed a small box with a smiley face in it in the upper left hand corner, which indicated she had received a text message. Clicking the box, she soon discovered Blaise had not given up, and the message read, "Hey, I am calling but u won't answer. sorry I got mad. let's meet somewhere. we can talk this out."

Jezalyn threw the phone back onto the bed, without responding, and grabbed a pair of jeans, a cute blue-green v-cut tee, and a pair of flats. She was pulling her hair back out of her face when she heard a knock at the door. Her heart sank and an ill feeling came over her as she thought, *Blaise! I should've responded*, but when she realized Blaise did not have enough time to drive from Monroe to Transylvania, she rushed to the door hoping to find Larkin on the other side. Relief and excitement overwhelmed her. It had only been thirty minutes or so since she received Blaise's first call, and now she felt a different kind of emotion as she peered at Larkin, who stood in her doorway holding two cups of coffee and a little white bag, the type you get when you pick up your medicine at the pharmacy.

"Come in," said Jezalyn with a welcoming grin on her face. Larkin strutted in and handed her a cup and the bag.

"What's this?" asked Jezalyn graciously accepting the items.

With a beaming grin he said, "I thought you would like a cup of coffee and a bear claw to get you started this morning."

Another large smile crossed her face, and she moved closer giving him a half hug and a peck on the lips. She enthusiastically pulled out the pastry and took a bite, and raised her hand to her mouth before muttering the words "Thank you."

"You're welcome. So what do you plan to do today?"

"Work, and. . ." the sound of her phone ringing interrupted her. Although Jezalyn paused for the initial ring, she ignored it and continued her sentence, ". . . write a paper for my online class. What are you doing?"

"Do you need to get that?" asked Larkin as he pointed to the phone in her pants pocket.

"No, it's just Blaise. He wants me to meet him later to talk about things."

"Okay, so, what time are you doing that?"

"Um," she shifted uncomfortably, "I didn't agree to go yet."

"I see," was the only response he made.

"Do you think I should go?"

"Kind of. You need to make an official decision. Don't you think?" asked Larkin.

Jezalyn nodded her head, and said, "Come on let's go downstairs before I am late for work."

He toddled toward the door and as he passed her, she kissed him adoringly. They went downstairs; she picked up a stack of books off the counter to stock on the shelf. They discussed a date for later that night while she placed the books on the shelf, but when her phone rang, they instantly knew who it was. Larkin excused himself with the claim of checking in on Wyler and Ana so that Jezalyn could have some privacy. Although Larkin wanted Blaise completely out of the picture, he knew that it could not happen without closure. Besides, Blaise did not intimidate Larkin since he could still read Jezalyn's mind and sense her emotions. Larkin surprisingly hoped her emotions were pure, and until he knew for sure, he would be unable to have a more intimate relationship with her. Although he longed to seduce her the previous night, he needed to feel the full conquering and thing with blaze needed to be settled first. Larkin was reminded from frequent instances of observation how lust can drive people to merciless madness. Yet, it was unclear if Larkin clung to his antiquated sense of propriety simply out of habit or out of nostalgia for his humanity.

"What do you want?" questioned Jezalyn as she placed another book on the shelf.

"Hi, I just want to talk."

"So, talk."

"Can I see you?"

There was a long pause before Jezalyn said, "I don't know."

Blaise found hope in the break and requested, "How about a cup of coffee, tea, or whatever you want?"

She made no response, so he continued, "We can talk this out. I know we can."

Jezalyn picked at the wood on the shelf as she finally replied, "Okay."

They decided to meet at a little coffee shop in the shopping center a few blocks from the university at three o'clock. After the arrangements to meet were in place, Blaise told her he loved her and hung up the phone.

chapter 21: astonishing responses

*YLER WAS GETTING in his vehicle when he saw Larkin entering Julius's house. Irritation soon followed this observation as Wyler thought, *If I knew Larkin was going to visit, it could have saved me a trip.* Then again, never being informed about things until after they turned south was part of his life as a Keeper. It was not in his power to demand the knowledge of Larkin's every movement much less Julius's. Besides, he found himself worrying more if he did know, so he never pressed the issue. He knew if either truly needed him then they would inform him, so as not to disturb their meeting Wyler checked his watch and backed out of the driveway. Jezalyn was supposed to get off in twenty minutes and he was still thirty minutes out. Wyler tried to speed, but he was stuck following a Parish cop, so he called the shop to inform Jezalyn about his delay. He became startled as he heard a male's voice say, "Hello."

Wyler checked his phone to make sure he had dialed the correct number before he intensely demanded, "Who is this?" Wyler could not imagine what man would be answering the phone at the shop with both Larkin and himself out.

"It's me," respond the manly voice on the other line.

"And who is me?" but before the voice could respond, Wyler asked another question, "Where is Jezalyn?"

"Monroe. Why?"

Wyler shook his head in disbelief as he recognized the familiarity of the man's serious tone. An overwrought Wyler slammed on the breaks and bellowed out, "Larkin!"

"Yes, what is wrong with you? If it's about the shop, don't worry I got it covered."

"We have a serious problem," replied Wyler as he turned his car around and drove back in the other direction.

"Now what?" responded an extremely aggravated Larkin?

"First off, you're at the shop."

"Yes," broke in Larkin with a condescending tone, "thanks for stating the obvious. I'll let you know if I burn down the shop."

Larkin could hear Wyler take a deep breath before he continued, "Secondly, I watched you go into Julius's house less than twenty minutes ago. Unless you developed the ability to be in two places at once we have a serious problem."

Wyler heard the crackling of plastic and knew Larkin was clenching the phone with his fist as he mumbled one name, "Theron."

"Don't worry; I am only about ten minutes from Julius now."

"Wyler, don't enter when you get there; it's too much of a risk. If Theron is back, it's only to wage a vendetta against me."

"I know; it includes me too, but am I supposed to let him rip Julius apart?"

"I'm on foot, so I'll meet you there soon. Don't go in, wait outside for me!" was the last demand Wyler heard accompanied by a loud clang. Wyler had gathered that Larkin had dropped the phone since the clang was followed by silence and not a dial tone.

It had been a long time since he had broken a law, but now he found an acceptable reason. Wyler felt free and invincible; the adrenaline pumped through him as he sped down the highway back to Julius. Soon he found himself in Epps, and Wyler spotted Theron getting into an old black car parked almost a block from Julius's house. Wyler pulled into a parking lot across the street and waited for Theron to drive off. Wyler exited his car as the tail lights disappeared around the corner. He ran up the driveway, not waiting for Larkin. Wyler felt he was in no danger since he had personally witnessed Theron's departure.

Wyler abruptly entered the house to find it filled with smoke. The air he let in upon entering the house fed the fire causing the smoke to grow thicker. Wyler covered his mouth and nose with the top of his shirt as he dropped to his knees and crawled across the floor. He crawled toward a figure lying on the floor. When he reached the body, he discovered it was not Julius. The body was female; it looked like a bear had attacked her. She had deep scratches and torn tissue where her jugular vein used to be. Wyler hunted for Julius, trying not to rub his burning eyes as he crawled toward two more bodies that lay motionless.

When he reached the bodies, he discovered one was Julius and the other another female. Wyler pulled Julius onto his back to discover a large hole in his chest. He coughed as he examined Julius, but Wyler found himself stunned to discover Julius holding his own heart. He pried the heart from his hand and shoved it back into his chest cavity. Wyler knew from experience that he needed blood if he had any chance of saving Julius, so he checked the girl lying next to him. She had a pulse, although it was faint. He opened Julius's mouth, pulled her arm over it, and slit her wrist with Julius' protruding fang. He watched as the blood slowly drained into his mouth. Wyler realized she did not have enough blood left in her to revive him, so he laid the girl's open wrist in Julius's mouth.

The fire blazed all around them. Even though Wyler's face and lungs were completely exposed to the smoke, he continued as if he was immune but all the while coughing uncontrollably. Still trying to block out the clouds of gray smoke that flood around him, Wyler pulled off his shirt and gathered it into a bundle and pressed it tightly over his face. With one last effort to save Julius, he grabbed a piece of broken glass hovered his wrist above the exposed heart and with one swift swipe slit his own wrist. The blood pooled up around Julius's non-beating heart as Wyler lay collapsed face down on his bundled shirt over Julius's chest.

***

Wyler awoke outside in an ambulance. An oxygen mask covered his face, and an EMT held out Wyler's arm bandaging it with two fingers. The EMT noticed Wyler gained consciousness and quickly asked, "How many are inside?"

Wyler stared at him for a moment trying to focus before shaking his head back and forth in the hopes to deter anyone from searching the house. Wyler was not concerned about them discovering Julius since vampires burned to ashes; it was the female bodies, which seemed unlikely to turn to ash, strewn across the floor that worried him.

Larkin interrupted them, "I am the owner of this house. No one else was inside, besides him."

"Well I will need to check you out also, sir."

"There will be no need; I am fine."

"Then you're denying treatment?" asked the medic.

"Yes," responded Larkin.

The EMT turned back to Wyler, "You should consider yourself lucky. It looks like you had minimal blood loss from your injury." Pointing at a monitor, he continued, "Also, your pulse oximetry test shows that you have a mild case of smoke inhalation."

"Ox- o- what?" asked Wyler pulling the oxygen mask off his face.

Placing the mask back over Wyler's face, "You see this little white piece attached to your finger? It measures the degree of oxygen in your blood; however, since you lost some blood I think it would be best to get a chest x-ray to make sure your condition is not worse than what it appears," said the EMT.

Wyler responded, "I am sure I am fine."

"Okay, but if you start wheezing or have trouble breathing, I recommend that you go to the hospital immediately."

Larkin interrupted, "I hate to break up this party, but, Wyler, I have to go." Turning to the EMT, Larkin asked, "Where are you taking him, so I can send his wife?"

Before the medic could respond, Wyler took the mask off and said, "Wait I am coming with you!"

The medic pulled out a piece of paper for Wyler to sign, before letting him get out of the ambulance.

***

While Wyler was trying to save Julius's life, Jezalyn was on her way to the coffee shop; it was almost three thirty before Jezalyn arrived at Rayne's Coffee Corner, where she found Blaise patiently but nervously waiting. She entered the shop and Blaise hopped up to meet her, "Glad you made it. I got worried you changed your mind."

Jezalyn responded nonchalantly, "Nah, just a little traffic."

He guided her to the counter. "What would you like?" asked both Blaise and the barista.

She ordered a small hot chocolate without whip cream, and she sat down at the table next to the window while Blaise waited on her order. Sitting quietly, Jezalyn there to formulate a way to tell him about Larkin. She did not know how to handle the situation. Courtesy of her over protective grandfather, Jezalyn had never been afforded the luxury of having to broken-up with anyone. She did not want to hurt or lead anyone on either, and her confusion soon turned to anxiousness. Jezalyn rubbed her moist palm on her pant leg as she watched Blaise take her cup from the barista and walk back toward her. In that moment, she decided she would break it off without telling him about Larkin.

"Here you go," said Blaise as he pushed the cup toward Jezalyn and took a seat.

"Thanks." They sipped their drinks occasionally staring at one another waiting for the other to speak.

After a couple of minutes, Blaise asked, "How was your drive up?"

"Okay."

After taking another sip of his drink, he asked, "So, how's your hot chocolate?"

She replied, "Good," but when she tried to take a sip, the hot steam met her lip, so she placed it back down in front of them creating an invisible barrier. "You said you wanted to talk; what do you have to say that I haven't already heard?"

He sat there trying to construct a response. After a moment of empty silence, Jezalyn grabbed her bag and said, "Well, if you're not going to talk, I'm leaving."

Putting his hand out as a gesture for her not to get up, he said, "Wait, it's just that I can't tell you where I was last night. I am sorry."

She placed her bag back down, "Why not?"

"Because, I just can't, but I promise you it has nothing to do with me being with another woman."

"Well if you don't tell me, then this is the end," said Jezalyn who felt somewhat relieved that she was breaking off the relationship without having to tell on herself.

He grabbed her hand, "Even if I told you, you wouldn't believe me."

Somewhat intrigued at his secrecy, she urged him to tell her. "Well, your silence is resulting in the same outcome, so why don't you just come clean, tell me the truth, and let the chips fall where they may."

Blaise took a deep breath, leaned forward, and said, "I am a hunter. I was out hunting."

"At night?" responded Jezalyn in disbelief.

"Yes."

"Oh really, isn't hunting at night illegal?"

"Yes."

"Well, did you at least kill anything worth ruining our relationship over?"

"No, she got away."

"She! I knew it! Where were you really at last night?"

He released a long sigh trying to hide his aggravation, "I was hunting," but he was interrupted when Jezalyn mumbled under her breath, "Um- hmm, hunting for other females," as she sat back in her chair with her arms crossed over her chest.

Blaise read her defensive posture and knew he had no choice but to tell her even if it was unbelievable.

Her eyes grew big as he said, "Yes, I was hunting a woman, but the truth is she is a vampire. I am a vampire hunter."

Jezalyn glowered at him with her big green eyes and began to cry, but it was quickly snuffed out when she thought, *He is absolutely insane, that is the lamest excuse in the whole world. How dare he insult my intelligence with this stupid lie?* "It is one lie after another with you! Why is it so hard for you to tell me the truth?" she asked sharply.

Blaise retorted, "It's the truth!"

Listening to him vigorously defend his claim made her glower. "Yeah, like it was the truth you were going home to work on your paper, or stayed at the library until three, or maybe the truth was what you told your roommate about staying at my house, but no, I guess you would rather me believe you were crazy than tell me the truth. Besides, if you're not going to tell me the truth, at least you could do is come up with a more believable lie than hunting vampires."

Blaise could only nod his head as he heard Jezalyn dismiss his claim with a mix of laughter and anger. "Well, what do you want to do?" he finally asked.

Overwhelmed, Jezalyn choked out, "I am sorry; I don't believe or trust. . ." Jezalyn's response lingered off because she knew not only could she not trust him, but also she could not trust herself. The schoolgirl crush she once had on Blaise was now replaced by an intensity she had never felt before with Larkin. She patted her face, composed herself, and scowled at him with disdain as she said, "Vampire slayer? Really!"

She shook her head as she got up and said, "Good-bye Blaise; I wish you all the best with whoever she is."

Blaise watched her bolt out the door but did not follow. He knew any chance of them getting back together was over. He became angry with himself for not anticipating the depth of her reaction. He had thought perhaps she would believe him or would just get angry, but eventually would get over it, yet he never dreamed she would truly abandon their relationship.

CɦAᴩᴛeʀ 22: Cʀʏꙅᴛ oʀ Cʀaᴩ

JEZALYN WANDERED ALONG the shopping strip mindlessly glancing into the windows. She had re-composed herself rather well after the disintegration of her relationship with Blaise. The only semblances to her previous distress were the cherry splotches under her eyes that had not yet faded. She had wandered several blocks from her vehicle. When Jezalyn realized the distance, she abruptly spun around stumbling directly into someone. "Excuse me," she said trying to catch her balance as she clutched onto him for stability. Once Jezalyn regained her poise, she pressed her body and lips against his.

After recollecting they were in public, she pulled away and asked, "Hey, Larkin, I thought you were at the shop?"

He smiled and before he could answer, a clerk ran out the shop and interrupted them. "Mr. Drythe, you forgot your walking stick."

"Thank you," he said, taking the elegant stick out of the clerks grasp. Jezalyn's eyes fixated on the stick, taking in its magnificent details. The body of the stick appeared to be carved out of a dark wood, but the part of the stick she gawked at was the top, where the hand would rest. The top was a silver ill-shaped ball with something engraved in the center of it. Jezalyn's inspection of the engraving revealed that it was a crest with two symbols in the center; however, she could not quite make out the shapes.

He broke her gaze, when he forcefully tapped the ground before thrusting the stick under his arm.

"Wow, that's a nice walking stick," said Jezalyn.

"I am glad you like it."

Trying to avert her eyes, she asked again, "So, what are you doing here?"

"I came to get this," he said as he held the stick out for her to examine.

"It looks remarkably detailed," said Jezalyn. She raised her finger, to match her focal point, and asked, "What's that symbol on top?"

"Oh, nothing," he replied pulling the engraving back out of view. "Are you busy? Can we go somewhere?"

"Um," with a short glance at the coffee shop she responded, "Sure. Let's go. I'm done here."

She held his hand as he guided her to an old black car. He opened her door, and she remarked on his vehicle, "What kind of car is this?" as she willingly climbed in.

Entering the driver side door he responded, "It's a 1973 Chevy Corvette."

"It's really nice."

"I obtained it fully restored."

After giving him a smile she asked, "So, where are we off to?"

"It's a surprise," he said holding up a handkerchief.

Jezalyn said, "What's that for?" as she pointed at the blindfold with an alarmed expression on her face.

"It's so the surprise isn't ruined," he said trying to hide his irritation at having to convince her to comply.

She reluctantly agreed as he slipped the blindfold over her eyes. Blaise trudged out the shop, just as the old black Chevy passed before him. It was not the model of the vehicle that caught Blaise's eye, but the sight of the woman he loved blindfolded and being kidnapped. He strained to see, but could not make out the driver, so he ran behind the car screaming Jezalyn's name as they sped away. He pulled out his phone as he ran toward his truck. "We have a problem. I think she has been kidnapped, permission to follow in pursuit."

The masculine voice on the other end replied, "Granted, but do not engage. Check back in, when the alleged kidnapper arrives at a fixed destination, on how to proceed."

"Yes, sir," was his response and the line went dead.

They rode in silence for a while, before Jezalyn said, "Drythe, I can't believe after all these months I never thought to ask you your last name."

"I guess it wasn't important to you."

Jezalyn nervously laughed at his response before continuing, "It does sound familiar though."

"Perhaps, you heard someone at the shop mention it," was his only response.

He cranked up the radio and said, "We'll be there in about forty minutes."

She sat there silently trying to process the opera that blared in her ears, and when they finally reached their destination, Jezalyn happily welcomed the overwhelming silence when he killed the roar of his engine. She had always assumed she liked all music, but today she discovered that opera was almost as unbearable as her grandfather's constant protective hovering.

Soon, Jezalyn heard the phrase "Here we are," so he reached up and ripped off her blindfold. There was a decorative sign to the left that read, The Fowler House Country Inn.

A bed and breakfast, how sweet, she thought and kissed his cheek.

As they entered the full front porch, she said, "Maybe, we could have some tea out here later."

He barely cracked a smile as he guided her into the house.

"I wonder where everyone's at," Jezalyn pondered aloud.

"They are gone. I rented out the place for the night. Do you like it?"

"Yes," she said with a beaming face that faded once she found herself unintentionally deliberating on the sleeping arrangements. *I wonder if we are going to be in the same room. Should I be spending the night with him on technically our second date? Maybe I should ask if we will be staying in separate rooms, but I also don't want to come off uninterested. Perhaps, I should wait and see how I feel later tonight,* was her last thought as she heard him ask her if she would take pleasure in a tour of the inn.

"Yes," she said as she slipped her arm around his. She noticed the old wood frame gray couch as they passed through to the kitchen, where she rubbed her hand down the island bar, before being guided back and around to the hall that led to the bedrooms.

He said, as he opened the door, "This is your room." She was happy to hear the words 'your room' and not 'ours'. Now she wouldn't have to feel awkward for the rest of the evening wondering about the sleeping arrangements. *Besides*, she thought, *I could always ask him to spoon with me later, if I change my mind.*

Jezalyn charged into the room, beaming full of relief, and immediately noticed a hutch in the far corner of one wall and on the other was an old fashion washbasin elegantly placed under an antique mirror. Jezalyn found the inn charming, which made her feel relaxed and comfortable. She checked her watch. It was close to five-thirty, so she suggested they go outside and watch the sun go down.

"Go ahead up front to the porch swing; I'll meet you out there," he said.

Jezalyn grabbed the throw off the end of her bed, and bundled up on the swing.

"I got us some tea," he said as he handed her a glass. She lifted the covers, and he slid in next to her. They watched the sky streak long rays of pink that faded into a dark purple, which inevitably turned midnight blue before becoming a shade of dreary obsidian.

Their tea dwindled with the sun. "Beautiful," she whispered hugging up next to his arm.

"Here take some covers. Your arm feels frosty."

He snickered at her and pulled the covers higher as she rested her head on his arm and he whispered something into her ear, Before long, she was sound asleep.

***

Earlier that day, while Jezalyn was meeting with Blaise, Larkin had arrived at Julius's house before any emergency personal came on the scene. He had run carefully into the house avoiding the flames. After Larkin discovering several bodies, he ripped open the metal trap door and hurled several corpses down the shaft before dragging Wyler out to safety. Out on the lawn, Larkin had discreetly fed Wyler some blood so that his body could recover faster. After his medical release, Wyler drove Larkin back to the shop.

"I am sorry, I didn't wait as you ordered. When I arrived, I spotted Theron leaving and I saw smoke. I don't know what happened. All I can conclude is that my war response took over and before I knew it, I was inside battling smoke and slitting wrists," said Wyler never taking his eyes off the road.

"It's okay. I understand," replied Larkin.

"I don't," said Wyler shaking his head. "I just put my life in jeopardy for someone who was already dead. We can't tell Ana; this has to be our secret."

"Your defiance might have saved Julius."

"Not likely! When I arrived, he was motionless gripping the heart that was torn from his own chest."

"There is a possibility Julius can make it, since you stuffed his heart back in his chest and drained your blood over it."

"I don't understand. I thought once the heart was removed that was it for vampires."

"Not exactly. The only way to truly kill a vampire is to destroy the heart."

"So Julius is still alive?"

"Yes, but he is vulnerable. We need to get him some fresh blood and close up that hole in his chest." With that last response from Larkin, Wyler forgot about the speed limit and drove directly to the bookstore.

It was almost five when they arrived. They needed to pick up some supplies and return to Epps before anyone could discover Julius.

As they entered the underground apartment, Ana rushed hysterically toward them. "Word is your brother is in town, and we need to find him before he finds us. We need to retreat to another safe house!"

"Too late," replied Wyler as he snatched his medical bag off the refrigerator.

"What do you mean?" asked Ana nervously rubbing at her hands.

"He torched Julius's house earlier today."

Ana gasped as she cupped her hands over her mouth, and shook her head in disbelief. "How touching," said Larkin, "I didn't think you cared for him much."

Wyler cut his eyes at Larkin and thought, *now's not the time for this shit*, but in all actuality, Larkin was not wrong. She gasped not out of sympathy, but because she knew if Theron got Julius, he could just as easily get them also.

"Let's go," said Larkin as he grabbed several pouches of blood from the refrigerator.

"Where are we going?" cried Ana.

"We have to go back and check on Julius."

"Where is Jezalyn? I don't think we should leave her behind with Theron on the loose."

Wyler and Larkin stared at each other. "Is she still silent?"

"Yes," responded Larkin as he dashed up the stairs into the shop.

"What does that mean? I thought the connection couldn't be broken."

"It can't," replied Wyler.

"Then, why can't he hear her?" asked Ana with intensity bordering on anger. She did not know how attached she had actually gotten to Jezalyn until that moment.

"Perhaps she is asleep, Bunny. Don't worry I'm sure he'll get a read on her soon." With that response Wyler ran upstairs to meet Larkin.

After gathering some supplies and Ana, they rushed back to Julius's house. Ana stood silent as she realized a charred shell was all that remained of Julius's house. The cindered walls smoked as Larkin and Wyler tossed the debris off the steel flap that led to Julius's body. After clearing the debris, Larkin looked at Wyler and said, "Take Ana and go to the old Epps Memorial Graveyard. Walk toward the back and down to the left. There will be several burial vaults. Search for the one titled Grimshaw; I will be waiting inside with Julius."

Wyler and Ana ran back to the car, and Larkin flipped open the lid and jumped into the hole. He cradled Julius in his arms like an infant and ran down the narrow shaft. When he reached the end, he pressed with his right shoulder against a rectangular stone that arched at the top. Once the secret passageway opened, he gently laid Julius down and unbolted the crypt for Wyler, but his speed afforded him enough time to retrieve the other two bodies and seal the secret passage before they arrived.

Larkin stood in a defensive posture as the door swung open to the burial tomb. "Where's he at?" asked Wyler going through the motions as he rushed to Julius's body.

Ana's eyes grew big. "Who is that?" questioned Ana as she pointed to the two lifeless female bodies resting next to Larkin's foot.

"Casualties," replied Larkin. "Inspect those crypts over here and see if there is any room."

Ana did as Larkin requested and turned her flashlight toward the wall. "No, not the wall crypts, those over there." Larkin pointed to several stone coffins positioned against the far left corner where darkness embraced them.

Ana edged forward, until she reached the first tomb. She pushed on the lid, but it would not budge. "I can't get it open," replied Ana as she threw her hands up in frustration.

Grabbing one of the corpses, Larkin said, "I got it." He pushed it back releasing an overwhelming stench, and

Ana instantly brought both her hands to her face dropping her light into the crypt.

Ana held her nose as she tried to retrieve her light, but with every attempt she gagged. It was not until her third unsuccessful retrieval that Larkin said, "I got it," before demanding that she go get the other body. Consequently as he brought the light up, he saw a shimmer. He tilted the light forward and discovered that the glint was a large diamond engagement ring on the finger of a somewhat decomposed body. Upon seeing the ring Larkin mumbled dryly, "Figures, Julius always had fine taste." After retrieving Ana's flashlight, he resealed the concrete tomb since there was not enough room to store another body. Larkin moved on to the next, all the while insisting that Ana drag the other body over while he lifted the lid and threw the body in. Larkin had resealed the stone coffin, and waited with the fourth open for Ana to bring him the body.

After dumping the remains, Larkin returned to Wyler. "How is he doing?"

Wyler, almost done closing Julius's chest, said, "I need more blood."

Larkin's animalistic nature took over, as he snatched up a bag of blood and tore it open, but before he could hand it to Wyler. Julius's piercing-blue eyes popped open.

"Look! He's awake," cried Ana.

At the sight of Larkin, Julius used all his might to push his body backward. Once out of Larkin's grip, he used what energy he had left and jumped to his feet. Blood gushed out of the two-inch hole that remained open in his chest. Julius stood in a defensive posture, even as Larkin identified himself as he moved closer, but it was not until he saw Larkin's scar-free hand that he relaxed and collapsed in his arms.

"Hand me another bag of blood, Ana," demanded Larkin.

Ana twisted off the cap, making sure not to spill the fluid, before handing the bag over to him. Larkin snatched it and said, "Don't move. Wyler is working on you. I need you to drink this; you already lost some of the blood he pumped into you." Julius, too weak to hold the bag, let Larkin hold it to his mouth the way a mother would hold a bottle for her baby.

With Julius conscious and all stitched up, they had to wait until dusk before they could move Julius into the car.

"What happened?"

"Your brother happened. How could you not tell me about your brother?"

"I thought he was dead, but once Wyler told me that he had seen me at your house, I knew that fact to be untrue. Did he say anything?"

"He asked for a drink, so I provided one. You know that should have tipped me off, since you haven't drank from a human, since me. However, I thought you were being pretentious for once, so I retrieved a red and a white aged about twenty-two years." Julius grabbed his chest as he chuckled at referencing the girls as wine.

"Then what happened?" urged Larkin.

"He ripped her throat out, so I asked you, I mean him, to stop because blood was spraying all over my vintage rug. That's when he informed me of whom he was and his plan to destroy everything that you hold dear."

"Jezalyn," blurted out Ana.

"Probably, her too," said Julius. "Odds are if he knew about me, he knows about her, too."

Ana jumped to her feet. "Larkin, concentrate, try to see if you can find Jezalyn."

"Don't you think I've been trying since I found out Theron was here? What time is it?"

Wyler checked his watch, "It's five fifty-seven."

"Ana, go see if it is dusk yet," ordered Larkin.

She cracked open the gate and peered out into the abandoned cemetery. "Yeah, and we're clear to move him. The plots are empty."

"Wyler, grab his legs! Ana, you go open the back door." Everyone moved on Larkin's command, and they packed Julius to the car undetected. They had barely backed out of the cemetery parking lot and onto the road, when Larkin said, "Pull over! And don't speak."

They quietly watched Larkin, and surveyed the area until Ana broke the silence, "Babe, I don't see anything."

Larkin cut his eyes at her. "Let me see your hand."

Ana timidly extended her hand toward Larkin. Disregarding the inconvenience of having another person's thoughts in his head, Larkin tightly clutched Ana's wrist and sank his teeth into her tanned skin. She jumped as his fangs pierced her skin, but soon found herself overwhelmed with a euphoric sensation and she did not want him to stop.

Larkin released his grip, licked his fangs clean, and closed his eyes.

Wyler, who was looking on extremely concerned, grabbed his wife's wrist, applied pressure, and reached for his medical bag. He pulled out the clotting powder, sprinkled it over the piercings, and continued the pressure until the powder dried. When he released her, the clot remained and the blood flowed normally through her veins. It took several minutes before the lilac tint of her fingers returned to normal.

Larkin's eyes remained closed for about ten minutes, before he opened them.

"I found Jezalyn. Theron has her."

"Where at?" asked Wyler.

"He is holed up with her at a little bed and breakfast in Winnsboro."

"Is she safe?" asked Ana cradling her wrist in her other hand.

"For now." Somehow, Theron had reestablished their brotherly telepathic bond; it had been a long time since Larkin had heard his brother's voice ringing in his head. "He took Jezalyn to ensure that I would stand and fight."

"We can set a trap and get her back," replied an optimistic Ana.

"Watch your words around me; Theron can still read my thoughts. Your blood should help muddle them, but it may take a while." Larkin pointed to Julius. "Ana,

Take our supplies and secure them safely in the bookstore stockroom."

Ana acknowledged his command with the tilt of her head, and looked to her husband for protection. "Honey, are you staying with us?"

Larkin answered for him, "Yes! It's too much of a risk. The plan is to remain in the shop, until I return and give you the signal."

"What's the signal?" asked Ana.

"The usual," replied Wyler, and Larkin nodded at his response.

"Do not under any circumstances go downstairs," warned Larkin.

When they arrived at the shop, Larkin punched into the computer the address Theron had provided him. "I'll go on foot; it will be just as fast."

Larkin cut through the woods and fields, as he rushed to Jezalyn's aid. He opted to leave off the threat of her imminent death to the others if he did not show up alone. The location was almost over an hour away, but by taking a detour through the woods, he would shave about a quarter of the time off. Consequently, the more ground he gained the stronger his link to his brother became. Larkin was about to jump a creek, when he heard Theron in his head, *I am getting bored, brother. I wonder if Jezalyn could help keep me entertained, but for how long will be up to you.*

Chapter 23: A Brotherly Squabble

THERON, IMMOBILIZED BY Jezalyn who was slumbering on top of him, decided to make good on his threat and use her as his entertainment. He leaned over and whispered something in her ear.

Jezalyn stirred at his words, and before she knew it, she found herself in the bedroom with Larkin. She pulled off her pants, reached for his hand, and silently guided him to the bed, but when she did, she felt something rough. Jezalyn flipped his hand over and examined it, "what happened?"

"Oh, I burnt myself a long time ago."

"A long time ago? It wasn't there last night," said Jezalyn.

He gave her a sinister smile and said, "Perhaps on Larkin it wasn't."

She jumped back against the headboard out of his arms as she realized that it might not be Larkin sitting in front of her, but to ease her fear she exclaimed, "Larkin, this isn't funny!"

He produced a snarling laugh, and she cried out, "Stop, Larkin! You're scaring me."

"Well, I suppose I could, if I was Larkin," replied Theron.

Without hesitation, she jumped out of bed and twisted the doorknob, but before she could get it open, Theron grabbed her by the waist and flung her onto the bed. She watched as his fangs extended, and she tried to squirm away; it was in that instant she knew Blaise had not lied to her— vampires were real. She cringed as she felt his tongue moisten her right thigh before he let his teeth penetrate her.

Theron heard Larkin approach, so he whispered into Jezalyn's ear once more, stood up, and waited for him.

When Larkin finally arrived, he spotted a truck parked across the way. He snuck into the yard, but found Theron waiting for him on the front porch.

"Nice of you to show up, brother," said Theron in a taunting tone. "We were just getting to the exciting part."

"Well, I like to oblige," replied Larkin, ignoring Theron's last comment. "Where's the girl?"

"You request her as if you have no interest in her," he responded with a sinister smirk that Larkin could not see.

"Please, you need something more concrete to lure me in," replied Larkin.

"Then perhaps, if I drug her out into the yard by the head of her hair and snapped her pretty little neck. Would that get your attention?"

"Certainly not, you would be doing me a favor."

He let out a robust laugh, "What do I owe the pleasure of your company?"

"Curiosity, I suppose."

"What could you be curious about?"

"For starters, where have you been?"

"Well, let's see, I think we parted back in 1906, and I last read your mind in 1907; I thought your mind had betrayed you when I heard you request everything to be shipped to Transylvania. I even laughed to myself as I thought how cliché it was for a vampire to retreat to Transylvania."

Larkin quietly chuckled. "Let me guess: not quite the betrayal you had hoped."

"I went to the dock to ambush you, but instead I found an unwelcoming surprise."

"I suppose that surprise wouldn't be the Hunter, now would it?"

"He thought he had the best of me, but I showed him. Then I hopped the next available ship to Romania thinking I would beat you across, but I waited for a week and nothing. Neither you nor your belongings had arrived. I quickly realized my error in presuming I had made it over before you. I ventured into the city, checking every castle and cave, but it had been several years since I received a connection from you, so I gave up my pursuit on the thought that you might have perished in the icy waters as you made your voyage to. . .," he paused and finished with a mocking tone, "Transylvania." With a loathing air, he said, "I retreated to the Carpathian Mountains, where I made an old kingdom my home. Unsure of your demise, I sat on my throne listening for the day I would find you again."

"I haven't been anywhere near Romania. How did you find me after all these years?"

"That girl, she reawakened some intense emotions within you, so don't tell me you care nothing for her," demanded Theron.

"That girl, you think means so much to me, stumbled onto my Memoirs. While reading them, she reawakened old feelings that I buried deep within."

"Admit it; she made you feel alive again."

"In a sense she did. Our bond forced me to recall my most intimate accounts with Isadora. It was those accounts that reawakened my soul."

"How dare you speak her name?" raged Theron.

"I see. She is still the reason you search for me and call me out."

"What if she is?" asked Theron.

"Brother, you really need to let this go."

"You would say that, you coward. Anything else you would like to ask me before you meet your ill-timed fate? Perhaps, you would like to hear an account of your dear friend Julius."

"One last question, since one of us is about to meet our demise," said Larkin.

"If you wish, since it is you who will meet your doom."

"How do you turn our telepathic link on and off?" asked Larkin.

"Well, there's no risk in revealing it now, since I know you will not soil your honor by fleeing."

Larkin tried to choke back his laughter. "I never ran, not even when you sent several men. Answer the question, so we can get on with it."

"Getting cocky I see," said Theron. "Do you know why spider lilies were Isadora's favorite flowers?"

"Because they looked exotic," shrugged Larkin.

"Hardly. I discovered you can mask any link by grinding spider lily whiskers and a pinch of white snakeroot into a powdery mixture. Not to mention as an added bonus the white snake root serves as an aphrodisiac, which Jezalyn is soon to discover."

"What have you done to her?" demanded Larkin.

"I only gave her a slight sedative," and an eerie smile crossed over Theron's face. "It's a shame you won't be alive to watch me really seduce her."

"What do you mean really seduce her?"

"That little picture of me biting into her thigh was a hypnotic suggestion; it's seemed terribly realistic didn't it?" Without waiting for a response, Theron leaped off the porch landing a few feet from Larkin. "Let's get on with it, so I can get on with it; a little herb, a little blood loss, will certainly make for an orgasmic delight. Don't you think, brother?" asked Theron as he rolled his tongue over his razor- sharp dagger.

Larkin brandished his fangs back at his brother, and they darted toward one another each hoping to send a significant blow. Theron, gaining more speed, pushed Larkin back several feet upon impact, yet Larkin's stance remained grounded. Larkin swiftly grabbed Theron around the waist and tossed him into a tree. The force of the impact caused the top section of the tree to topple to the ground.

Theron, back on his feet, lifted the fallen portion of the tree and flung it at Larkin as effortlessly as a twelve year old would skip a rock across a body of water. The blow sent Larkin flying backwards. He reemerged unshaken, but a blood trail staining his sleeve suggested he was injured. They lunged at one another again, this time trying to lock one another in a death grip, but each time one thought they had the upper hand, the other would slip away. Finally, Larkin was able to secure both hands around Theron's neck and body slam him into the ground. The hard earth caved in around his brother's body. Now on his knees hovering over Theron, Larkin reared back to send a fatal blow into his chest cavity, but he was distracted before he could propel his fist through the cartilage to Theron's heart.

***

Wyler had arrived to find Blaise standing in the middle of the road watching two vampires fight.

"What are you doing here?" asked Wyler.

"I followed Jezalyn here thinking she got kidnapped, but when she got out of the car with Larkin, I watched her body language and discovered she was with him by her own free will. I stayed not really knowing why, perhaps hoping she would change her mind, but this other guy showed up. I thought it was Larkin."

"That's his twin brother."

"I moved closer to hear what they were saying and after a while they started fighting."

"I see that," said Wyler as he moved toward the fight.

Blaise caught his arm. "You can't interfere with that. Those creatures are not human! They'll rip you to shreds."

"I am not concerned," replied Wyler as he yanked his arm free.

Wyler could not distinguish the difference between them, so he called for Larkin, which distracted him, as he ran toward the fight.

Theron used this distraction to his advantage, for in that critical moment Larkin, with his fist raised above Theron's chest, flinched at the sound of Wyler's voice allowing Theron a split second to twist his body to the side so that the punch would glide past him into the already sunken earth. Theron retaliated and elbowed Larkin in the side causing him to propel several feet. Both vampires instantly leaped to their feet. Theron, not even somewhat amused, said, "You brought a human to the fight. I told you if you didn't come alone I would kill her." He bent backwards to realign his spine.

"He came on his own accord," replied Larkin popping his shoulder back into place.

"Now instead of an execution, it will be a slaughter," said Theron letting out a menacing cry as he ran toward Wyler, but before he could reach him Theron felt a sharp pain in his back that ran through to his chest. Theron stopped, glanced down, and saw a wooden arrow with jagged edges sticking out of his chest. He turned to find Blaise releasing another arrow, but before it could make contact, Theron snatched it out of the air. Upon catching the arrow, he flung it back like a dart guided at a bull's eye, but it miraculously bounced off Blaise's chest as he reached for another arrow.

"What's this, brother? Now you have a hunter on your side?" asked Theron as he took a step back to let Blaise's next arrow glide past him.

"He is not with me, but it looks like the odds are on my side tonight."

"You will reap the consequences for this betrayal," roared Theron as he dashed off into the nearby woods. *Everyone will pay for your cowardice, brother,* was the last thought Larkin heard from Theron.

Larkin darted over to Wyler, "What are you doing here?"

"You left the address on the computer, so I took it as a sign to follow you. Are you alright?" inquired Wyler taking note of blood dripping from a gash on his forearm.

"It's only a scratch. Did you bring your bag?"

Before Wyler could retrieve his bag, Blaise ran up to them with his bow still drawn in Larkin's direction, "Where is Jezalyn?"

"I suppose she is on the porch or in the house," replied Larkin.

"I have sworn to protect her, so I suggest you stay out of my way while I collect her," said Blaise stepping around Wyler, placing him three feet from the porch.

Larkin's first response was to Wyler. "Go and get the bag," he said, and after turning to Blaise he continued, "oh really, you think so?"

"Don't move," ordered Blaise.

Wyler put his hands up and froze.

"Look, boy, you don't know who you are dealing with," announced Larkin. Again, Larkin commanded Wyler to get the black bag, but this time he told Wyler not to respond to Blaise's demands.

"I said, don't move," bellowed Blaise as the bow released with a snap. Blaise had targeted Wyler's calf, but before he could blink Larkin had Blaise pressed against the porch railing with one hand and holding the tip of the arrow in another.

"My patience is running thin with you, boy," said Larkin clenching his teeth exposing his fangs. A clinking sound was heard as Larkin tapped Blaise's chest with the arrow, "You don't seem scared," said Larkin as he released him.

Blaise taking the arrow replied, "No, not particularly. Hunters in our division are well trained."

"I figured as much from the first day I met you. The smell of lighter fluid and poison gave it away."

Blaise grimaced at him, and Wyler interrupted them as he returned with his bag. Wyler rarely gave commands even to his own wife, but the war medic side of his life made him more forceful. He sharply instructed Larkin to sit down and roll up his sleeve.

"How can you help such a monster?" Blaise questioned.

"I think you have him confused with his brother," replied Wyler.

"All vampires are monsters."

Wyler did not even acknowledge him as he responded, "Really, do you care to explain why he saved Jezalyn's life twice in a month and a half? Since he is a monster I suppose he's going through all this trouble to devour her later."

Larkin released an enthused howl as Wyler finished sewing him up. "Perplexed, are we?" uttered Larkin rolling his sleeve back down over Wyler's sloppy stitch work.

"Maybe, but I am not leaving here without her."

"You could take her now and expose me, but if you do, it will shatter her innocence. She will never be able to trust anyone or anything again," replied Larkin.

"A cruel awaking to this harsh world might be just what she needs," retorted Blaise.

Larkin shook his head and said, "Maybe your world, but not mine. She will live the rest of her life looking over her shoulder fearing that everyone and anyone is a monster, if you expose me here tonight."

Wyler closing his bag said, "There is an easier way to secure her safety and innocence."

"How?" asked Blaise.

"She thinks she came with Larkin, not his brother, so we will leave them here until morning. With Larkin she will be safe, and remain in the dark about vampires and of the kidnapping."

Blaise had listened to the proposal, but was not ready to concede. He designed several scenarios in his mind, but nothing would allow for Jezalyn's mental state to emerge unscathed in some way. He knew they were probably right that if he exposed any part of the night's events, then Jezalyn would never feel safe again. "I don't like this plan, but it might be her best option for now," said Blaise finally agreeing with Wyler. In a way, Blaise wanted Jezalyn to discover the truth so that they would have a shot at getting back together. However, at the same time, he did not want to destroy her sense of security for a chance at regaining her affection, so he drove away on the agreement that Larkin would return her to the bookstore and Wyler would send her home the next day. Wyler was happy to suggest such a scenario, for he had wanted to evict her for some time now, ever since Larkin showed signs of interest.

"I am going to go, too," said Wyler as he watched Blaise's truck drive off down the street. "Do you need anything else, before I go?"

"No, I am good. I will drive Theron's car back into town in the morning."

"Are you sure? What if he comes back tonight?"

"He won't. That arrow Blaise shot into him had serrated edges from tip to feather. He will be too weak from blood loss to do anything else tonight."

Wyler said, "Oh," as he turned and sprinted to his car.

Larkin stepped onto the porch and found Jezalyn asleep on the swing with her legs still covered by the blanket. He scooped her up, brought her into the room, and laid her down on the bed. He stood there elated watching her chest slowly heave for several minutes, which reaffirmed that life was circulating in her lungs before lightly lifting her to remove her pants as a necessity to check her for bite marks. A feeling of gladness overwhelmed him as Larkin found none. Instantly, he concluded that his brother was not lying to him about manipulating her mind. Flinging her jeans to the end of the bed, he knew that his joy was only secondary to the euphoria he had felt upon finding her still alive.

After a moment of staring at Jezalyn's quiet, petite fair face, Larkin felt a deep pang in his heart. His face twisted as the pain brought back the faded memory of his beloved Isadora, for the knowledge of her death was the last time he had experienced such an emotion. Not able to discern if this current sensation was for one or the other, Larkin bent over and kissed Jezalyn's check. His lips drank in the warmth of her being and the agony began to dispel. Rising from the depths of his ardor, Larkin slightly lifted his head and whispered passionately in her ear, "I think I love you, too."

ChApteR 24: Che Oevil's CheRRy AnD black bat SuRpRise

THERON RAN THROUGH the woods until he started to lose speed. He stopped at a large boulder near the creek to rest. Theron inspected the barbed arrow sticking out of his chest, took several large steps forward, and hurled his body backward. A loud thud radiated in the air accompanied by a pop. It took Theron a moment to pick himself up out of the rubble that was once the boulder. Looking down, he saw a large portion of the arrow had broken off, so he grabbed the tip, being sure not to grasp the barbs, and pulled. He let out a gut-wrenching wail that echoed through the foggy forest as he stumbled into the frigid creek water, stirring up the mist that rested on top before he collapsed. As the water settled down, so did the haze covering the exposed portion of Theron's body. Several minutes after Theron's cry, which felt like an eternity to him, someone grabbed his leg and pulled him out of his frozen watery grave.

"What happened to you?" asked the somewhat stocky figure.

"Maurice!"

"Yes," he said bending down to offer Theron his hand.

Taking his hand, Theron divulged, "A hunter—shot me."

"Where is the arrow?" asked Maurice.

"Over there," he replied pointing to the broken boulder.

He walked over and kicked around the ruble until he spotted the arrow. Maurice squatted down, picked up the arrow by its feather, bought it to his nose, and inhaled. He sprung up and spun around holding the stick away from his body as if it was a snake ready to strike. "Boss, we got a problem."

"What's that?" said Theron.

"The arrow has been poisoned," replied Maurice dropping the broken arrow at his feet and quickly moving toward the creek to wash his hands.

"I suspected that when I could no longer keep my speed. I need you to tell me what kind of poison and how to cure it," replied Theron edgily, but trying to come off coolly.

"It looks like Devil's Cherry."

"Are you sure?"

"Yes. I couldn't pick up on a scent, but there was a blue tinge to the wood. Whatever they added to the poison must have masked the smell."

"Clever," replied Theron in a rather exasperated tone, "but not clever enough. Do we have what we need to draw the poison out?"

"Yes, all it takes is some Broom Snakeweed and Calabar Beans, but that's not the problem."

"I know the poison will make me susceptible to light, but if I stay in the murky shadows of the night, I'll be fine."

"True, but that's not it."

"What! Stop beating around the proverbial bush and lay it straight," replied Theron.

Taking a deep breath, Maurice said, "The problem is the hunter wrapped the barbs with tentacles from a Black Bat flower."

"Impossible," roared Theron. "That flower has been extinct for centuries; I destroyed them myself." Theron picking up the broken arrow that laid next to his foot in disbelief. He tossed it into the creek and mumbled under his breath "There is only one man that could know this lethal combination."

"Who?" questioned Maurice trying to extract more information.

"Luther," bellowed Theron in a fit of rage and shook his head as he found the thought incomprehensible.

Watching Theron's unfathomable response at his own conclusion caused Maurice to question his declaration. "Well, is it Luther or not? Whose house do we need to visit?" said Maurice with a menacing smile as he kicked the stick baring the arrow tip into the water.

"It has all the tell-tale signs of Luther, but it can't be. I left Luther for dead, bleeding out at the shipyard."

"He must have survived. I heard he was a resourceful man," responded Maurice.

Grabbing Maurice's arm for support, he said, "I got a good view of the hunter and it was not Luther."

"Well, looks like not only did Luther survive, but he has undertaken an apprentice." Feeling the heat rise on his skin where Theron's hand lay, gave him cause to worry. "We need to move now. The bat flower is keeping you from healing, and your temperature is rising."

Theron released Maurice's arm and jumped back into the water.

"What are you doing?" he screamed, leaping in the water after him.

"I have to slow down the process," replied Theron. "The flower reverses our ability to heal, thus causing our body to go into shock and run high fever. It is a death sentence because the fever triggers a chain reaction making the blood boil, and we burn from the inside until the heart explodes."

"What's the cure?" said Maurice pulling him back out of the water.

"Broom Snakeweed and an ancient herb called Wood Avens."

"Wood Avens?" replied a confused Maurice.

"Don't worry. I think I know where to find some. Go retrieve the Broom Snakeweed and get some Saltbush too. I will meet you at location B in an hour."

"The herbs are already there; I never removed them from cargo."

"Alright, then it's on me," replied Theron as he tipped his head to his companion and ran off.

Theron ran back to the town of Transylvania, and when he reached the town's water tower, he propped up against it clutching his chest. He grimaced at the heat he felt inside, closed his eyes, and fell to his knees. Trying to compose himself enough to regain his footing, a breeze blew past, and his nose caught a whiff of aged blood. His eyes sprung open, and he found himself staring at a black and white dress loafer only a few inches from his face.

Looking down upon a familiar shoe, Theron smiled and said, "Maurice, you followed." He let Maurice help him to his feet after which a loud clatter arose as he stomped the ground. Pointing down at the shrouded metal entrance, he said, "We need to go that way." Theron followed the smell of old blood, with the aid of Maurice, down an underground tunnel, which lead them to the secret door into Ana and Wyler's underground loft. Maurice opened the door, and Theron entered.

"Where are we?"

"Find the herbs," said Theron moving toward the kitchen. "Tear this place apart, if you have to. I am going to see if I can get an invitation."

Maurice nodded and raked his arm across the counter, and with a loud crash, the overfilled dish drainer fell to the floor. The sound caught Ana's attention upstairs. She covered Julius and lightly tiptoed toward the center of the stockroom. She jumped when the door burst open, and in front of her was Theron or Larkin, she knew not which, crouched down holding his chest.

"Ana, help me."

With wide eyes she observed his broken physique and found herself alarmed at the thought of Theron's strength verses her husband. "Where's Wyler?" cried Ana trying to hold back the hysterics in her voice.

"He is downstairs frantically searching for his herbs. I am in too much pain; come help me."

Ana gritted her teeth at his command as she moved closer, "Wait! Show me the sign."

He lifted his blood stained hands, and said in a more authoritative tone, "Help me, now!"

Ana, being used to Larkin's demands, cried out, "Wyler, I moved the herbs to the vault behind the fridge."

She was about an arm's length away when she heard a voice not of her husband's cry out, "I got it; let's go." Fright crossed Ana's face as she turned to recoil, but it was too late. She was already too close. Theron popped up, reached out with his bloody right hand, snagged a fist full of Ana's hair, and pulled. Theron's withdraw was quick and effortless. He had Ana, but only a piece. He looked over to find Ana laying on the floor holding her head while Julius's eyes burned into him.

Theron shook the toffee brown hair from his hand, "Julius, what a nice surprise. I thought I left you heartbroken over your old carpet."

Julius's body had not fully recovered yet, so he did not let his temper flair. He let out a chuckle and said, "Perhaps."

"Come on, Theron," Maurice called out from behind.

Theron bowed, "Until next time."

"Next time we meet, it will be your heart I feel pulsating in my hand," said Julius.

The words "Not likely," accompanied by a snarl was Theron's final response as he rushed back downstairs.

"Let me see," said Theron. Maurice silently held up the bag. "That's it," responded Theron as he flung open the freezer, grabbed several ice cubes, and pushed them into his wounds. With every insert, Theron let out a teeth-grinding grunt.

"Let's go! This ice is going to melt fast," said Theron. By the time they re-emerged at the surface, Theron was clasping his chest again.

Maurice grabbed Theron and threw him over his shoulders. "We are only ten minutes away. We can make it; just hold on," said Maurice as he sprinted through the woods toward the Mississippi River.

＊

Wyler returned home to find his weeping wife huddled up next to Julius, and to his surprise, Julius was genuinely trying to comfort her. Upon seeing her husband, Ana raced to him squeezing his torso as hard as she could, refusing to let go. She finally released him, as she unfolded the events that took place while he was gone. Finally, she bent over to pick up the hair Theron had torn out. After discovering that Theron was not alone, Wyler did the only sensible thing he could. He first obtained the inn's number, and afterwards he relayed the events that had unfolded at the shop to Larkin. As Wyler retold Ana's story, she huddled against his back. Wyler urged Larkin to come back regardless of the previous plan since they now knew Theron was not alone and did not know how many co-conspirators Theron had brought with him. Larkin agreed it would be the best course of action and cautioned Wyler about going downstairs. "I'll inform them to stay in the storage room," replied Wyler, and as Larkin hung up the phone, he debated on how to awaken Jezalyn and return her to the shop without suspicion.

Instead of waking Jezalyn immediately, he paced back and forth in front of her door trying to come up with a suitable reason for departing in the middle of the night. Unbeknownst to Larkin, Jezalyn had awakened, her head foggy from the remnants of the sedative that Theron gave her. She glanced around the room a moment before quietly sliding off the bed. Jezalyn crouched down next to it, as if to hide, all the while peeking under and over it to make sure she was alone. Once she discovered she was alone, she checked both thighs. She had found no blood or even one mark on them, so she slowly stood up and sat back on the bed, took a deep breath, and concluded that she must have fallen asleep. "It was all a dream," mumbled Jezalyn as she slid her bare legs back under the covers. She found herself trying to piece things together. She remembered, *I felt fear, pain, and then pleasure, but what could it mean? There was Larkin who really wasn't Larkin, Blaise, and aggression. I am missing something*, thought Jezalyn as Larkin lightly rapped on the door before entering.

"You're awake," said Larkin as he entered the room with a wooden tray.

"What's all this?" said Jezalyn pointing for him to place it on the nightstand next to the bed as she pulled the covers up to her chest.

After fulfilling her direction, he sat down next to her, "I made you some eggs, grits, French toast, and bacon." He reached up to brush a few strands of hair out of her face, but she winced at the approach and reached for his hands.

"What's wrong, Jezalyn?" asked Larkin.

"Nothing," she responded with a smile as she saw two smooth hands. She certainly knew she had been dreaming when she found no scar, so she leaned in to kiss him.

As she pulled away, she said with a giggle, "It's a little early in the morning for breakfast, isn't it?"

"I know," kissing the hand that clasped his, "but Wyler called and requested that we come home as soon as possible."

"Is everything alright?" said Jezalyn with her body sitting up at full attention, letting the covers fall into her lap.

"Wyler said, 'Ana had some kind of incident with a patient at work.' He felt it would be better for Ana if we were to come back, but I didn't want you to leave here without receiving breakfast at the bed and breakfast inn."

Jezalyn giggled again at his reference before allowing her facial structure to form serious features, "Is Ana okay?"

"I think so, but we can't be sure until we get all the facts."

"Well, let's go now then. Ana might need us for emotional support," said Jezalyn pulling back her cover to get out of bed forgetting she had no pants on.

Larkin tried not to stare at her exposed panties, but he could not help it. When Jezalyn realized her pants were missing, she jumped back in the bed and quickly covered up her naked legs. Her countenance mixed with confusion and embarrassment. "Um, where are my pants?" she asked.

He moved to the bottom of the bed, lifted up the pants, and handed them off to her. "I'll take this food back to the kitchen while you get dressed."

"Wait!" exclaimed Jezalyn, pulling a piece of bacon off the plate as Larkin moved back toward the nightstand to recover the tray.

He picked up the plate and held it out to her, in a butler fashion, "Anything else?" Larkin lingered a moment waiting for Jezalyn's extended hand to pluck a piece of food off the plate. He was somewhat surprised to find her hand had extended beyond the plate and onto his. Jezalyn did not flinch at the clattering of the plate hitting the floor as she pulled him into the bed with her.

Ϲʜᴀρϲeʀ 25: A Ϲoϲκϲᴀιl ᴀɴᴏ ᴀ Ϲoɴfliϲϲ

LL TOO SOON, Larkin and Jezalyn found themselves back at Wyler's bookstore. Soon after entering the shop, they happened upon Wyler and Ana sitting next to a man with jet-black hair. It was short and stopped at the nape of his neck like most clean cut men's hair, but the top was several inches long with no part. He styled it down toward the face and the back of the neck; Jezalyn could not see any sideburns. However, she assumed that if he had some, his hairstyle probably covered them. She noticed he wore a black tee and denim, but regardless of his fashion, she concluded he seemed well put together, almost like a model. Although she knew she should find him attractive and interesting on appearance alone, she did not.

Jezalyn completely by-passed everyone and ran up to Ana, swung her arms around her neck, and squeezed, "Are you okay? Larkin told me about your patient. What happened? Do you feel up to talking about it yet?"

Hugging her back, Ana said, "I am okay now. I am glad you're back home safe."

"We are all safe," replied Jezalyn, and Ana could not keep herself from wishing she was as innocent and trusting as Jezalyn.

Wyler introduced Julius, who stood up and shook her hand. Jezalyn shuttered at the iciness of his hand. "I'm sorry; I got here only moments before you. I couldn't find my gloves, so I jogged over without them anyway."

"It's okay; it's unusually cold out tonight. How about I make us all some tea?" replied Jezalyn running water into the kettle before anyone could respond.

"Good idea," said Wyler. Then jerking his head toward the downstairs door he continued, "Larkin, we're all upstairs because the heater went out downstairs, do you think you could come take a look at it with me?"

"Sure," replied Larkin somewhat hesitantly. "Perhaps Julius should join us, too."

Julius responded to Larkin's request with a mischievous smile as he said, "Nah, my fingers are frozen as popsicles; I won't be any help to you. I think it's best if I remain upstairs with the ladies," lifting his eyebrows playfully to taunt Larkin.

Jezalyn and Ana blurted-out simultaneously, "I agree!"

As Larkin headed down the stairs to the underground apartment, he found himself perplexed by the emotions and thoughts garbled up inside his head. He needed to find a release of all these bonds, his brother, Ana, and at this point even Jezalyn.

He cleared his own thoughts long enough to survey the premises. Theron had done a good job of ransacking the loft; he had left the space broken and trashed.

"Scan for missing things; we need to find what he was searching for."

"We don't have to; Ana told me what Theron was after," said Wyler.

"What?"

"Herbs! Theron made her think he was you, so she told him where to find them."

"And where would that be?" asked Larkin.

"In the safe, behind the fridge."

Larkin pushed the fridge to the side to reveal a mangled safe; the door hung down by one hinge exposing a large hole in the wall. Wyler rushed past him and grabbed the remaining contents and brought them over to the counter.

"Looks like they took the Saltbush, Wood Avens, and some Lavender," said Wyler glancing over his herbs again. "What do they need this combination of herbs for? I understand the Wood Avens because it's difficult to find, but Lavender, really!"

"I figured he would come after them," replied Larkin. "After he scampered off into the woods, our connection was still linked. His body was slowing down, and he started staggering about and hallucinating. When he stopped at the creek, the connection was lost until an intense pain radiated through my chest. His intense emotions reconnected us long enough to discover that the arrow Blaise shot him with was poisoned."

"Poisoned!"

"Yes, poisoned."

"What kind of poison would need Lavender?"

"It's not the Lavender that concerns me. We need to get our hands on some more Wood Avens."

Wyler darted into the bedroom stumbling over clutter as he went. "Ah-ha!" called out Wyler as he removed the bed knobs. He ripped them off and ran into the kitchen with Larkin, "Look," he said twisting off the stub that fit into the bedpost. He shook the contents out of each one in front of him. Larkin dug through the small bags and discovered they had two bags of Wood Avens, one bag of Snakeweed stems, and several bags of other miscellaneous herbs used to ward off maladies.

"Put these in your medical bag and have it at arm's length at all times," commanded Larkin holding several bagged herbs out for him to take. Wyler shoved them into his pocket, since he had left his bag upstairs.

"Okay now. How are we going to secure the door so that Ana will come back down without alarming Jezalyn?"

"We don't have to worry about that tonight with the type of poison Blaise used on Theron. Besides, there are three of us here now."

"What am I to tell Ana?"

"Tell her that we are setting up security perimeters, but before we go back up I need you to make me some special tea."

"Okay," replied Wyler moving to the cabinet without second-guessing his request even though Jezalyn was upstairs also making tea at that very moment. He filled one of the only remaining cups with water, put it in the microwave, and pressed the beverage button.

As the microwave counted down, Wyler asked, "Which flavor you want tonight blackberry, chai, or AB positive?"

"Neither, I need a special concoction. Grab a bowl and spoon," said Larkin as he bent down to pick up several flowers off the floor. With the bowl next to him, he asked Larkin to search his pockets for some Snakeroot. The microwave buzzed as Wyler flipped out a baggie on the table.

"This is Snakeweed; I need White Snakeroot. Check again."

Wyler carefully tip-toed through the debris to bring the hot cup of water over to the table. He sat it down next to Larkin before searching his pockets again. He placed the correct bag down next to Larkin and watched him pluck the tiny whiskers out of several flowers while he waited for his next order.

Larkin scooped the flower whisker into the bowl, added a pinch of Snakeroot, and ground it together. Once it was minced, he placed the mixture in the hot water and stirred.

Larkin blew into the cup before requesting Larkin to hand him a cube of ice since the steam burnt his lip as he blew. Wyler did as he requested, "That's funny. We don't have any."

"No ice! Now I am certain that one of the poisons inflicted on Theron was Black Bat's Flower."

"Those plants were supposed to be extinct," responded Wyler.

"I know, but when these flowers and vampire blood intertwine, one's condition becomes extremely volatile."

"So that's why Theron attempted to come here. He was desperate."

"Perhaps," said Larkin, "but he could have had ulterior motives. My brother is not to be trusted."

"Oh, I know all too well. I have not forgotten," replied Wyler. "Do you want me to go upstairs and see if Jezalyn has some in her apartment?"

"No, I will chug it like this. If it burns going down, my body will restore after a while. I only wanted to avoid the irritation."

After guzzling the hot tea, they sprinted upstairs to find Ana and Jezalyn laughing and joking with Julius. They were having such a good time that they did not even notice that Larkin and Wyler had returned. Wyler strolled over to Ana and wrapped his arms around her neck, kissed the top of her head, and quietly whispered in her ear, "I love you, Bunny," but not quite loud enough for the rest of them to hear. Jezalyn watched Ana's face beam with merriment before getting up to get Larkin a cup of tea.

"Here you go," Jezalyn said handing him the cup of tea. "Two sugars, right?"

"Right," replied Larkin taking the cup. He brought it to his lip and pretended to take a sip, his throat had not fully recovered yet, but he found himself not wanting to offend her by rejecting the tea, so he did what he had never done before and faked it to oblige someone else.

"Did you get the heater fixed?" asked Ana.

"Yes, darling, I do believe it is," replied her husband, who then walked over to his medical bag to deposit the remaining herbs.

"How about a game of cards before bed?" asked Larkin trying to take the attention off of Wyler. Not to mention, he longed to know whether his concoction was as success for him as it was for Theron. Moreover, he needed both Ana and Jezalyn awake. Seeing how there was an odd number of players, pairs were out. Because not everyone knew the rules to other games, they finally decided to resign the cards and play dominoes instead. They decided to set a limit, two games to five-hundred before heading off to bed.

The thoughts running through Larkin's head began to become vague about an hour into the first game. Larkin may have been losing his hand, but he was overjoyed to be winning his sanity back. Furthermore, as time ticked past, the intrusive thoughts grew vaguer until they were so indistinct that he could no longer distinguish who thought what or even what the thought was. Larkin pondered as to how such a cure was not unearthed throughout his extensive years of existence. Yet, he could only blame himself for such a lack of wisdom, seeing how it was he who had suppressed himself from the world whenever the loss of Isadora became too painful to bear. For a moment his happy grin slanted into a melancholy stare, but Larkin quickly regained his smile when Jezalyn played the five-two to gain herself fifteen points.

He became increasingly irritated with the attention that Julius had shown her all night. Larkin knew he was doing it just to get under his skin, so he flashed him a smile and laid down a domino out of his hand.

When the last game finally ended, Jezalyn helped Ana pick up the dominoes while Larkin pulled Wyler to the side.

"The mixture is working. There's haziness in my head, and I can't hear anything that is going on in either of their heads."

"That's good," replied Wyler.

"Now I need you to make Ana feel something, so I can determine if the emotions are blocked as well."

Uncomfortable at the suggestion Larkin gave him as a test to heighten Ana's feelings, Wyler still put the plan into action. Larkin slid a forgotten domino toward Ana, with the aim of missing her and when she bent over to pick it up Wyler gave her a playful, but rather painful smack on the bottom.

"Wyler!" Ana exclaimed as she popped up and rubbed her bottom. "What in the hell is wrong with you?"

Jezalyn tried not to laugh as a shell shocked Wyler stuttered the word, "S-s-s-sorry, Bunny, I was just goofing around." Larkin was rather amused, but not at the conflict but at the assurance that he felt nothing. He did not feel the sensation of the slap on his buttocks or the embarrassment and anger Ana felt toward Wyler.

"Let's head to bed, and I will rub it for you," joked Wyler trying to ease the tension.

"You will not be rubbing anything tonight mister," replied Ana angrily.

"Good night everyone; I'll see y'all in the morning," said Jezalyn as she grabbed her sweater.

"Hey, let me walk you up," said Julius beating Larkin to the punch.

"Okay," replied Jezalyn as she glanced at Larkin, who was trying not to show much attention to the situation. Larkin was furious at Julius for requesting to accompany Jezalyn upstairs, but also at himself for drinking that stupid concoction that now blocked all Jezalyn's thoughts and emotions. As Julius and Jezalyn navigated up to her apartment door, Larkin could not tell if Jezalyn wanted Julius to walk her up, or if she was just being polite. Wyler and Ana had gone downstairs leaving Larkin in the shop impatiently waiting for Julius to return. Julius did not directly return downstairs, and the fury mounted in Larkin with each passing moment.

Upon his return, Larkin exploded at the sight of Julius when he finally emerged downstairs with a devious grin plastered across his face. He rushed at him, but Julius deflected the move, and Larkin crashed into a bookshelf.

"Why all the hostility, friend?" Julius asked somewhat intrigued and cocky.

"Tell me what you were doing up there for so long?"

"You should know. I am sure you read her every thought."

"I can't read her thoughts anymore."

"Really?" responded Julius fairly surprised and yet amused at the situation.

Julius's refusal to tell him immediately along with his newfound amusement over the situation re-invoked Larkin's rage. Sprawled out all over the floor, books lay beneath his feet, so Larkin bent down, picked one up, and flung it at Julius. Larkin was not quick enough because Julius ducked and the book flew past him embedding itself in the wall.

"You should calm down or our little girlfriend will hear us," Julius teased. "What will you tell her?"

After several minutes of trying to calm himself, Larkin finally replied, "I told you to stay away from her."

"I must say, I can see why you're so keen on her now."

The implications of that one statement caused Larkin's blind rage to get the better of him, and he charged Julius. The force of the impact shoved Julius back into the stockroom where Larkin firmly gripped Julius around the waist; and power drove his body into the solid concrete floor. Still recovering from his prior wounds, Julius spat up blood.

"You are starting to piss me off, so I suggest you back up before this gets serious," warned Julius.

"It wouldn't have to get serious; if you would not chase after …"

Jezalyn ran in interrupting them, "Hey is everyone alright? The building just shook. I think we might've had an earthquake or something. There are books scattered about all over the floor in the shop."

"We felt it too," said Julius whipping his mouth with his sleeve.

"Oh my gosh, you're bleeding," said Jezalyn as she clasped her hand to her mouth only a second before pulling herself together to give demanding instructions. "Larkin! Go get Wyler; he's coughing up a lot of blood."

Larkin did not have to move because in that instant both Wyler and Ana were flying through the door.

"What happened?" cried Ana as Wyler ran to his medical kit.

The phrase, "I'm fine," spurted out of Julius's bloody mouth as he took a seat at the little table where they had played dominoes before adding "everyone go back to bed. I just bumped my lip on the table."

"I'll go pick up the books before heading back to bed," mumbled Jezalyn as she turned to leave the stockroom.

"Books?" asked Wyler.

She stopped and responded, "Yeah, the earthquake shook several of the shelves."

Wyler knew there had been no earthquake, and it was Larkin and Julius that had caused the ruckus she heard or felt. Wyler also knew the first course of action was to get Julius downstairs so that he could examine his chest wound. There were no way the wounds Julius had sustained earlier that day had enough time to completely heal, so Wyler scarcely expressed any concern over the books as he encouraged Jezalyn to go back to bed.

"I'll pick them up in the morning," said Ana following her husband's lead.

Jezalyn nodded her head, but as she turned to go back to her loft, she stopped once and asked, "Larkin, would you mind walking me back up?"

Larkin smiled gingerly at Jezalyn and agreed, although he was rather irritated at her for allowing Julius to accompany her up earlier. As Larkin escorted her up, he felt something new; it could not be a reflection of Jezalyn or Ana feeling, since he drank the potion, but his own emotions that occupied his thoughts. He realized that he was not only mad at himself for losing his temper with Julius almost to the point of exposure, but that he was genuinely concerned about the potential injuries that he might have inflicted on his friend.

Chapter 26: Exposed

JULIUS REMOVED HIS black tee so that Wyler could examine his chest. His shirtless body exposed an almost eight inch makeshift suture. As Wyler examined his work, he requested Ana get some water and rags. Reluctant as Ana normally would have been at the thought of her kitchen turning into a trauma room, she moved swiftly to get all the items Wyler required never once complaining about the bloody state of her kitchen as Wyler burst Julius's suture stitching every few inches. Julius gritted his teeth at the sound of each stitch popping under the pressure of Ana's cutlery knife.

"Watch the edges of that thing!" blared Julius as one of the jagged edges of the cutlery knife nipped his skin near his nipple.

"Only a couple more to go," said Ana trying to calm him. Wyler stared at her with eerie displeasure as he observed the unusual attention she displayed toward Julius. It was not the time to deliberate on the reasons of her sudden change of heart because right now Wyler needed to make sure whatever little tiff Julius and Larkin just entangled themselves in did not re-rupture his heart valve connections. Of course, he knew Julius could still go on even if the valve was severed, but Wyler needed Julius to heal fast so that he could help Larkin protect them efficiently when the time came.

Almost prepared to cut open the last few sutures, Wyler snapped, "Ana get a spoon." Following his command Ana rummaged through her kitchen drawers. A few moments later, a black plastic ladle disrupted Wyler's view as Ana let it dangle in front of his face. "Get a

wooden one, something Julius can bite down on," said
Wyler disapproving of her selection. Ana dropped the ladle
in his lap and ran back to the drawers.

"I don't need something to bite down on."

"I am about to remove the last few stitches, and
when I do, your chest will spring open faster than an
overcooked, dehydrated Thanksgiving turkey. I suspect it is
going to hurt, and we need to muffle the range of your. . ."
said Wyler as he slid the cold jagged steel under the last
few loops holding Julius's chest together. Ana returned
with the wooden spoon, placed it into Julius's mouth, and
Wyler pulled the knife upward. Julius face contorted from
the pain, but he barely released a cry at the jolt of his chest
splitting open.

Wyler mumbled under his breath, "Now to find and
check the heart," as he placed his hand into Julius's chest
cavity. When Wyler found the heart, he pulled it into the
gaping opening and examined the valves. He inspected the
superior pulmonary veins before moving on to the arteries.
The veins had fused back together without any problems,
but the left aortic valve seemed to be partially separated.
Larkin washed his hands and threaded his needle. "Ana.
Keep him quiet," was his only response as he dug around in
Julius chest once again to retrieve his heart. A vampire's
heart shifted around inside them much like a snake's heart
so that penetration of the heart with an animate object
became difficult. The elasticity of a vampire's heart
provided them with a great defense against their adversary.

Ana moved to Julius's head and pressed down on
his shoulders as he writhed in pain. The grip of his
clenched jaws broke the spoon as Wyler inserted a needle
into his cusp trying to stitch closed the hole. A sound of
agony burst out Julius's mouth and Wyler, with a look of

wildness in his eyes and face covered in blood from griping the needle between his teeth every now and then, said in an earnest tone, "Keep him still and quiet."

Ana somewhat terrified at the expression in her husband's face braced her knees around Julius's head and placed her hand over his mouth to muffle out the cries. When that attempt to stifle the sound did not work, she shoved her wrist into his mouth and gagged him. Julius bit down on her wrist, as he had the spoon, and Ana winced at the sharp pain that ran up her arm. Blood trickled down into his mouth, and Julius tried not to swallow, but his lust for blood overwhelmed him. The thirst was uncontrollable and he swallowed until Wyler screamed out, "I got it."

Julius released his grip as his heart recoiled back into his chest. Ana holding her arm clenched to her chest barely heard her husband's command to get some blood out of the refrigerator.

"Ana! The blood now, Ana!" demanded Wyler. Ana opened the refrigerator pulled out two bags and dropped them next to Wyler. Without noticing the pasty hue of Ana's skin, he picked up the bag ripped it open and emptied it into Julius's chest. The pain was less intense and Julius was able to stifle his own cries, as Wyler re-stitched the open chest cavity closed. Wyler prepared to knot the last stitch, when he heard a loud thud behind him. He turned to discover his wife's body sprawled out on the floor behind him.

***

Several hours later, Larkin returned downstairs to find the loft dark and quiet. He snuck up behind Julius, who sat on the edge of the couch sipping a cup of blood, and put his hand on his shoulder; "You okay?"

"Hmm, the question is, are you okay?" replied Julius turning to face him.

He exhaled deeply with a sigh. "I am sorry about the Jezalyn thing. I don't know what happened."

"Jealous much?" was the only taunting response he gave Larkin.

Gritting his teeth, he said, "Perhaps, I don't know what came over me. I guess my problem was that I was not ready to find out if Jezalyn's interest in me was as superficial as yours usually is in women," said Larkin trying to goad him back.

"And is it?" he said ignoring Larkin's womanizing statement.

"No, but you already knew that. Jezalyn is still uneasy about your test and her uncontrollable compulsion to retaliate."

Julius motioned to rub his cheek. "That one is a fire cat all right."

"I should not have assumed your motives dishonorable."

"Well, I did test her," replied Julius with a rather tantalizing smirk as an image of him kissing the nape of Jezalyn's neck materialized in his mind.

Larkin ignored Julius's provoking attempt. "Either way, I am glad there is no need for concern."

Somewhat irritated at Larkin's deflection of his prodding attempt, he icily responded, "Your problem is called love, and my current interest is not in Jezalyn. It is, however, in your brother and why he attacked me."

"He attacked you to get at me."

"Tell me something I don't know, like, why you kept your sadistic twin a secret?"

"Theron was not a secret; I thought he was dead so that's where I left him. As twins, we were bonded together from birth, but when I turned, the bond broke. My feud with my brother goes back centuries, before I entered into this being."

Julius felt he was owed more of an explanation, so he dug for a motive, "And the cause of the rift?"

With sadness in his eyes, he responded, "It was a long time ago. Let's just say my brother and I have been at odds since. . ."

Sorrowfulness crossed Larkin's face; it was only for a moment, but that was a moment too long and Julius's expression hardened. "He ripped my heart out over a woman," said Julius as he tightened his grip on the porcelain cup. It took him several minutes to realize the pressure had shattered the cup before slowly opening his hand letting blood and glass trickle to the floor.

"Calm down," said Larkin, "I'll go get Wyler."

"No! I am fine," replied Julius bending down to pick up the broken cup.

"Looks like a lot of blood. Wyler will stitch it up for you."

"I'll wrap a towel around it; I will be fine. Wyler has too much going on with Ana right now."

"What's wrong with Ana, now?" asked Larkin a bit irritated thinking about the way the night had played out.

His aggression was not with Ana, but Theron. Larkin feared that Ana was too weak to handle the intensity of assuming the role of Keeper, but he agreed to take her on to oblige Wyler. Had he known his brother was still alive, he would have never consented.

"Our little romp created a tear in my heart, and Wyler had to go back in and close it up."

Larkin tried to hide his tone of annoyance, "Okay—and the problem with Ana?"

Julius became irritated at Larkin's annoyance and blurted out, "She passed out?"

"What?" cried Larkin.

"What a weakling I initially thought, but when I realized we both fed on her tonight; it was understandable that she was unable to maintain her balance."

"You fed on her! Why? You do realize you will be bonded to her forever."

"I did, and that's why I forced my blood down her throat."

"You didn't!"

"I did," he said mischievously.

"Did she transform?" asked Larkin with a horror stricken face.

"Unfortunately, she did not," he said as he placed his hands on his head while mimicking a face of agony before blurting out, "She vomited. I don't know how you do it!"

A feeling of relief swept over Larkin's face, and he disappeared into the kitchen, boiled some water, and added a bud of Wood Avens and other herbs, the same herbs he had used to block Ana's and Jezalyn's bond a few hours before. "Here drink this; it will help your body heal faster."

Julius took the cup off the saucer and placed the shatter pieces he collected on it. "Why have you not given this to me earlier?"

"Because it's difficult to obtain. Besides, there is only one wound our bodies won't heal from, and that's what it's saved for."

"What wound?"

"Black Bat Flower is lethal to us, if we ingest the tentacles."

"What?" a wave of anger took over his tone.

Larkin responded with calming news. "The flowers were destroyed centuries ago by Theron," he said watching Julius's harden features relax, "I suppose I should warn you that Blaise found a way to acquire some, which he wrapped around the arrow that injured Theron, so do not underestimate him."

He lifted the cup to his mouth and gulped down the last bit of the concoction before he responded, "Who? Blaise or Theron."

"Both."

Julius said nothing else as he laughed all the way to the couch where he closed his eyes and tried to block the low rapid beat of Ana's sleeping heart.

***

When Larkin closed Jezalyn's apartment door behind him to go downstairs and check on Julius, Jezalyn dove into her bed sprawling out across the foot of it rubbing her red irritated eyes. She held her fingers pressed tightly against them trying to relieve some of the pain. She had not experienced this type of exhaustion since last December when she stayed up all night cramming for finals. Without opening her eyes, she fumbled for the edge of the blanket and folded it over her. She quickly fell into slumber where her unconscious mind took over. By the time she entered the dream realm, her mind aimlessly bounced through that nights images. She thought of Larkin and his tender kisses, and her hand connecting with Julius's face for kissing the nape of her neck as he requested to come in, but that image turned from her hand to Larkin's hand. She ran her finger over his scar and instantly found herself being drug to the foot of the bed. As she kicked and wiggled to get free, she felt a pinch on her thigh. With the sting sensation, her body awoke startled and sweaty.

Jezalyn's heart raced; panic-stricken she flung back the blanket and hunted for marks. Upon finding none, she brushed her partially damp hair back out of her face and strutted into the bathroom. As she splashed water onto her face she repeated to herself, "It was just another nightmare," and to prove it to herself she checked her legs once more before retreating to bed. She tossed and turned trying to get the dream out of her head, but it was to no avail, so she reached over picked up a book, and read. She thumbed through her book trying to remember where she left off, reading a bit here and there and every so often closing her tired eyes. By the time Jezalyn found her place, her eyes were too tired to read, so she let the book close with her finger still as the marker. She intended only to rest her eyes for a moment. However, when she re-opened them she found the red numbers on her clock blurry. Once her eyes became alert, Jezalyn was stunned to discover she had slept through most of the day. She heard a loud thud as she energetically swung her rested legs off the bed.

After opening the drapes to her window, Jezalyn spotted her book lying on the floor and soon realized the thud she heard earlier was her book. *Hmm, I must have knocked it off the bed*, she thought as she picked it up and sat down on the bed to read. Even though the drapes were open, it was too late for the sun to brighten the room, so Jezalyn reached over to turn on the lamp. The light illuminated the nightstand drawing her attention to the memoir. Jezalyn put down her book and cradled the memoirs in her arm like a baby as she scooted backward until her back rested against the headboard. She removed the pages from the hard case cover, tossing it to the side with the old twine still nestled inside. Jezalyn glanced at the first page, but before she could turn it, something caught her eye. It was not a word or a phrase; it was a name, Drythe—Theron Drythe. Without care or gentle ease she spread the papers out frantically nudging and scanning several papers from the center. She stopped suddenly and stood on her knees letting the papers slip off her lap as she read,

Julius is like a Greek God embodying beauty, dominance, and valor. He breaks every law except the gentlemanly invitation. It is the only rule he is bound by except the elusive golden ray. The allure of his stature and the soft kiss to the nape of their necks is too great for them to resist. One by one, they invite him in. He always

entertains them before entertaining himself.
Beware world: a Vampire God is born.

Jezalyn let the page slide out of her fingertips, as she grabbed the back of her neck. She went still as a wave of nausea swept over her and fear set in. Jumping out of the bed, she fumbled through the papers for her phone. Jezalyn paced back and forth, trying to cope with the unbelievable circumstance she found herself in. "Vampires can't be real, they just can't." As the phone rang and rang, she thought, *Come on answer, where are you?*

Finally, she heard his voice, "Hey, Babe!"

Her voice cracked as she responded, "Hey."

"Are you okay?"

"No," said Jezalyn grabbing her suitcase out of the closet and launching it onto the bed. "I believe you! Vampires are real! I am too scared to go downstairs; can you come pick me up?"

She heard a level of concern enter Blaise's voice as he asked, "What's wrong. Did Larkin threaten you?"

"Larkin! No! Why would he threaten me?"

"Didn't he tell you he was a vampire?"

"No! I was talking about Julius. Larkin's a vampire, too?"

"Do not invite them in."

"Them? You knew they were vampires?"

"Well. . . just don't invite them in."

When Blaise got no response, he reiterated with the most serious tone he could muster, "Jezalyn, are you listening to me? It is imperative that you do not invite them into your apartment."

"I won't," replied Jezalyn frantically throwing clothes into her suitcase.

"I am about an hour away; don't leave the apartment until I get there."

"Alright," mumbled Jezalyn peering at her watch as the line went dead. It was a quarter after five, and only about an hour of day light remained. She closed the suitcase and sat down next to it trying to process the information. For thirty minutes, her mind raced around the facts until she finally concluded that Larkin and Julius were vampires, and Blaise knew it. Not to mention the latter claimed to be a vampire hunter.

Finally she thought, *Wait! Blaise knew that Larkin and Julius were vampires and yet he didn't warn me! Can I really trust him?* And with that notion, paranoia set in. *Perhaps, I'll test him. If he is not one of them, then he will not be able to enter, seeing how I never invited him up. But, what if they are all working together? The only people that have been up here are Ana, Wyler, and Larkin. Larkin, I can't believe I let him in. He can't be a vampire, but. . . Blaise said. . . he must be. I am not safe here, I can't wait. . . I need to get out of here—Now!*

Jezalyn grabbed her partially filled suitcase, ran downstairs and out the door to her car, where she threw it into the trunk. She recklessly backed up nearly hitting another car and sped away without even so much as an apologetic wave or nod. Jezalyn pointed her vehicle in the one direction she had felt safe all her life, home. Jezalyn was on the road less than fifteen minutes when her phone rang, it was Blaise, but she did not answer. She let it go to voicemail since she felt like she could no longer trust him or anyone.

Blaise calmly spoke as he left her a message. "Hey, I am here. Come on down or if you're too scared, I can come up." He punched the dash as he hung up, realizing he had not brought much of the gear required for a vampire fight. Blaise had left Monroe ill-prepared because he was overwrought with concern for Jezalyn's immediate safety, so when she did not answer or come down, he did not barge in confident and unannounced. Instead, Blaise snuck up to the shop door and lightly pulled. Amazed to find it unlocked, he slipped through and quietly tiptoed up the stairs only to find Jezalyn's apartment empty. Nervous for her whereabouts, he hurried back downstairs so fast that he stumbled on the last stair and fell. The loud thud stirred Larkin and in a flash, he was upstairs helping Blaise to his feet.

"What are you doing here?" demanded Larkin.

Blaise yanked his arm away from Larkin, and Blaise helped himself to his feet. "I am here because Jezalyn called me frightened. She knows about you— vampires, and somebody named. . ."

Larkin ran upstairs glanced around and was back standing in front of Blaise holding several sheets of paper before Blaise had a chance to complete his sentence, ". . . and now she is gone."

Larkin glared at Blaise wildly, "You exposed us? I thought we decided it was in her best interest to keep her innocence intact."

"No, she already knew when she called; I might have inadvertently confirmed it. Who is this Julius? Do you think he grabbed her?"

"She does not have to worry about Julius; he is far from interested in her. Besides, he is still downstairs. "

Blaise held his ears as Larkin bellowed in a deep animalistic growl for Wyler, and seconds later Ana and Wyler appeared before them. With alarmed faces, both simultaneously asked, "What's wrong?"

"Jezalyn, she is gone."

Wyler gawked at Blaise in fright, "Do you know where she went?"

"If I did, would I be standing here talking to you?" responded Blaise in a rather haughty tone.

Larkin's body jerked forward then backward, but too quick for the human eye to notice the preemptive attack. They only saw a flinch as if he may have stumbled a bit, "Watch how you speak to us, boy."

Wyler was trying to defuse the situation and with one hand up he said, "It's alright, I am sure he didn't mean any disrespect. I am sure Blaise is just as concerned about Jezalyn."

"And with good rights he ought to be," said Ana.

"What does that mean?" requested Blaise as a wave of uneasiness took over.

"Theron!" said Larkin.

Wyler glanced over, "Has the potion wore off yet, can you sense or hear either of them?"

"Wait, what do you mean—sense?" interjected Blaise, but they ignored him. He watched as Larkin closed his eyes and after a while his eyes reopened, and he shook his head no.

"Great, we have lost her," was Ana's response, and she began to weep.

"Ana, go get a bag of blood; it might counteract the blocking potion." Ana, wiping the tears from her face, did as they requested and rushed back with a few bags in hand. Blaise grimaced at the sight of Larkin downing the bag of blood the way a frat brother would a keg of beer. When he had finished, he closed his eyes again. Blood ran down the corner of his mouth and dripped onto the chest of his shirt.

"Anything," said Wyler.

"No!"

"Perhaps, you need fresh blood," called out a voice deep in the shadows. Ana held her arms clenched tightly to her chest remembering the repercussions of last night's ordeal.

"Who's there? Make yourself visible!" demanded Blaise in a defensive stance.

Wyler answered his question, "It is Julius; he cannot emerge. He is bound by the light to darkness."

"Which will be for only ten more minutes," inserted Julius playfully.

"Ana's blood did heighten my connection to Theron last time, although it also jumbled up my thoughts as well."

"That wouldn't happen this time, if they were not alive to interrupt your thoughts," concluded Julius inaudibly directing the statement toward Blaise. Ignoring Julius's comment, Ana held out her arm revealing several bite impressions.

"It's worth a try," said Ana.

"No," said Wyler and pushed her back before exposing his own wrist. Larkin grabbed his arm, sank his fangs in, and drank. Although Larkin tried to pierce the skin with as little pain as possible, Wyler still flinched and the sight of the whole experience sent Blaise running upstairs to seek refuge in Jezalyn's apartment. Larkin released Wyler, closed his eyes and tried to reconnect once again with Jezalyn.

"It is unclear," said Larkin as he opened his eyes silently taking note to the absence of Blaise's presence.

Julius stood next to Larkin and with a teasing tone, he announced to anyone that would listen, "Maybe it was eight minutes, a minute too late to get my hands around that chicken's neck."

"Perhaps, it is good that he ran," said Ana not advocating violence.

Julius peered at her for a moment before he said, "Or perhaps, Larkin should go up and quench his thirst so that we can find Jezalyn before Theron finds her."

Ana shrieked at the thought, but Larkin agreed with Julius. Although he knew Julius was playing the emotion card to get him to do his bidding, it worked. Larkin and Julius flew upstairs and rapped on the door, but there was no answer, so Julius kicked the door off the hinges. It only took one extension of the leg and the door flew back, hit the wall, and eventually rested catty corner in the couch.

"I know you cannot come in, so what do you want?" said Blaise pushing his phone back into his pocket.

"We request a small donation to help find Jezalyn," responded Julius.

"You already tried that with Wyler. If it did not work then, there is no reason to suspect it would work now," replied Blaise.

Larkin held out his hands in an inviting manner, "If my brother gets a hold of her, she will definitely die. Are you not willing to risk a little blood to save her life?"

Blaise pulled at his face and fidgeted with his clothes, as he paced back and forth, "No. I called for backup. Once I am out, I will save her from all of you."

Julius made the sound of a buzzer, "Wrong answer."

"Enough of this!" blurted out Larkin.

"I will not and do not invite you in," said Blaise laughing aloud.

"True. I never received an invitation," said Julius, "but Larkin has."

Before Blaise knew it, he found himself clutched in Larkin's mighty grasp. Blaise struggled against the restraint even after having knifed Larkin in the side, the vampire's grip did not loosen as he plunged his tiny but lethal daggers into his shoulder; it was in that moment that Blaise realized he was too powerless to escape. With every violent thrash, Blaise made, more blood gushed into Larkin's mouth causing Larkin to guzzled faster and faster until Blaise went limp in his arms. After releasing his limp body,

Larkin pulled a short serrated pocketknife out of his left side and closed his eyes.

Larkin opened his eyes and cracked his neck to the side before he announced, "Let's go, the hunters will be here soon." They zipped back downstairs and stressed the importance of their immediate departure, "Quick, we have to go!"

Ana ran to the car, "Did you find Jezalyn?"

"Wyler, did you get the bag?" asked Larkin ignoring Ana.

Larkin glanced at Julius, and he nodded. "Put this thing in drive; they will soon be upon us!" he shouted.

"Who?" replied both Wyler and Ana?

"Hunters," responded Julius with an enlightened grin. As they sped off, Ana noticed in her rearview mirror several trucks pulling in the bookstore parking lot.

"Drive normally so they don't suspect anything," said Larkin.

They drove silently west for a while before Larkin directed them south.

"So you did find Jezalyn," asked Ana again as she turned south.

"No!" replied Larkin, "but I found Theron."

Chapter 27: The Chase

EAR ENVELOPED JEZALYN the same way darkness had swallowed the sky; it slowly crept in until it invaded every nuance of space. Jezalyn nervously checked her cell phone every few seconds for a signal. She wished and prayed that one little red bar would illuminate in the right hand corner of the screen. After staring at her phone for nearly twenty to thirty minutes after darkness fell, Jezalyn saw not one, but two bars; however, they quickly faded. Luckily, there were no vehicles traveling behind her, because she slammed on her brakes bringing her car to an abrupt halt before guiding it off the road. Now out of the line of traffic, Jezalyn slowly backed up, all the while imploring the cell signal to return. When it had, Jezalyn put the car in park and frantically punched at her phone. She had to re-dial the number several times before getting the right combination.

"Hello," said a voice on the other end.

"Grandpa, it's me. I am coming home for a visit," said Jezalyn as coolly as possible.

"Okay, I will put some extra food on for you. Where are you at now?"

Staring at her GPS, Jezalyn said, "I am on Hwy 65, but I don't recognize any of these towns. I think I just passed through Islington."

"Jezalyn, you're driving south. You need to re-direct so that you are going southwest or you will be on the road for hours."

"I don't know where I am. These GPS directions suck!"

"Okay, when is your next turn?"

"Hwy 84 and it's like a million miles away."

"Okay, so here is what you are going to do: when you get to the town of Newellton turn west on Hwy 4 to Gilbert. Now, Hwy 4 will turn into 128, but keep going, and when you get to Gilbert turn left on to 15. After several miles turn right back onto Hwy 128. Take 128 until it runs into Hwy 4 and take a left. Once you pass through Fort Necessity, stay the course and Hwy 4 will lead you to 165."

"Wait! I can't remember all that, why can't I just stay on 4 and skip all the turns."

"Because Hwy 4 turns north and goes up past Winnsboro before turning back south to meet 165; it's several hours out of the way. You need to come west so that you don't spend all night out on the road. You know how I feel about you driving at night."

"I know, Grandpa. Tell me again," requested a frustrated Jezalyn releasing a heavy sigh.

Her grandfather requested that she write down the directions, but Jezalyn did not have a writing utensil, so he spoke in short phrases so she could remember the directions. "Turn on Hwy 4 in Newllton. Stay strait until Gilbert."

Jezalyn repeated the directions back, "Okay, I go to Newllton, Hwy 4, and then Gilbert; is that right Grandpa?"

"Yes. The GPS should take over and do the rest. Call me, if it doesn't."

"I will. Thanks."

"Be careful, and don't stop for anything except gas."

"Yes sir," said Jezalyn as she hung up the phone and drove toward Newllton.

She drove with the radio blaring, trying to keep her mind off Blaise and Larkin, until she came to a sign that read, *Newllton ten miles; Waterproof. . .*, her attention was drawn, before she could finish, to the flashing red light on her dash prompting Jezalyn to get gas. Tightening the grip of the wheel, she sat up strait and thought; *a car can usually go 20 or 30 miles before running out. I am only ten miles from Newllton; I can make it.*

She breathed a sigh of relief as she pulled into a full service gas station. A middle-aged man in blue jeans stepped to her window. Jezalyn thought, *God bless paw-paw's paranoia,* as she dug in her glove box, fondling around for a small match box. The sudden tap at the window startled her, and she sat erect in her seat. Peering slightly over her shoulder, she saw a middle-aged man bent down peering into her window. "How much, ma'am?"

Jezalyn opened the matchbox, took out two twenty-dollar bills, handed them to the man, and said, "Fill her up, please." The man nodded, took the money, and treaded to the back of the car.

As the attendant proceeded to pump gas into her car, Jezalyn rolled the window up tight and checked the doors. After securing her doors, she assessed her surroundings, letting her gaze bounce from mirror to mirror making sure no one approached. She had never been paranoid. That was her grandpa's trait, but with all that had taken place in the last thirty-six hours, she now felt insecure in the world. An object, flickering from side to side, caught Jezalyn's eye as she glanced out of the rearview mirror. She watched as it grew closer and closer until it stopped behind her car. Jezalyn anxiously stared out her passenger side mirror, but after viewing only the road, she immediately turned her head. Now gazing into the driver side mirror, Jezalyn saw Larkin standing behind the gas attendant holding his neck between both hands.

Larkin smiled at Jezalyn when her glare caught his eye, and he bit into the gas attendant's neck similar to the way she would bit into a pork rib. Jezalyn's heart leapt at the sight and a wave of nausea swept over her as she cranked the car, put it in drive, and stepped on the gas. She sped down the highway trying to keep both her eyes on the road ahead and the road behind her. Her head jerked when she heard a loud thud, but felt at ease when she discovered it was only the gas pump hose hanging from her gas tank. Scared and on edge, her eyes reverted to her gas gauge as she grabbed for the phone. *Good, I got almost a full tank. I should be able to make it home without stopping.*

Although she had three-fourths of a tank of gas, Jezalyn tried to call home.

"Ah," screamed Jezalyn as she heard a beeping sound letting her knew her signal was not strong enough to place a call. She pushed the send button repeatedly, until the call finally connected.

"Hey, where's grandpa?" demanded Jezalyn.

"He left to go meet you a long time ago" said a male voice.

"What? No!" hollered Jezalyn as tears welled up in her eyes. She felt helpless out on the road alone not knowing where she was or what she was going to encounter next.

"Look, don't freak out. He took my cell when he left." Then under his breath, the same voice said in a sarcastic tone, "Like he even knows how it works."

"Thanks, Reed," said Jezalyn as the wave of helplessness fell away and a glimmer of security took its place. Jezalyn scrolled down to Reed's number; it was already in her phone, since her grandpa would have her call him regularly, whenever her grandfather needed help with the fencing or other chores around the farm.

The phone only rang once, before Jezalyn heard her grandfather's voice.

"Grandpa," said Jezalyn sobbing at the sound of his voice.

"Where are you?"

"Still on 65, I think I missed my turn," choked out Jezalyn who was sobbing so hard she could barely see the road.

"You are too upset to be driving. I think you should pull over for a few minutes until you've calmed down. There's no need to get upset over being a little lost," said her grandfather hearing her cries.

"No, I have to keep driving or he might get me."

"Listen, Baby Girl, I need you to stop crying and do the speed limit or you are going to wreck."

She wiped her face with the cuff of her sleeve and slowed down, putting the car on cruise control as she tried to choke back her tears. Jezalyn's heavy breathing had stopped and only sniffling remained when she heard her grandfather continue, "Who is after you?"

Still trying to control her emotions, she responded in fragments trying to keep the tears from returning. "This guy. . . Larkin. . . he killed the gas attendant. . . I sped away."

"Listen, everything will be alright; he is not going to get you. Stay on 65, do the speed limit, and I'll meet you in Waterproof."

"But how will I find you?" asked Jezalyn.

"Just call me. . ." was the last thing Jezalyn heard as the phone signal broke up and the line went dead.

Jezalyn had driven only a few miles after talking to her grandfather when her car jerked almost to a stopping speed. She checked the emergency brake, but it had not been pulled. The car was now at a full stop. Jezalyn pressed firmly down on the gas pedal. The engine roared, but the car did not move. Instead, it seemed to be sliding backwards, so she scanned her surroundings. Through the rear-view mirror, Jezalyn saw Larkin standing in the middle of the road clutching the broken gas pump line. He was hand over hand slowly, inch by inch, pulling the vehicle and her toward him. Jezalyn did all she could to stop the vehicle from sliding backward, but nothing worked. She quickly decided she had only two options: The first, to abandon the car and make a break for the woods; or secondly, she could slide the gear in reverse, stomp on the gas, and try to run him down. After little consideration, Jezalyn held her foot on the gas and slipped the gear into reverse.

The car hurled itself backward with the added force of the vampires pull, but to no avail did the car strike

Larkin. He jumped strait up, letting the car pass beneath him, but as he did, the end of the nozzle dislodged from the car. Jezalyn slammed on the brakes trying to regain control of the vehicle, stopping a few feet from where Larkin had landed in the middle of the road. As the car roared to a screeching halt, Larkin lashed the broken gas line forward like a whip and the nozzle lodged in the windshield. The car jerked forward and the windshield shattered from the force of the makeshift whip as it recoiled backwards. Jezalyn's eyes slanted with a self-preservational air as she gazed out of her busted windshield. She intensely gripped the wheel as she put the car in drive, pounded the gas pedal with her foot, and let out a roar as she barreled toward him.

Once again, Larkin leaped into the air, but this time as the vehicle passed, he landed on top. A loud thud sounded above her head, and she instinctively glanced up to see a fist imprint denting the roof. Jezalyn weaved and swerved from side to side trying to knock him off. During this terrible nightmare, the phone rang. She pressed the answer button, but when she did Larkin's hand came through the roof and grabbed the wheel causing her to lose control. She and the phone flew forward as the car came to a screeching halt when it fishtailed and slid off the road into the embankment of a small bridge. Jezalyn moved to the passenger seat when she saw Larkin jump down next to her window, but she unfortunately discovered the bridge, parallel with the door, had her trapped. After realizing she was pinned in, Jezalyn tried to scramble over the back seat of her car. She heard a crash and then felt a hand wrap around her ankle. She tried to kick free, but with one small tug, she was lying up against the dash trying to catch the breath she had lost from the impact of her bouncing against it.

"Sorry, sometimes I don't know my own strength," he said with a wicked chuckle.

"Larkin, why are you doing this?" said Jezalyn as she tried to inch as close to the passenger door as she could.

He raised his hand up violently at her and said, "My name is Theron, and if you try to jump out I will break that pretty little neck."

"Okay," said Jezalyn. "I will do anything, please don't kill me!"

Theron did not even glance her way. Instead, he put the car in drive and slowly drove toward Waterproof. Jezalyn rode silently, happy to be keeping her original course. Although she was panicked, she wondered why he drove slowly.

Theron answered her question without her having asked it, "So that Larkin can catch up with us."

She watched him in alarm as she thought; *He answered the same question I was pondering. I have not said anything, so how did he know to answer it? --- Perhaps, he just assumed I was thinking it and offered up the information; it's not like he can read my mind.*

"Or can I?" said Theron and horror consumed her as a grisly smile took over his face.

CHAPTER 28: REVELATION

THERON SLUNG THE car to a screeching halt at the border of the woods, where he forcefully grabbed Jezalyn's wrist and drug her through trees for about a mile. Stopping only when they reached his vessel, Theron smirked as he heard Larkin crashing through the foliage in pursuit of them. Theron clinched his grip tighter around Jezalyn's neck as Larkin jumped from a makeshift dock onto the deck of Theron's barge that he cleverly hid on the bank of the Mississippi just five minutes from Waterproof, Louisiana. Jezalyn stood motionless, scared his grip would tighten further, trying to comprehend the image that stood before her. She had thought Theron to be lying about his name whether he had misinformed her in the beginning or now, but she never considered that Theron was not Larkin. Jezalyn soon came to the notion that *they must be twins*. She felt at ease as she contemplated and concluded, *this man must be the vampire and not Larkin*; however, that hope flickered away, when she witnessed Larkin demand her release all the while brandishing his fangs at her captor.

"Ah—brother, so nice of you to grant me an audience once again," said Theron sporting a malicious grin.

"Well, I like to indulge," replied Larkin as Wyler snuck up behind Theron positioning himself behind a large barrel. Unfortunately, Wyler's presence had not gone unnoticed, and Theron demand for him to reveal himself.

As Wyler moved into sight, Theron showed his dominance. With his right hand, Theron grabbed Jezalyn around the waist; with his other, he tightly gripped her hair. Her arms and legs thrashed about when he first subdued her, but his harsh hold became more forceful with every flail. Soon she was unable to struggle against the unbearable pain. Jezalyn quickly resigned to the reality that his hold was too tight for her to wiggle free toward Wyler. Her head throbbed from the tight hold that he had on her, so she tried to keep her head as still as possible in the blind hope that he would loosen if not release his grip.

Larkin had attempted to move closer at the sight of seeing Jezalyn squirming and writhing in pain as her arms and legs flailed about, but both Wyler and Larkin froze as Theron announced her immediate death if anyone took another step. He abruptly cocked Jezalyn's neck to the side and sunk his teeth into her to prove he was capable. The horror of Theron feeding on Jezalyn was too much for Ana, and she sprung out of her hiding place and rushed toward him with a knife. Her response was not quick enough to take the vampire by surprise, and he released his grip on Jezalyn's head, blocked the blow, and captured Ana. Theron held them tightly around the waist, squeezing them tighter with the slightest muscle movement the way an anaconda would crush the life out of its pray.

Wyler fell to his knees and pleaded for Theron to release Ana, but his pleas fell upon deaf ears.

"Let's play a game shall we?" said Theron pleased with his allotment.

"Enough! Release the girls; they have nothing to do with our quarrel," replied Larkin.

He gave a queer smirk at this response and said, "Alright, but I think a parting gift is in order—"

"No! Let us go!" screamed Ana. She knew that someone would no doubt lose their life before he would release them. Ana knew she could not sit idly by and let

Jezalyn's light be extinguished at such a young age, so she hesitated only a second before she added, "I'll be your prize if one is necessary."

Theron's grip on Jezalyn tightened and she found it too grueling to breathe, much less respond to Ana's sacrificing gesture to save her. Although Jezalyn could only inhale sharp gulps of air, it was not the only reason she could not bring herself to thwart Ana's attempt to surrender to the vampire. She hung her head and watched the blood that rolled to the front of her throat, drip to the ground in front of her. She almost felt ashamed that her self-preservation instincts kept her silent. Jezalyn felt some relief when Theron loosened his grip, allowing her to intake larger breaths of air so that he could glance around the hull of the ship.

"Julius, what a miraculous turn of events. You look nothing like the shattered vessel I had last seen doing his best to rip Ana from my clutches. Do you think you will succeed this time?" asked Theron with a patronizing smile.

"Wood Avens, what a lovely herb," said Julius as he licked his lips ignoring the challenge; he was never the one to be provoked into blind rage when generally it was he who did the provoking.

"Brother, how clever of you to have an abundant stash," said Theron as he remembered raiding Larkin's herb supplies.

"One can never be too careful with the Hunter about," replied Larkin.

"Luther! I thought I dealt with him long ago. No need to hash that up now; I will take care of him and his patsy once I dispense with you." Glancing at the girls, Theron announced, "Now back to business. Which one shall I liberate from this cruel world?" He waited several moments for a response before he continued, "One must die; brother, you choose?"

Although Theron directed his question toward Larkin, Julius responded, "Kill them both; either way, you are mine."

"No! Take me," screamed Wyler. He frantically ran his fingers roughly through his hair as he shot a pleading stare at Theron.

"Oh, how self-sacrificing," was the only response Theron gave as he spoke over Wyler's exclamation. He thought nothing of the pain he saw in Wyler's face, and he continued, "Looks like a tie, two for two."

"So which will it be: this human toy, or your loyal companion's lover?"

Wyler glared at Larkin with a sincere plea, but Larkin showed no emotion, and he immediately feared the worst. He knew Larkin's infatuation with Jezalyn was strong, but he was praying his devotion to himself, Larkin's faithful servant and Keeper, was stronger.

After a few moments passed, Larkin responded with confident vigor, "Neither! You will release both of them or I will rip—"

Theron did not let him finish his threat. In one swift motion, he released Jezalyn, snapped Ana's neck, and flung her to the side like a rag doll. He quickly re-seized Jezalyn before she had the chance to flee. The only thing Jezalyn comprehended during that episode was the piercing pain she felt in her neck when Theron re-punctured her throat. Jezalyn did not even realize Theron's first attack was on Ana and not on herself.

"No!" screeched Wyler as he ran toward his wife's lifeless body that lay strewn across the deck of the barge.

As Wyler bellowed at the loss of his wife, Larkin felt his pain. It was a powerful ache that struck his chest before radiating through his body with such an effect that he almost plummeted to his knees. Larkin had never realized the depth of Wyler's love for Ana until that moment. Wyler's pain was familiar to him, for it was similar to the agony of losing his beloved Isadora. Larkin did his best to push the emotional intensity that was thrust upon him to the back of his mind, since the circumstances had gone from dire to aghast. Ana was dead, and Jezalyn's life would soon slip away. Theron continued to drain her until an arrow clipped him in the back as Larkin and Julius flew upon him. Theron dropped Jezalyn in defense of their collaborated attack.

Jezalyn, too weak to move, was left crouched in the fetal position to watch as the fight ensued around her. Julius and Larkin took turns punching at Theron, but he deflected most of the blows. Jezalyn covered her face praying not be trampled beneath their feet as they stomped around her trying to box Theron in so that he would have no choice but to surrender. However, surrendering was not an option for him. Theron was considerably quicker than Julius, considering he had nearly four hundred years on him, making it difficult to trap him. Although Theron was able to escape the cleaver moves of his opponents, he was not quite prepared for the wrath of a grieving husband. Wyler, in a fit of rage over the death of his wife, ran up behind Theron and kicked the arrow burying it deeper into Theron's back. Wyler landed on his hip while Julius and Larkin jumped back as the arrow punctured through to the front of Theron's chest. He let out a sinister growl as he fell to his knees clutching the arrow; it had barbs around the rod similar to the last one bearing the same deadly poison that had already attempted to take his life once.

Larkin grabbed his brother, being careful not to grasp the prickly arrow, and hurled him across the barge. Theron landed against the cold steel wall, and Larkin's face was emotionless as he sauntered up to him, bent down, and buried his fist into his brother's chest. His hand lingered for a moment before he pulled it out empty, "I cannot kill my own brother."

Julius pushed Larkin to the side, bent down and pushed his fist deep into the open chest cavity. "It's okay—I can," he said as he dug around for Theron's heart.

Theron pleaded for his brother's help. "Brother, if you let him kill me, Isadora and Ana will suffer a harsher punishment."

"Isadora? Isadora is dead, and thanks to you so is Ana," blasted Larkin angrily.

"No, she is still alive. She imprisoned herself, refusing to live a life without you. If he kills me, you will never find her and both will rot for all eternity."

"I care not," replied Julius, and he pulled the organ from Theron's chest.

"No!" screamed Wyler, who overheard Theron's proclamation to save his wife as Theron's accomplice, Maurice, was escorted at arrow point onto the barge. A hunter held him captive.

Julius showed no interest in their presence and held the heart high above his face letting the blood drip around and in his mouth. Wyler, who had landed only a few feet from Jezalyn, froze with a terror stricken face as his last opportunity to save his wife laid heartless against the edge of the barge. His gaze broke, when he heard Jezalyn faintly crying out, "Help! Wyler … Help me! … Please, anybody."

Wyler checked her pulse and called out to Larkin, who had not flinched since hearing the news that Isadora was alive, "Larkin, I don't think she is going to make it."

Larkin let the thought of his old love wither as he ran to the aid of his current. Upon reaching her, Larkin scooped her up in his arms and pressed his hand against her chest. The beat was not faint enough to turn her, but faint enough for her to go into cardiac arrest. Without any contemplation, he pulled her injured neck close to his lips and extracted enough blood for him to turn her.

"Drink," said Larkin as he punctured his own wrist with his fangs. Jezalyn refused to drink his blood and tried to push him away, but she was only strong enough to thrust his wrist backwards. Larkin thinking not of the consequences threatened, "If you don't willingly take it, I will be forced to make you." Julius watched as Jezalyn denied his arm once again.

"You can't force her, or she will hate you forever," Julius cried out. Without waiting for a response, Julius bent down and placed Theron's heart in his right hand and lightly whispered, "Whose brokenhearted now!"

"I can't lose her again," retorted Larkin.

"She's not Isadora," whimpered Wyler as he stroked and cradled his dead wife's head.

"Snap out of it," yelled Julius.

"I'd rather her live then love me," was his only retort. Ignoring Julius's caution, Larkin lifted her head to press it to his wrist. Then suddenly, an arrow caught him in the chest forcing him to release her. Jezalyn's head fell against the metal flooring when Larkin gripped the barbed arrow. "A hunter's signature," mumbled Larkin, and his eyes fixated on the little black tentacles wrapped around the sharp hooks.

"Luther," he growled in an ominous tone over the babbling Jezalyn, who mumbled the word grandpa. He controlled his anger and picked Jezalyn's head up once again to finish his desperate act of saving her even if he would soon die himself.

"Don't do it, Larkin," said an old familiar voice that he had not heard in a century. Larkin turned to find himself confronted by the Hunter. Larkin did not have to ponder his challenger's physical appearance, his aged features and snow-white hair with silvery tones, to conclude who stood before him. Larkin knew by his stature and the way he held his bow drawn upon him that it was Luther.

"Luther, it's been ages," said Larkin still cradling Jezalyn's head in his lap.

"It has," said Luther nonchalantly, before forcefully demanding, without letting his voice rise, "Give me the girl."

"I can't," replied Larkin. "I have to save her."

"You did well with your brother today, but let me take over here."

"No! I won't risk it. Besides, you owe me, old man."

Julius listened with great interest, *a hunter indebted to a vampire.*

"Maybe I do, but she owes you nothing, so you will release her."

"Don't give me demands! I saved your life when Theron left you for dead at the shipyard. It is time to cash in a favor, so you are going to walk away and let me save her."

"You did, and it's one of the reasons why all of you are still alive."

"But not for much longer," replied Larkin as Julius thought, *one, what is the other? How scandalous this is all turning out to be; a vampire saving a hunter and a hunter indebted to a vampire. There has to be a deeper connection!*

Luther ordered Falken, the hunter who detained Maurice, to throw a bag of Wood Aven's to Julius, which in turn broke Julius's thoughts as he instinctually extended his arm to catch the bag that was hurled toward him. Luther also ordered Falken to release Maurice to Julius for Larkin to deal with in whatever way he saw fit.

"Now hand her over, and don't worry. I have survived for centuries as a human. I think I can help her safely sustain her human life better than you," replied Luther.

Larkin nodded in agreement even though he did not want to release her. Luther's logic was too great for him to deny, so he toddled over to Luther and gently relinquished Jezalyn.

Jezalyn who slipped in and out of consciousness blurted out as she left Larkin's arms, "Grandpa, help me! He's a vampire!"

Everyone stared in disbelief as Luther responded, "Just hold on, Baby Girl; everything is alright."

Luther produced a vial from his pocket and as he popped the top off, Jezalyn whispered, "I wanna go home."

"We are going home, but first you need to take this medicine," replied Luther.

He hoped she would not deny herself the one thing that could keep her alive, and he knew she had consented to take the potion when she opened her mouth like a baby bird for him to pour it in. Relief moved over everyone as she closed her mouth to swallow.

Upon swallowing it, she responded like a child, "All gone," sticking out her tongue, "can we go home now?"

"Yes," he said as he cradled her in his arms. Pointing at his bow, Luther ordered, "Falken, gather my things; it's time to go." Falken obeyed, picked up the bow, strolled over to them, and stood defensively.

Larkin stared at Jezalyn's face and saw no resemblance, and even so he could not deny the regard in Luther's eye or the feeling of safety that swept over Jezalyn when Luther held her close, so he stepped aside and let them pass.

Wyler was the first to break the silence as they watched the hunters climb the levy with Jezalyn's body. "Julius, toss me the Wood Avens. I need to make a mixture for Larkin."

He tossed the baggy across the ship, but Larkin caught it in his hand, tore open the bag, and emptied the contents in his mouth.

Julius watched him gag on the herb as he tried to command them on what to do next. "Take the bodies below."

"And put them where?" asked Julius.

"If I know my brother, there are several crypts or cells below. We need to voyage this barge up river away from society until we decide what to do with them and him," said Larkin pointing at Maurice.

Wyler's gaze drifted toward Maurice as he cradled his dead wife as gently as possible. "Good idea! We can torture you over and over until you tell us how to find Isadora," he said, before lightly kissing Ana's head, like someone would a sleeping infant, not ready to acknowledge she was gone.

Julius was surprised to hear such spiteful words escape Wyler's mouth, but then again he could understand the reasoning, so he nodded in agreement. Maurice tried to flee, but his attempted was unsuccessful. Julius had caught him by the neck and snapped it to incapacitate him for awhile so that he could move Theron's corpse downstairs.

While they moved the bodies downstairs, Larkin closed his eyes and took a deep breath letting a smile slide across his face as he felt Jezalyn's once faint heart beat increase to a steady pace.

Wyler's voice broke Larkin's meditation as he called out, "Julius, keep the heart. We may need him if Maurice doesn't talk."

Julius nodded and as he strutted over to the body and thought, *Someone must know the secret! What could connect Luther and Larkin? Why would they try to save each other; it's not as if they are blood. I must know how they ended up bonded.* Julius plucked the heart out of Theron's hand before mumbling, "You might come in handy after all" as he drug the heavy, limp body across the stained deck and into the corridor.

The announcement of Isadora's death as a sham coupled with the possibly that she could save Ana was all the hope Wyler needed and he clung to it fervently.

"Let's go," said Larkin and as he walked to the helm to take the wheel, he knew that not only had Jezalyn survived his brother, but she had also survived him. He only prayed that her revelation of this cruel world would not alter her spirit. However, his thoughts did not linger on Jezalyn's potentially shattered innocence for long, for he still sensed Wyler's overwhelming sorrow, an agony that radiated intensely through every fiber of Larkin's body. He could barely move and at that moment he acknowledged the internal strength of his faithful servant, for Larkin could hear Wyler's determination to find Isadora and resurrect his sweet bunny. Larkin knew Wyler would not be quieted.

Need More?

THANK YOU FOR reading the first instalment of Sabrina Street's new series *The Vampire Keeper*!

Blog: There are two ways to follow Sabrina's blog: visit her website www.sabrinastreet.com.

Email: You can join Sabrina's email list at www.sabrinastreet.com or write email list in the subject line.

Facebook: Like Sabrina's author page at www.facebook.com/AuthorSabrinaStreet or stop by and post a shout out about *The Vampire Keeper* or any Fantasy Realm related interest.

Google+: Sabrina actively reposts genre relate materials, as well as anything she deems interesting, so search Sabrina out at google.com/+sabrinastreet to add her to your Google circle. She'll add you back.

Review it: You can write or read a review about *The Vampire Keeper* on www.goodreads.com and www.amazon.com.

Twitter: Follow and message Sabrina at @snstreet. She would love to hear your thoughts about her books.

Vote for it: If you enjoyed *The Vampire Keeper,* you can vote for it at www.goodreads.com and www.amazon.com.

Website: Check out www.sabrinastreet.com where you'll
be able to stay up to date with Sabrina's creative
progress, reviews and interviews.

About the Author

SABRINA STREET IS a Secondary Teacher in Louisiana. Street earned a BLS in English at Louisiana State University at Alexandria before obtaining her Master of Arts in Teaching from Louisiana College. Street added author to her list of accomplishments with her debut novel, *The Vampire Keeper*. She continues to educate adolescents as she works on her next novel.